Tax Revolt
An American Insurrection

by

K Mike Hill

iUniverse, Inc.
New York   Bloomington

Tax Revolt

An American Insurrection

iUniverse books may be ordered through booksellers or by contacting:

iUniverse
1663 Liberty Drive
Bloomington, IN 47403
www.iuniverse.com
1-800-Authors (1-800-288-4677)

Because of the dynamic nature of the Internet, any Web addresses or links contained in this book may have changed since publication and may no longer be valid. The views expressed in this work are solely those of the author and do not necessarily reflect the views of the publisher, and the publisher hereby disclaims any responsibility for them.

ISBN: 978-1-4401-0940-9(pbk)
ISBN: 978-1-4401-0939-3 (ebk)

Printed in the United States of America

iUniverse rev. date: 11/21/2008

Dedicated to the Next Generation

Shana

Rachel

Stefanie

Amanda

Nicholas

Kraig

Koty

Kara

Robby

Rita

That they may have the wisdom to build a better world

PREFACE

Maybe the time for this cautionary tale has passed. It was begun in 1996 when a besieged president had to contend with an opposition majority in congress. When President Clinton sent cruise missile into Afghanistan, many saw the necessity of punishing the Taliban sponsors of terror. Others, seeking political advantage, yelled 'Wage the Dog', in reference to the movie in which a beleaguered president used military action to distract the country. Unfortunately, this project wasn't released in enough time to warn about the possible abuses of a manipulative administration. Fortunately, the country was not incensed enough to result in the kind of social collapse that this tale envisions. But many manipulators are still out there, and this may be a warning of what could be if citizens lose their faith in government and Democracy loses its' way.

Contents

INTRODUCTION

"No Taxation without Representation," is a slogan that helped spark the American Revolution. The founding fathers realized that taxation was needed. The New Deal electrified America. The interstate highway system bound it together. The armed forces protected it and the space program made us proud. All of this is accomplished by a government financed by the people.

Taxes have been levied and collected, often by force, since ancient times. But even in a government 'By the People' some taxation is needed to maintain a safe and sane society. When the American Revolution won the right of self-government, the founding fathers continued to see a need for taxation; if self-imposed.

Many, though, are alienated from their government and do not see the benefits of taxes. Where would we be without an army? People complain about the tax burden without considering what their tax bill buys. Taxes at some level pay for police, firemen, highways, the diplomatic corps, armed services, food and water safety, garbage disposal, utilities, the criminal justice system and a host of good and necessary services.

But suppose the social fabric tore. Suppose uninfomed or misinformed citizens, detached from the direct use of taxes for public services, chose not to support their government. Suppose a party, out of self-interest, who felt burden and restricted by government, used this frustration to actively conspire to let the institutions wither away. What might that society look like?

It might take years to reestablish the infrastructure of a modern society. And the task would be all the more difficult in the absence of an organized military force to maintain order while representative government is re-invented. What if people did not acknowledge the authority of their government? Suppose trust in government was destroyed. Citizens of a state in anarchy would soon discovered that all elements of society were very much inter-dependent; that a shared tax burden is preferable to chaos.

Michael Corbett is a number cruncher working with government data when the Ultra faction comes to power with a veto proof legislature and a lame duck president. He sees how narrow special interests, in league with party loyalists, are manipulating information to siphon off the resources of the country. He sees a coming day of reckoning that he is powerless to stop.

Restricted by his security oaths, he attempts to use public information to expose the abuses of a deceptive promise to America; the 13-States Rights. To the Ultras, this is conspiracy. The party starves the government and strips it of enforcement capabilities. The speaking point, "No more taxes", is repeated and taken literally by a large part of the population. Corporations, in cynical self-interest, withhold quarterly tax payments for short term benefit of the few.

Too late the puppet masters discover that, encouraged by the Ultras' distain for government, the general public have lost confidence in public institutions. Tax with-holding crusades, intended to starve big government, escalate. Federal employees are furloughed. In a domino effect state, county and city workers follow. Government medical and subsistence systems fail. A government voucher system, instituted to heal the crisis, fails. The electronic banking and financial systems evaporate; the victim of cyber attacks by disgruntled citizens. Pensions, utilities, trash collection, police and fire agencies collapse with the failure of public finance. Could order survive?

Grass roots communities emerge; where a farmer is more valuable than a merchant, and a Wall Street fund manager is worthless.

Can the people of the United States restore order and emerge from this new Dark Age? Is an American Insurrection possible and how might it happen?

FOREIGN SERVICE

It's hard to tell when it began. The way things are. It wasn't Michael's arrest. That he handled as just another day at the office. Someone wanted to squelch his vote, or revoke his security clearance or collect a civil reward. That was common enough. Yes, he evaded the tithe; the Government imposed ten percent flat tax that was supposed to make everything fair. Everyone tried to cut their tax bill. But his thinking had changed and the Ultras knew it.

The charges were tax evasion, fraud and conspiracy. 'That's how they got Capone,' Michael mused to himself. This was just a publicly acceptable excuse. He used barter labor. Ironically, that was set up by the Ultras themselves to benefit their loyalists.

But the Conspiracy charge. What kind of crime was that? Not influence peddling; that the Ultras did with gusto. Conspiracy! That could mean anything. They made it sound like backroom dealing to swindle grandma out of her pension.

Michael did his time in the military and understood that sometimes you were asked to 'take one for the team'. But this felt different. The team was corrupt.

Up until now life had gone according to plan. For Michael, most of the race had been won at birth; born white, middle class, in the United States, in the second half of the 20th Century. Though Michael's father died in his youth, his mother was able to depend on an adequate Railroad pension to raise her son. Other than that, it was well laid plans, brains and breaks.

Michael, seeking adventure, had enlisted in the military. He joined up to do his time even before coercive recruiting became law. He had even considered a career. Since he was a boy he had thrilled at the adventures of generations of soldiers for America. He wanted the training; he wanted the adventure; he wanted the chicks. Great-grandpa Lewis had served in France during 'The War to End all War', Grandpa Harry had done time in the belly of a B-17 in WWII, and Pop had trained Asia allies in special weapons during the Asian War. Michael felt he had to pay his dues to take his place with the venerated Armchair Generals. (Though not generals in the literal sense. None actually rose above captain.) Captain Corbett would take his turn at war. He was disgusted with those who hadn't served feigning military expertise. He wanted to learn for himself. He couldn't comment authoritatively unless he'd been there. He would not be a 'Chickenhawk'.

He has spent eight years as a junior officer in overseas hot spots. Clandestine service on the borders of the Iraqi Republics and in the jungles of South America had bought him the choice assignment to diplomatic security. All the time he was learning. He took every course that the army had to offer from code breaking to dog handling. It was an excellent inside view of the workings of power politics. A fly on the wall at diplomatic functions, he mingled with East European power brokers and Arab sheiks. He got drunk with their security details and slept with their secretaries.

He got some interesting, sometimes blood curdling variations on world history from the foreign staffers. "When your President Reagan was trading missiles for hostages in the Middle East," the thoroughly drunk Russian agent was saying, "the militants grabbed a Russian and tried to strike a deal. We grabbed one of their operatives and sent him back to them in mason jars," the Russian commando made a hand gesture as though screwing a lid on a jar. "No discussion. No national whining," He nonchalantly downed his vodka, "We asked for nothing; we demanded nothing. They got the message. Our man was returned unharmed. They never dared to take another of our people."

Michael was impressed by the cold blooded efficiency of some foreign regimes; not that he would wish America to be similarly efficient. Soldiers understood killing, but wars are not won by killing every last enemy soldier. The Ultras applied the symbolism of war to every issue. It didn't always make sense. Criminal justice, for example, blurred the line between criminals and soldiers. When war did come, every enemy soldier and civilian was perceived by many Americans as criminals. Every last criminal captured and punished, yes; every last soldier, no. If the activity is criminal, then treat the perpetrators as criminals not soldiers; call the response crime-fighting, not war. Ultras gave everything a WAR label to expand and justify their administrative powers. It made everything they professed black n white. It made Michael uncomfortable, but he went along to get his ticket to the fortunate fraction. Soldiers could be a little more emotionally detached in their profession. They didn't make policy.

A generation of SciFi blamed military bad guys for secretively seeking better ways to kill, breeding monsters and using alien technology or developing new improved weapons that render the enemy's useless. There were plenty of lethal ways to kill. Disease and starvation were a couple of the most efficient.

The war winning dimension was often intelligence; something Michael found a remarkable lack of in the Ultras. Every piece was a cog with only knowledge of their function. Those who could have stitched together the 'Big Picture' instead choose to close their eyes, or worse, paint a misleading picture for political security. Soldiers generally didn't think that deep.

The secular dictatorships in foreign countries had been replaced by more democratic governments. Unfortunately for America, when left to the democratic process, the successors of the pro-Western dictators were radical Moslem extremists, Latin American nationalists and Asian warlords. Selected by a majority of their people, most were decidedly anti-American. They now controlled the bulk of the world's oil reserves. The new people's governments did not share the same greed for American dollars as their predecessors and were content to settle for less to make America suffer.

On the security team of the Columbian Ambassador, Michael saw an ally without a clue. The American Embassy warned, "We don't want to see a 99% electoral victory." Maybe a cliché, but the ambassador thought that the host government got the message. The

United States wanted to recognize a friendly government that had credibility around the world. The vote count came in at 98.7%.

The Ambassador was incensed as he announced that the United States would accept the results. What else could they do to avoid anarchy? He tried to keep a straight face; a diplomatic facade.

"What's the problem?" the allied envoy asked. "We allowed an opposition vote. It is below what you suggested and we have shown that we have great support among the people." The local junta strongman was very pleased with himself. He was only considering internal politics. Fear was more relevant than fair. In the dictators' opinion, everything had worked out just right. The foreign administration felt that they had followed the letter of the U.S. request, but they had missed the meaning entirely. In their desire to show support and appease the Americans, they had actually achieved the worst of both worlds. It was obviously not a legitimate election, but cynical manipulation. No vote would achieve that level of support; yet the Americans could hardly withhold support of the corrupt puppet regime. The internationally short sighted Junta could not see anything wrong with what they had done. Michael made a mental note, 'don't talk to foreigners in clichés. They might translate it literally.'

During the Iraq war, America continually proclaimed that it would not negotiate, but then offered $20,000 for information on lost soldiers. What was this, other than an incentive for further abductions? It was easy enough for the opposition forces to arrange a, seemingly, innocent third party to collect the reward for a piece of the take. If the hunt got too hot, they would kill the hostage and dispose of the body. In the meantime, several thousand soldiers involved in the search were diverted from the real mission of stabilizing the country. And even worse, the search had just further endangered the hostages' life and cost the lives of some of the searchers. Don't tell mom back home, but a soldier has to be prepared to be written off for the good of the service, the mission and his country.

The Latin border war was not going well. It had begun as a Columbian drug interdiction, advanced to a war to liberate the

Venezuelan oil fields. Expanded to a hunt for South American terrorists across the borders and, eventually, was just called the Latin War.

The United States backed the local right-wing stongman and his pro-American policies over the nationalist Elian Sanchez in Venezuela. Sanchez won a popular election fair and square, in spite of widespread fraud by the opposition and American threats; or maybe because of them. Elians' anti-American, war-like action was to nationalize the oil fields. The American puppet in Columbia dutifully declared war on his neighbor on a trumped up border incursion charge.

Citizens were incensed by widely reported stories of American citizens abused by the Latin militia bands who supported Elian. 'He would poison our kids with drugs. He would send waves of illegal immigrant across our borders. He would starve us of oil. He had mad-cow disease and the flesh eating virus to unleash.' Not since Hurst had incited the country to war with Spain a century earlier had war fever run so high in the American public. The only solution offered by the Ultras was war.

After the political maneuvering and manipulation of the Bush, Chaney, Rumsfield debacle in Iraq, the Veto Proof Congress demanded that the political leadership leave the war fighting to the military. By 'political leadership' they meant President White. The American oil companies, concerned with the large oil reserves in South America, convinced the Ultra congress to force President Whites' hand. The Congress dutifully issued a declaration of war and the game was on.

America responded to appeals for military aid by the ousted Venezuelan dictator using Columbia as a staging area. The Columbian people, however, resented their country being used by the Gringos to attack a fellow Latin neighbor. Politically, it was the old 'with us or against us' Bush bravado. The old axiom of 'the enemy of my enemy is my friend', which built alliances, was reversed to 'the friend of my enemy is my enemy', which built coalitions of enemies. Most countries did not want to face the U.S.

militarily, but disengagement, alone, worked financial hardship on America.

Unfortunately, the Ultras had not learned the lessons of history. The world had matured beyond the point when a foreign power could move in and decapitate a country's government, install a more friendly regime, and assume the levers of power. During the colonial period, a foreign interest could assume power and the military, police and civil service of the occupied country may carry on under new management. That changed as indigenous people realized the power that they had by simply refusing to cooperate. The military could achieve military objectives, but a country's people could not be ruled by an outsider, if they didn't conform. As Iraq had shown, there was no cheap oil in a sweetheart deal for the intruder; just heartbreak for military families.

American Special Forces took back the Venezuelan oil fields in the name of U.S. oil companies. Called restoring American property, it was grant theft on a national scale.

TV commentators began using military terminology in an attempt to sound informed and patriotic, but no one knew exactly what capability the enemy had. And it suited the Ultras to keep people in the dark. Military contractors rejoiced. In the absence of war, their profits had suffered. What's a few boots on the ground compared to millions in the bank. The limited offensive military capability of the Venezuelans was analyzed and routinely disregarded by self-appointed experts. 'We would beat them in a matter of days,' media chickenhawks boasted. The generals hated the idea; the Ultra politicians loved it. It would divert the people while the Ultras picked their pockets. It didn't turn out to be the kind of war they expected.

Elian did not fight fair. He did not stand and fight in his capitol. He took to the border regions between his country and Columbia, out of the reach of the massive conventional military forces. He delegated independent command to a number of competent lieutenants. Then mobilized his population and began to bleed the Americans. Bolivia, Panama, Ecuador and others sent what they called peace keepers. By that they meant keeping the peace by presenting a united front against the American bully.

The American military's sophisticated weapons systems were routinely sabotaged by computer experts operating with nothing more high-tech than a laptop computer. A number of hackers had taken a page from the Chinese Olympic playbook and figured out how to block internet sites. Others followed the example of the Russian invasion of Georgia. They overwhelmed servers and blocked electronic communications in a high tech refinement of radar jamming. Not only military communication and weapons control were infiltrated. The entire internet became unstable. Those who depended on technology, from the banking system to those making a living on internet auctions, saw their connections failing in South and North America.

The Columbian puppet remained holed up in his capitol bedecked in medals he awarded himself, protected by his bodyguard. Militarily he was insignificant. The U.S. Embassy was an armed camp. Marines guarded the gates against the irregular forces of Elians' guerillas. Captain Corbett and a select few Special Forces troops labored over the maps and intelligence reports that flooded in from American military advisors and Columbian forces in the field.

"Here is an interesting one, sir," Captain Corbett held up a troubling fax that had arrived from a remote outpost. "It seems a primary enemy asset has been dispatched on a mission and his location has been confirmed."

Colonel South, the on the scene military advisor, did not even look up from his computer screen. "Well, send out a Hellfire and neutralize him."

"But he's in an urban area. There will be collateral damage. Maybe up to fifty meters. There would be civilian casualties," Michael responded.

"So? This is war. People die," the Colonel was getting impatient. Many Venezuelan civilians had died in the preceding months. This did not even seem worth mentioning. As a matter of fact, all of the enemy, all of the casualties, appeared to be civilian.

7

"But this collateral damage would be AmCits," Michael used the military abbreviation that indicated American citizens. "This safe house is in San Antonio."

South looked up with a blank stare, then regained his composure. "The military doesn't have jurisdiction inside the States. Send it off to the FBI."

"By the time they act on it, he'll be long gone."

"Nothin' we can do about that," South sighed. "We got bigger problems. Gitmo has fallen."

In a show of solidarity, most of Latin American had started to give the Americans trouble. The Panama Canal came under fire and traffic was suspended. Guatemala, El Salvador closed the American embassies and ejected the staff. Mexico cut off oil shipments and called off the American inspired war on drugs. The Columbian people, if not their unpopular rulers, enlisted for service in Venezuela. Fighters poured in from every Latin neighbor. The Cubans surrounded Guantanamo Bay with lightly armed forces that didn't present a large enough military target to warrant massive B-1 bomber strikes. The United States could not use its sledge hammer to kill all the flies that swarmed around them.

Cuban forces were armed with light, mobile mortars and Rocket Propelled Grenades (RPGs) that made landing and take-off dangerous. Light artillery could fire a few rounds and disappear under a jungle canopy. The generals compared it to punching a bucket of water. It gave way before them and closed in around them. Then, as soon as they withdrew, the Cubans filled the vacuum. Casualties were mounting and there was no way to evacuate the wounded. Threats to bomb Cuban cities went unanswered. World War II had shown that people were not demoralized by bombing; it made them furious. The threat of civilian bombing was roundly condemned by the nations of the world.

Swarm of speed boats, packed with explosives, sealed off the sea lanes. The siege had lasted for several months. American military analysts had assumed the base could be held against anything that the Cubans could throw against it. Air drops had provided necessary supplies, but the strain had taken its' toll and the

Generals in charge, to spare their troops, had agreed to a cessation of hostilities. Eventually the Cuban offer of evacuation was accepted. The Ultras claimed credit for bringing the boys home. President White took the scorn.

Surrender was not something that the American people considered feasible. But in the cold reflection of history, most people didn't want American troops to die to the last man. In retrospect, the men on Wake Island and the men at Bataan were recognized heroes. Surrender allowed them to survive to witness the ultimate victory and return to their families.

Michael discovered diplomacy was not weakness that emboldens the enemy; that's how countries do business. Mankind has been engaged in this activity with friends and enemies, in war and peace, for thousands of years. Even a superpower, with just five percent of the worlds' population, can not threaten all the rest of the world into cooperating. Michael rubbed elbows with adversaries as soldiers in a less-than-battlefield assignment. They would have killed each other with no remorse in combat and would understand each other brutal motivation.

Michael found himself explaining friendly-fire, collateral-damage, unprivileged belligerent and the use of a term like terrorist to Special Forces troopers of foreign countries over vodka and cigars. Frankly, they never did understand the degrees of death that the United States insisted on recognizing. General Powell reintroduced the 'K' word (Kill) to the military vocabulary. Michael thought the human interest stories would give way to better military understanding. But people liked the human element and every action was broadcast as dramatic and relevant; like the score of a sporting event. Up and coming journalists flocked to interview the families of dead and missing soldiers. On a superficial level it seemed patriotic. But it was just what the enemy in a low intensity war wanted; overestimate the significance of casualties. And most journalists thought that was the way you covered war; on the personal level. They didn't know any better. Journalism schools were teaching the emotional, the superfluous.

Most of the public were satisfied with clichés that military men knew weren't true. Leave No Man Behind emerged during the cynical Nixon administrations' attempt to keep the American public emotionally attached to continued commitment to Vietnam. Americans had become use to being left in possession of the battlefield and being able to recover the fallen. Possession of the battlefield felt like victory. Thus, 'Leave no man behind' was more easily accomplished and cited as a long standing military axiom, which it was not. Leave no man behind was a public position to ease the fears of mothers back home. Special Forces knew that the first priority was the mission. The mission is never put at risk, and recovering a corpse did not justify further casualties.

These colours don't run was a much cheered propaganda slogan but anyone with a view to history knew it wasn't true. The Bladensburg races, the various skid-daddles on both sides during the Civil War, the Chosin 'attack in another direction' and the Mogadishu Mile had shown that. Sometimes it would be militarily irresponsible not to run. From the beginning, General Washington ran to keep the Revolution alive.

Problems came when pronouncements for public consumption are enforced literally on the military. It is disingenuous for politicians to say, 'the decisions are left to the generals', then firing generals in the chain of command until a yes man rises to the top. The situation is not altered. That policy just insures that a political ally, often an incompetent, is placed in charge.

Semantics can be a stumbling block. Acceptable dates are time horizons, milestones or benchmarks for accountability; political opponents' dates mean tipping your hand to terrorists, preaching cut-n-run or surrender or waving the white flag, emboldening the enemy. Never negotiate would not have served the Iranian hostages. All were returned alive because President Carter was willing to face the wrath of American hard liners. Reagan made bold public statements, then negotiated with terrorists and secretly traded arms for hostages; yet hostages were held for years and treated like commodities. Clinton achieved the return of hostages in Yemen in eleven days, from Mogadishu in four days and British commandos freed another from Pakistan. Bush II saw Americans captured and executed due to self-righteous tough talk. Michael had supported the ultras because they seemed tough internationally. Only later he had discovered that that toughness was selfish financial manipulation; political posturing for the folks back home.

Soldiers knew sacrifice. Individuals may violate the rules of war with the understanding that they would have to answer for it. Spies are hung. The mother country would not publically acknowledge such actions or write them into law and hopefully the operatives were intelligent and committed enough to know when to bend the rules; and be willing to suffer the consequences for their country's position of deniability. It boiled down to the old Mission Impossible cliché, 'the Secretary will disavow any knowledge of your actions'. He may be congratulated by some public elements but disavowed by legitimate government officials; and rightly so. A soldier cannot allow his country to be blackmailed emotionally or militarily for his sake. War used up dollars and soldiers. The balance sheet doesn't always result in victory. Soldiers are used up killing and being killed. That's what soldiers were for. No need to be that blunt to moms back home, but policy needs to be clear about the cost/benefit. The wisest strategy is a realistic assessment of the likely outcome; not wishful thinking or the politically acceptable.

Michael was fascinated by the unconventional tactics of General VonRiper in his wargames against the American Middle Eastern Command in 2002. The exercise called 'Millennium Challenge' saw the U.S. team losing 16 ships sunk, in spite of the American high-tech advantage. The American team expected a routine round-up. What they got were uncooperative mustangs. VonRiper was able to assault the American team with more missiles from more locations than the Americans thought possible. Rubber boats, RPGs, independent command authority at the ground level; the data was there but at times fools make policy through rose colored glasses. These were exactly the tactics that the Latin forces were using against the Americans. It is what the American military should have been training to counter; rather than tank battles. Elians' Venezuelans learned what the Americans had not.

This exposed the inadequacy of the Rumsfield Doctrine regardless of the victorious pronouncements from the press office. Special Forces and technology can defeat armies; but they can't defeat a society. Michael, and anybody that paid attention to public information, could see the holes in the policies, but most Americans were just trusting. After all, we are a super-power. Special Forces defeated the Taliban and conquered Afghanistan in 2001. Then the Army profiteers and contractors moved in and made themselves targets.

Another shock in military planning was that there is such a thing as an army being too big for the task. General Powells' doctrine may have made sense in the first gulf war against Saddam, or Monday morning quarterbacking Vietnam, but it did not apply to violent, state-less thugs seeking soft targets. The oversized Military was forced to farm out many logistical duties like food, transport, and supply. This left an army in the field dependent on corporations that measured success by the bottom line. Truck driving contractors did not have to follow orders. Soldiers could not decline a convoy that they felt was too dangerous, contractors did; and soldiers might be left without food, fuel and water. (Or worse, dependent on foreign suppliers for parts, from computer chips to boot laces.)

Real terrorist converts encouraged by U.S. foreign policy, numbered in the millions. With us or against us policy meant, by default, many on the fence were pushed into the enemy camp by definition. 'I don't support you, so by your definition, I'm an enemy.' Even long time European allies took on the mantle proudly in protest of U.S. shortsighted international policy. For an administration devoid of historical understanding, the old socialist tactic had worked beautifully. Through acts of violence, force the government to act repressively until the people reject their own government excesses. George the Second had said, 'Bring it on'. Those oppose to America had brought it on and destroyed the Bush presidency and Americas' reputation. The bastion of liberty in the world became a closed society of fear; isolated from former friends. Even Dubyas' 'Mission Accomplished' could not disguise the truth and return things to normal.

Planners were at a loss to figure out how to prosecute war on an abstract noun; terror. Political insiders thought it was a stroke of genius. All bad effects attributed to the enemy; all good effects attributed to those in power. Almost dictatorial control abdicated by two branches of government. President White as the Commander in Chief was relegated to executive supervisor, while the generals ruled war. As in the old joke 'when all you have is a hammer, everything looks like a nail', every problem seemed to warrant a military response. The congress took their constitutional Advise and Consent role to the extreme. The legislators, that is to say the Ultras veto-proof senate, decided which generals were acceptable. The vague 'War on Evil' was no treat to the military services. They were handed such misjudgments as police duties in Iraq, planned by think tanks full of people with no military experience. Rosy theories rejected accurate analysis. It was wishful thinking, rather than analysis, to support pet projects. Enemies abounded; both overseas and at home. 'Anyone who disagreed with the Ultras empowered the enemy and is therefore an enemy'; akin to a terrorist.

In his overseas assignments, Captain Corbett learned to appreciate American liberties. He spent time in repressive and terrorized societies and was disgusted by the cavalier use of the military by less honorable regimes for political, economic and religious ends. Foreign lands dealt with poverty and destitution unknown to most Americans; and often it was dealt with it brutally. Michael could safely observe; made immune by his American citizenship.

With study and planning there were better ways to apply diplomacy and force. Information was the key and Michael found himself drawn to the data; past, present and projected. At times unbiased analysis was uncannily accurate.

THE FORTUNATE FRACTION

After eight adventurous and exciting years he just wanted to work the home front; the security and tranquility of the States. He would not wear the label 'Chickenhawk'. It was the dues you paid to be able to criticize on international affairs. With his interest in research, Michael transitioned to data management in the civilian world. He went with what he knew and worked research contracts with state and federal government, providing policy makers with the information they needed to make the decisions. His work brought him into contact with many of the power brokers of the Ultra movement.

Michael began his civilian career as a data analyst and knew the messenger of bad news was often expendable. Honest analysis was a threat to some. The political types and the business types found that the data did not always support the policy they wanted, and they had perfected the art of shaping perception. If you brought them bad news, they were as likely to shoot the messenger as change course; especially if it meant keeping the secrets that kept them on the gravy train.

The average Joe believed that hard work and good sense meant success; that being innocent kept you off the farm. Michael knew that only a fraction of the population had any chance at success. He wanted to be in that fortunate fraction; to the point of criminal complicity. But that wasn't the basis of the conspiracy charge. Though illegal and immoral, conspiracy to benefit the fortunate fraction was perfectly acceptable to the Ultras.

Most of the Ultras seemed to harbor the secret of the fortunate fraction with no feelings of guilt, but Michael was not yet that cold. The others lack of remorse struck Michael as more a fear of not being among the fortunate; pure survival. The fear was real and you don't apologize for self-preservation. The Ultras controlled the party, and thus the country, using divide and conquer tactics. Each faction supported the party line in order to insure support for their particular faction. With unlimited funds and media control, a small fortunate fraction of the population ruled; the Ultras.

The Ultra-conservative wing of the Republican Party had stepped further and further to the right until they were just one step away from the philosophy of complete party control at the expense of the individual. With no sense of history, many saw nothing wrong with this view; as long as they were included in the ranks of the favored.

Psychologists had show that normally respectable people would carry out instructions by authority figures, even to the point of morally reprehensible acts. Something as simple as a white lab-coat could convey an aura of authority. Far from being dismayed, the Ultras were encouraged and inspired by the excesses of blatantly unconstitutional activities of former administrations. Shared and convoluted responsibility was hidden in the Machiavellian workings of a veto proof congress, with an impotent president of the opposition party to hold accountable. Opposition was disoriented and silenced.

Through fear, intimidation and character assassination the Ultras ruled. Those who stood in their way were eliminated; politically or legally. Enemies might not be physically harmed, but were just as effectively neutralized; say, with a trumped up conspiracy charge. Those who were an inconvenience to the Ultras had nowhere to turn.

In the early days of America, the frontier beckoned to the disenfranchised, offering them a fresh start. But the pressure valve had closed. From sea to shining sea, every bit of America was now owned by somebody. There was no easy outlet for the unpropertied to move on to undeveloped lands or to migrate for subsistence. The ranks of the homeless and useless multiplied. Vagrancy laws provided the legal justification for arrest to 'Clean up the streets'. In effect, being homeless became a crime. Society accepted the out-of-sight out-of-mind solution. Fear of becoming one of the disenfranchised kept most people in line.

At the end of the 20th Century, a new generation of capitalists found productivity had peaked and markets were saturated. The only remaining way to wring more money out of a business plan was to bluff and deceive customers; or to cut workers benefits and taxes. The Reagan years had bred a culture of selfishness and cut-throat competition; the 'Greed is Good' generation. With every ounce of fluff wrung out of the business models, the new breed of executives sought a way to make the same windfall as their predecessors. The expand or die truism gave way to a new cliché that swept the top tiers of business; Downsizing.

Stories surfaced of CEOs that sold off company assets to boost stock prices and claim a bonus. The problems emerged later. The short term gain meant that they didn't have the equipment they needed to maintain production. Semi-trailers could not be built when the welding equipment had been sold and a skilled workforce pruned. The short term balance sheet showed an influx of cash and savings on labor costs. Only later, after executive bonuses had been paid, did the concerns arise about maintaining production. The only solution was to purchase new equipment at inflated prices, often arranged in sweet-heart deals that further enriched the abusing executives at the expense of the stockholders. It was a shell game that benefited very few; and it guaranteed that the company would crumble.

And mismanagement and executive abuses were not the only dangers. This new breed of capitalists saw it as their mission, not only to manage their organization, but to strangle the competition as well. Success was measured not by being better than the competition, but by being a survivor. Even their own employees were not safe from manipulation. With the fluff gone, the potential profit became the workers benefits and the share that state, local and federal government claimed. The health of the company was not an issue, just the short term personal gain of those at the top. The tactics would provide a gold-plated exit for the executives. As the company collapsed, those not well connected or legally distanced might go to prison. A show trail maybe served up to placate furious workers, pensioners, shareholders, and other trusting souls left bewildered at the paper shuffle that cost them their nest egg. They got the spectacle but they didn't get restitution. The protected members, the Ultras, didn't suffer. The insiders would say it could never happen to them, because it never came up before, but the possibility put a real fear on the faces of the Ultras. 'Never' was a word they never expected to be tested.

The Ultras, a minority in the party, could cobble together enough single issues factions to form a controlling block. They were well funded and were ready to condone any moneyed enterprise. They fought diligently to give business the tools they needed to manage the system, eliminate oversight, control their workers and reap the financial rewards.

As Director of Research, Michael tracked the data and performed targeted searches of vast government databases to synthesis need-to-know information for public officials and to a lesser extent, in edited form, to the public. Senator Dodge was particularly pleased with the competent researcher that could produce a variety of convincing facts to promote the Senators' pet projects. Dodge believed that the Ultras had a use for such a man.

Often the discussions were just word games. The cryptic and strategic sounding euphemism 'force enhancement' replaced surge, which replaced escalation. Surge had played well for George II, but was exposed by the end of his term as just another term for escalation. A new term had to be found. "Ramp up? Resizing? Right sizing!" This was politics and Michaels' function was to fight the public policy war with a computer, solving problems at the state level on the home front. Civilian leadership needed relevant data to exercise proper policy.

"No, that was used for the Saudi police action," the Senator Dodge said dismissively of the suggestion to use the term 'surge' to justify increased troop levels in the Columbian operation.

Previously bad guys were rational, capitalists with motives of self interest. They could be bought or intimidated. Religious and nationalist zealots, using terror tactics, were not inclined to diplomacy. They could not be paid off. Pain and imprisonment were not a deterrent but a recruiting tool. Suicide bombers were unfathomable to most Americans. As the Senator spoke, Michael was taken back to his college days. He remembered a World History professor at college who had told the class of the Aztec game of ball where the 'Losing' team was sacrificed to the gods. The class snickered along with the professor, agreeing, 'that would sure make you play your best'. The problem with the joke was that Michael knew better. In Anthropology he had learned that it was the 'Winning' team that was sacrificed as messengers to the gods. Incomprehensible to an American class, but perfectly understandable to a faith based society where the winners would be given their ticket to heaven. A people so strong in their faith that they wanted to win and be sent to their God as an envoy. Michael held his peace; Americans, even the professor, wouldn't understand. Michaels' Russian Special Forces counterparts would have understood. It made his classmates seem a little less worldly when it came to understanding a fanatical enemy. Yet, the Senator was asking the army to deploy its' soldiers on faith. He could not understand an enemy that did not act rationally.

Nukes or number of boots did not equal intimidation. This was an enemy who would rather blow himself to heaven and take you with him than say uncle. Cultural beliefs must be taken into account, such as interest on loans in the Middle East where interest is an offense to Allah. However, a gift (bribe) is a common method of showing gratitude for a loan. However, bribery could not be accommodated by American style banking laws. American fruit companies in Latin America paid tax to rebel groups, the same as they paid tax to a Junta recognized by the government, but they would run into trouble with government accountants. The American government may call it extortion, which is what it was, but it was not much different than foreign aid paid to tyrants. Michael had handed out hundred dollar bills from black accounts to Special Forces informants overseas. The CIA didn't concern themselves with accountants; just results.

Stateside things were suppose to be different. Michael had become aware of more insidious social structures. Political manipulation that subverted public security. He had an inside look at the priorities. Tax dollars did not return to impoverished areas. While suburban voters, well represented carefully gauged the goods and services that were provided by their tax dollars. Poor neighborhoods had little access to that kind of detailed analysis. Their tax dollars were not returned… period. The only government services they received were police patrols and prison.

A man could try to enlighten his fellow man; to empower the masses; to draw back the curtain and settle for less for the general good. But history showed that that was usually futile. Few voices were able to emerge from the crush of the masses. Those who try may end up as one of the deprived masses, shunned, or worse targeted, by powerful political warriors; and they didn't fight fair. Forget the odds; Michael did not fell that noble.

Ultras controlled no more than 20% of the GOP but they held the reins of power. That was 20% of a party that was composed of about 33% of voters; so, about six or seven percent of the country's voters ran the show. Frightened senior citizens and loyal troops, the devout and the deceived were corralled into a majority. They had little use for the opposition Greens, Socialists, Communists, Democrats or Panthers. Many one issue voters voted against their best interest and remained in poverty due to the Ultras' rosy, but deceptive, public image. The various opposition parties never seemed to master the art of coalition, as many Europeans had.

The fraction was so small that they had to spin a good story to stay in the saddle. People had to be convinced to vote against their own best interest. The defection of a number of voting blocks from the Democratic Party resulted in a Republican majority in most places. The Greens, Socialists, Communists and other small parties siphoned enough votes from the Democratic Party to relegate them to at best a watchdog of the Republican organization. The real political fight devolved to the power struggle in the Republican Party. Though there was disagreement within, they held together to vote as a block securing elective office. The Republican majority was pulled together from a number of interests. Such and such a percent anti-abortion, this much anti-gays, these gun owners and wannabe businessmen. Percentage point by percentage point the Ultras courted voters until they reached the critical mass, 50% plus one, then screw the rest. With the core fiscal conservatives, blind faith converts, big business interests and favorable redistricting, elections were assured.

The Ultras threw off any illusion of restraint. They flew all banners and embraced every factional interest that could insure their majority. To the victors go the spoils became acceptable policy. Old Eisenhower style Republicans with social sensibility were marginalized or intimidated. Democrats and rebel Republican senators and representatives saw their districts deprived of virtually all services and projects and blamed by their constituency for the austerity. Payback was the order of the day. Play ball... or else.

When the party began to subvert the system for the sake of victory, Michael felt that it was not paternalistic politics; it bordered on treason. He didn't agree with the starry-eyed proposals of the Greens, the utopias of the Socialists, the old politics of the Democrats, the anarchy of the Communists or anger of the Panthers, but it would be un-American to just hang them all. He liked the debate; as a researcher demanding, "Prove it". But some Ultra solutions seemed beyond self-serving; they were sociopathic.

The Executive branch had fallen out of favor after the abuses of Bush II. Acceptable judges manned the Supreme Court and the congressional majority held absolute power. Democrats were nothing more than a watchdog; and as events unfolded, not a very effective one. The Ultra congress lorded over an impotent Democratic president. Elected for his soothing, conciliatory attitude, President White was powerless, but a convenient focus for the Ultras scorn and blame. But the White presidency would survive. The Ultras were not interested in impeachment. That would have removed a convenient scapegoat.

Realizing that no Republican could be elected in a heavily Democratic state, a campaign style known as blue-washing emerged. In a number of states, Clay Raven had orchestrated campaigns that gave rise to candidates, progressive in name, but Ultra in democratic clothing.

Senator Richard Chancey was one of these candidates. Financed with Ultra money, he gave a pittance to the environmentalists and ran advertisements applauding his green credentials. He voted consistently with the party on votes where his votes didn't make a difference and abstained on close votes; thus his voting record looked clean. He paid lip service to seniors and blue-collar causes. He spoke in favor of government programs that were popular with workers, then subverted them. The result was the election of an Ultra style conservative Republican in a thoroughly blue state. In order to carry the conservative southern Democrats, independents and cross over voters, presidential candidate White needed to have a running mate for Vice President that would appeal to these constituents. Chancey fit the profile.

It was believed that his background would insure the support of southern and western states. He projected a populous enough media image to earn a wink from the Ultras. He was heavily promoted by Rob Patson, Russ Limpaw, Troy Benedict and other media heavy weights to independent and cross-over voters. He targeted NASCAR fans and promoted himself heavily on country music circuits. The result was, in effect, that President White was cursed from the beginning with an insider from the opposition.

The presidents' cabinet was a stacked deck. The Secretary of Education was intent on dismantling the agency. The Secretary of State didn't believe in diplomacy and the Secretary of Defense was a bully. The FBI engaged in political character assassination and the CIA spied on Americans abroad as enemies. The Secretary of the Interior intended to give out federal resources to political contributors. Agriculture represented industrial farming, and the Secretary of Labor was a union buster. The Department of Energy was headed by a petro-chemical lobbyist and Veterans Affairs was a cost cutter; which meant service cuts. Health and Human Services represented the pharmaceutical and insurance industry intent on siphoning off government money. Housing and Urban Development paid a hefty salary to a horse breeder who was an

Ultra fund raiser; hired to do nothing. The UN representative was determined to subvert international treaties and frustrate efforts at global regulation. Ambassadors were a collection of well connected tourists living in U.S. facilities on the taxpayers' dime. They were routinely ignored by foreign powers as ineffective and Americans abroad as unresponsive, except for Ultra internationalists; many of whom had escaped to overseas locations to avoid American taxes or prosecution.

Michael felt sorry for President White, burdened with problems not of his making. He took the blame and the electorates' fury at the lack of results. But Michael was powerless. He was a lowly state worker. Many voters viewed politics as a sporting event. Even when the party subverted the system and their interests, they remained faithful to the team. The President was left with the tough and painful decisions resulting from the abuse of the prior moneyed interest policies. Some thought the Ultra money-lenders had intentionally lost the election, so that the opposition party would be responsible for the unpopular choices necessary to repair the damage they had done.

Vice-President Chancey was added to the ticket to appease the conservative southern democrats and had become the power behind the throne. In backroom deals he had inserted himself into every aspect of the administration. It was an open secret that he was an Ultra mole whispering poison in the Presidents' ear. His ambition to 'come to the rescue' when the president failed, led him to actively conspire to bring about that failure. The Ultra long range goal might even include impeachment to bring it about. But they were in no hurry to accept the responsibility of the Presidency. The last thing they wanted was to be held responsible. President White seemed so desperate to be accepted by the people that, it was thought, he might even step down rather than fight impeachment if the time came.

Michael was the states hired gun when it came to research. The Legislature wanted to find ways to save money. Michael spearheaded the study that showed that combining administrative duties of state activities, with emerging information technology, would cut costs. Some jobs were lost, but Michael didn't feel guilty. This was just the cold efficiency of statistics. He prepared briefs that proved the benefits of prison transition programs and was frustrated that the same common sense solutions were not applied to prisoners returning to society. It wasn't politically acceptable; no matter what the numbers said. At least he had given the elected leaders an honest analysis. Wind and Solar energy projects that he conducted for the Department of Energy showed promise, but it was contrary to the interests of the Oil lobby in the party and was scrapped. This was more inexcusable in Michaels' view, as not in the interest of most people. It would have been politically acceptable if people understood.

The Ultras gave self-fulfilling prophecy a whole new meaning. It was amazing the way they spun out prophecies. Then with slick media saturation and deep pockets they made them happen; sanctimoniously proclaiming their own wisdom and foresight.

A chicken in every pot! A working stiff got a chicken; Mike got a Lexus. The oversimplified tag line worked. 'Money In Your Pocket for every taxpayer'. The railroad worker with a couple of kids got ten bucks; Michael got a pair of jet skies.

Public information requests from the Ultras gave Michael a view of outright abuse of his statistics. It was not just using the most favorable slant to satisfy friendly factions. It was abuse. 'How much welfare money is spent on cigarettes and alcohol?' A reasonable question. The answer, 'negligible. Very low and strictly monitored.' But the Ultras wanted to hear 'Big Bucks' to justify cutting entitlement programs. When it didn't materialize, they created the abuse argument anyway

The rhetoric would be sculpted as 'So many thooosannnds of dollars to justify righteously cutting another three percent, dooming another three percent of children to malnutrition. Even fiscal conservatives, like Michael, were not that cold, but it meant another pile of chips for a select few Ultras and the illusion of fiscal responsibility. Non-disclosure pledges kept Michael from passing the correct analysis on to those who monitored government actions in defense of the helpless.

The Ultras back home partied in white tie and tails. Michael attended as a useful tag-along. The Ultras were dangling membership to the fortunate fraction to the useful few. The Governors' mansion was filled to capacity by the insider crowd that felt compelled to attend such events. State officials mingled with the National representatives, lobbyists and party faithful. Michael was invited as the representative of the State Research Office.

Clay Raven, the almost mythical political power broker of the Ultras, was there.

Radio guru Russ Limpaw provided a media presence. Russ started out as a routine shock-jock, exaggerating news items for comic effect. When his following grow, he continued exaggerating, but presented himself as a legitimate journalist. Entertaining? Yes. Trusted with public policy? No.

Limpaw escorted the new Ultra self-appointed morality cop; Sarah Colt. Sarahs' claim to fame was the inspiration of putting frightening, but basically irrelevant, ballot initiatives on states ballots to bring out the votes during national elections. One gay rights item and the morally offended would turn out in droves. Keep gays from recruiting our kids initiative! Parent-phobia was a powerful tool. She called it family values, but it was party posturing. Actions were shuffled to the bottom of the deck after the election.

Sarah was busy flirting with various power-brokers, as she was between commitments just then. She had a habit of jutting out her front teeth. Somebody probably told her as a child that it looked cute and she just kept it up. She prided herself on being anti-abortion, anti-gay, anti-government, anti-most everything. She captured the cynical comic format of exaggerating for effect, but she took herself seriously. And her fans were just uninformed enough to take her exaggerations as fact. Her one man/one women diatribe was whisperingly referred to as serial monogamy. She was well known as one man (at-a-time) Sarah.

Women were increasingly breaking through the glass ceiling and, since Sarah had made it, she was determined to see that other women would not. That would make her all the more special. Her anti-feminist attitude seemed to indicate that she wanted to cut down the ladder so that she could stand out as an achiever in spite of, not because of, her gender. She could not claim to have advanced on her own merit, as long as the affirmative action program that she had used was in effect. The good-ol-boys claimed that her 'merit' had more to do with entirely feminine features. Behind her back, the attention of the good 'ol boys had more to do with cleavage than cleverness.

She was the newest of the Ultras' favorite cute-face-on-a-bad-cause defenders. She was paid backdoor by mass book sales to organizational supporters. Her last book 'Government Waste' sold 250,015 copies to 16 buyers; fifteen to individuals and 250,000 to an Ultra organization proxy. There was never even an indication that they had been delivered; just paid for. It provided a legal payoff and allowed them to book her on talk shows as a 'best selling' author.

Michael made sure to steer clear of that train wreck.

The conversations centered around policy. In particular, food stamp cuts and childrens' immunization. The talking points were being driven home, giving exactly the wrong perception of the issues being discussed.

Michael was forced to remove his copy of 'How to Lie with Statistics', the classic research tool by Darrell Huff, from his work area in his state research office. The management thought it projected a bad attitude. Researchers knew it was an invaluable reference guide on how to avoid mistakes; and how to detect errors when conducting peer review. A less than honorable person could use it to mislead, but why would a reputable research person do that and sacrifice his reputation? The Ultras would give him the answer; money. Professional researchers were expected to value their integrity. That was how you got jobs and research grants. But the Ultras demanded no such pledge as long as you followed instructions and remained loyal to the cause. Michael tried to fit in but the discussions seemed at best naive, at worst self-deceptive. They fiddled while Rome burned.

Senator Dodge, with whom Michael had worked in his capacity as a state research analyst, was discussing policy with Clay Raven, the Ultras political heavyweight.

"Inoculations for every child will bust the national health care budget wide open," Raven declared.

"So," the Senator said cautiously, "How do we argue against sick kids?"

"I understand there is a risk to the inoculations." Raven replied.

The Senator understood where that was going, "We insist on an opt-out clause while spreading around the worst case stories."

"Or, opt-in with a gag order to keep government data secure," Raven added. "We get sued, we settle and seal the case record."

"What were the figures Mikey?" Dodge turned to Michael a few feet away.

Michael was not part of the discussion, and didn't want to be, but felt obliged to answer. "About 3 per 1000 adverse reactions."

"There you see," Raven said triumphantly, "on a scale of millions of kids nationwide, we can say thousands of kids will get sick due to forced medical programs..."

"Socialized medicine," Dodge added triumphantly.

"Medical experimentation," Raven refined the threatening aspect.

"So be it," Dodge proclaimed.

"But, Sir," the Senator seemed surprised at Michaels' interruption. After all Dodge had said, 'So-be-it'. That was supposed to end any further discussion.

Michael continued, "about 50 per 1,000 will fall ill if the vaccine is not used, many will develop lifelong disabilities," he couldn't imagine a public servant would save six cents in preventive care and, allow a child to go blind; telling him to fend for himself. Wouldn't the cost of doing nothing be far higher? Unless they planned to dodge that expense down the road. Michael had seen the cost comparisons. "And adverse reactions to inoculation were medically irrelevant. Mostly, a minor fever for a few days."

Raven scowled; Dodge looked befuddled. This information was not welcome. Raven would have preferred to say that, neither he nor the Senator, were aware if asked by a congressional committee. Both walked away continuing their discussion out of earshot of the annoying bean counter.

As a reputable researcher, Michael grew tired of the policy maneuvering that distorted the relevant facts. He walked alone out into the well maintained garden and sat on the marble bench with his head in his hands. "How long can I keep up this charade?" he asked himself.

A gentle hand came to rest on his shoulder. "Problems?" a soft voice asked.

Before he remembered his party loyalty, he spurted it out, "Children will suffer."

"An Ultra with a conscience?" The question was sincere, not cynical. The young, blond womans' green eyes flashed an honest concern. "You 'bout to lose some of your Ultra privileges?" she gently joked, her features softening but remaining a little judgmental.

"Not me. Comes a time when you don't worry about yourself. You're free to think about other people." Michael wondered if he was being too honest. He fell back on a worn out Ultra speaking point, "Compassion is our prime concern."

"No, it ain't," the girls' eyes were again sparkling, but with amusement and heresy.

Michael was stunned by the candor. The Ultras' throw-away lines were a standard defense when a statement was questioned and a quick safe answer was needed. Nobody was rude, or honest, enough to doubt the basic premise. "Debutantes shouldn't talk like that. Especially at an event like this," Michael said.

"Then I must be the other type," she seemed to be reading Michaels' mind. The gala parties were attended by the emerging aristocracy, the political debutants and an assortment of trophy wives and gold-digging girlfriends. "Window dressing? Arm candy?" she asked.

"No !" that was exactly what Michael was thinking.

"From the fat cats point of view, those girls are toys. From the girls' point of view, they're Cinderella." She sat beside him, her lovely voice falling like musical tones in spite of the party blasphemy she so easily voiced. "Cinderellas' ugly sisters went to the Ball too. You suppose they got any action?"

Michael couldn't help by smile. She was natural, honest, perceptive.

"Whatever you Ultras think of yourselves, you're not all princes."

"I'm far from a prince. Not even really an Ultra. Just a staffer; a number cruncher. I don't get to think." It felt good to share an unguarded opinion; to speak honestly seemed a relief.

"Well, they haven't killed your conscience yet," she said.

"And you're no stereotype. You talk like you don't belong here," he answered.

"My daddy's the gardener. He probably grew that carnation you're wearing."

"I'm Michael."

"Suzanne."

"You want to have some coffee?"

She smiled and offered her hand.

Suzanne was neither debutant nor window dressing. Her father was invited to the event by the Governor as a courtesy for years of faithful service. He had started out as the capitol grounds keeper some thirty years before. He had risen to management by nature of his seniority but he still preferred to get his hands dirty. He had brought his daughter to the event to give her a taste of the formal functions, but her education and upbringing was strictly blue collar. She was more amused than star-struck. Her candid conversation was refreshing after all the Ultra double speak that rattled Michaels' reasoned researcher mind.

Those that mistook her for a trophy wife or window dressing in a policy debate often found themselves seriously outmatched. She was well informed and fearless in defending her position; more than likely in defense of the disenfranchised as oppose to the Ultras. Michael would have been in serious trouble with the Ultras for expressing such views, but Suzanne was seen as just a beautiful, if misguided, mere woman. Most Ultras weren't prepared to debate a well informed women with an opinion; especially a pretty one.

Suzanne would become the breath of reason in Michaels' life when the power brokers began to infiltrate every aspect of state and federal government.

THE ULTRA CAUSE

Michael worked for the state, producing accurate technical reports on a number of issues. His unbiased and accurate reporting brought him promotion in state service and the attention of the Ultra policy makers. When questions came up regarding criminal justice, entitlement programs, food stamps, labor statistics, Michael became the go-to guy for data. He did his best to be an honest broker of the data used by various factions that depended on statistical information. Policy was left to others; that was not his job. At the time his greatest fear was that he would not be accepted as part of the Fortunate Fraction. Occasionally, the data was misconstrued; accidentally or intentionally. That wasn't his responsibility. He kept his detached professional distance and earned a reputation as a solid source for even obscure data and astute analysis. He felt fortunate to be in a favored group and his fear of falling into poverty subsided. But some day the unfortunate masses might find out that the game was stacked. Then the Ultras would have Hell to pay.

Michael served the state faithfully until research contracts began to dry up with budget cuts. He had a ringside seat to how his own job was cut. The budget hawks declared the fiscal waste of paying a state worker $50,000 to collect data. Michael knew the data collected was eagerly sought by industry to plan building projects, bring in five million dollars to state transportation and construction projects. The budget cutters would save fifty grand on his salary but it would cost the state over one-hundred and fifty $30,000 family wage jobs. The workers would blame the state, blame the company, blame their own bad luck, but Michael knew the real culprits. Little did the unemployed construction worker know, as he applauded the fat being cut from state government, that the lack of the state income from that cut had cost him his job. Michael couldn't speak up about it because of confidentiality agreements and speaking up would constitute lobbying; something he was not entitled to do.

With little prospect of continued state service, Michael looked to the private sector for employment. The Ultras were interested. He was an experienced computer analyst with experience in Government data sources. Furthermore, he had a 'Secret' security clearance conducted by the military during his Army days. The Ultras could pay up to six figures to get that kind of background check on a potential employee for a sensitive position. Michaels' background had already saved them money. Further, he was white, well-dressed, presumably Christian; not a practicing Jew or a professed Moslem or anything.

Senator Dodge had served several terms and had loyal support for his pro-business, tough-on-crime, support-our-boy-in-uniform, guns, Christ and cash stance (whatever the topic under discussion, one of those would solve it). Prompt and accurate data from the data analysis section had brought Michael to the attention of the Senator. The Senator made him an offer he couldn't refuse; a staff job funded by the Ultra wing of the party to aid the Senator.

He was placed on the staff of the loyal Senator Dodge; paid by the party to do the Senators' bidding, therefore, not responsible to the public. The position included a plush Washington D.C. apartment, also covered by the Ultras. The house on the west coast, bought during his state service with honest money, remained the family residence. Thus he had a Washington and state home to be available for the Senators' projects.

Michael was even assigned an ambitious research assistant; Chip Libby. Chip had caught the eye of the Ultras' for his work on opposition research as a grad student. He had gained experience on state projects. He was a competent researcher but a little too pliable for Michaels' taste. He was willing to spin the twisted logic of the Ultra organization as long as he could get a foot in the door. This struck Michael as not entirely scientific, albeit reliable, by Ultra standards.

Chip was hired by the Ultras to assist Senator Dodge. Another data analyst had made it into the ranks of the Ultras as a member of Michaels' team of number-crunchers, but his sympathies were purely political; to the point of data manipulation. Michael hated it; the Senator loved it. On paper, Chip worked for Michael, but he was in the Senators' pocket.

As an insider, Michael was able to spend a few hours with the Ultras' wealth management guru, Thomas Hamilton. He learned the insiders' method of a marginally legal method to distribute assets. Retirees, using the Hamilton system, signed over businesses to the next generation without contributing to the tax base. Grandpas' house was signed off and rented back to him at the cost of his Social Security payments. The family corporation held the mortgage as an expense. The mortgage payments became deductions. Food and clothing become the responsibility of his sons and he became a dependent on their taxes.

Family business were advised to stop paying relatives; income zero. Social Security and Medicaid contribution; zero. The funds in the family cookie jar stayed in the family. Henry R. Parrots' mulit-billion dollar USA stores paid him a hundred bucks. Thus, the government imposed ten percent, his tithe, ten bucks.

Feeling that he had secure employment and having fallen unmistakably in love with Suzanne, Michael proposed and she accepted without hesitation. As a wedding gift, Michael gave Suzanne a secluded acre on Black Lake outside the city. Their hide-a-way was a long range project.

It would be fortunate that they had the house at Black Lake recorded under Suzannes' maiden name before their marriage. Michael was already involved in the property distribution plan developed by Mr. Hamilton, the Ultra wealth protection advisor. But 'the Homestead', as they called it, was apart from all the Ultra manipulation. It was immune from the financial web that the Ultras used to ensnare their faithful; the chains that insured loyalty.

Often they would host Suzannes' parents. James loved giving his opinion on landscaping and gardening and Ruth gloried in the kitchen. Suzanne seemed to know every tree and animal

In his new job as an Ultra technical, Michael found out very quickly that he could crunch the numbers but the interpretation was to be left to the spin doctors. And inconvenient numbers might be ignored altogether.

Michael could usually sit quietly in the policy and strategy sessions and jot down notes. He was expected to know what studies and reports were needed and if the information was available. He was not there for opinion; though at times he was called upon to interpret tables, graphs or percentages. Math was not the Senators' strong suit.

"We need black faces on stage. Maybe a Spanish accent. Find a black and a Latino that got a job. Somebody to praise and endorse the Right to Work statute," Dodge said.

"That'll be tough," Michael answered. The room burst into laughter. Michael didn't intend it to be a joke. He knew most of the low wage and part time jobs filled by minorities under the statute were a way for employers to dodge full pay and benefits and the workers were not happy about it. Most felt like forced labor. Everyone in the room knew that the 'Right to Work' was not in the interest of workers. To avoid benefits for full time workers, employers hired twice the people at half the hours. In this way they shed the inconvenience and expense of workers benefits.

Dodge glared at him. "I mean," Michael continued, "we can look at summary data and talk percentages, but we can't take a name out of the hat without violating confidentiality. Those government sources are protected information. Now if we have a volunteer that will give us permission to use his name…"

"Do we have fan mail?" Chip asked. "Find a thank you letter and follow-up?"

"Yah," Michael agreed. "If someone has contacted us, we can respond… and ask permission."

"Hispanic is easy, but how do we find a 'Black' name?" Dodge wondered.

"Location," Chip suggested. 'That may be marginally legal,' Michael thought, 'let Chip stick his neck out on this one.'

Chip was in charge of the Three-P project; the Perpetual Party Project. The project was divided into three major thrusts; enemy voter suppression, enemy disruption and enemy outing (more accurately called - Character Assassination). It was guerilla warfare, short of violence.

"Okay, look into it Chip," answered Dodge. Michael was relieved that this wasn't on his plate.

"Now about those precincts that might be trouble," Dodge turned to election politics.

"We have the edge on crime," Chip studied the charts.

"Any sex offenders released in the 24th?" the Senator needed a winning issue; one that wouldn't upset the status quo. "That will scare up some votes." Chip and the Senator laughed at the innuendo; Michael could not. The same fear tactics and tired joke emerged during every election cycle.

"There's always somebody being released." Chip said thoughtfully. "That's too common. We need a re-offender. The revolving door issue. You know, Willie Horton stuff."

The Senator studied the sheet of statistics that he would mine to victory, "So the rural 17th district will climb aboard with the gun issue. The fear factor is a net gain. We should gain 21% and loose maybe six or seven percent; crime victims and such."

"Right, sir," Chip confirmed, "Columbine and Virginia Tech. are a wash. Some want to limit guns; as many want to arm themselves... a wash. "

"The Urban 21st?" the congressmen asked about the more affluent section.

"No go boss," Chip shook his head, "gain eleven or twelve and we will lose about eighteen percent."

The Senator looked glum.

"But sir," Chip said, "If we play religion and the flag in the cities, go noncommittal on abortion, the urban precincts will show a 21% gain with a 17% loss to labor and liberals, and that is a big demographic. That's a big slice of the demographic pie. Four percent of those far outnumber ten percent of ex-hippies and Jews. We're going to lose most of them anyway."

"But can I afford to lose 10% of the Jewish vote?" the Senator looked doubtful.

"Sir, there's a high per capita church attendance. Not like L.A. or Chicago. We can take it with the religion. And the military base on the outskirts we can bring over on the flag flap." Michael still thought of victory in the best interest of all in spite of the manipulation of voter fears and emotions. Chip was pure strategy for victory, "All they want is a freeway ramp... Play to labor on AM radio. Urban sprawl in the suburbs. In fact we don't want a ramp, but after the election we can watch it die; blame the anti-growth crowd; call 'em tree-huggers."

"How do I court the Blacks?" the Senator asked.

"They're fightin' the wars and fillin' the prisons," Chip said coldly, "They're not going to vote for you in any case. Write them off. Best not to stir 'em up. Our best chance is to have them sit it out. Save your money." Michael was shocked that his protégé had developed such a cold attitude. "Maybe some suppression tactics, at best."

"Screw 'em," the Senator said venomously, "once we're in ethnics and rednecks don't matter."

Michael held his peace. Was this what it meant to be an insider? He was ashamed.

"We serve those who support me... and just the ones that have paid their dues get a seat at the table. Like Cheney said 'to the victor go the spoils' the Senator quoted ex-Vice President Chaney. The Ultras had disavowed this former Vice-President of an unpopular war, though they took his actions to heart. People reconsidered just who supported the military and who the spoilers were. The issue had become a loser. Many of the worst offenders of the former administration had fled into the ranks of the Ultras. "As far as opposition, we'll let 'em sit it out. Then bust their union and present ourselves as the good guys. Uniters, not dividers," the Senator joked mimicking the former President Bush, "...then divide and conquer."

Michael was shocked to hear a peoples' representative refer to political victory as conquering. Michael had naively believed that the best ideas would triumph. "Blame anti-labor union bosses... more money 'In your pocket'. The unemployed won't matter... sounds open and shut to me," the Senator continued.

Michael knew they were talking lost jobs. Taxpayers' money to maintain infrastructure, good for small business, was diverted; secreted in corporate accounts in the Cayman Islands out of reach of the tax man. The cost, just a few thousand in political contributions. The cold calculation of research crashed. This wasn't just feeding the people statistics and letting them misunderstand. This was pure manipulation, against the common good. Even against the good of the fortunate fraction that greedily sought every little favor. They wouldn't know until it was too late. And by dangling admittance to the elite, many would continue to cut their own economic throats; the lottery mentality gone political. Michael had never played the Lottery. The bean counters had a definition for the LOTTO. They called it a tax on the mathematically challenged. It didn't work unless the state won most of the time, minus advertising costs and a few lucky stiffs. Most people had to lose, most of the time.

"How about the military base? Can we draw on patriotism? You know support our troops?" Michael tried to change the subject.

"No, sir," Chip was ready with the numbers. "Focus groups show that, with extended tours and stop-loss, it sounds like 'stay the course' and that don't sell. Too many small businesses in the district are losing ground with the loss of GI dollars."

"And the loss of GIs!" Michael contributed.

Both the Senator and Chip looked irritated at the interruption. "Anyway, with a large Hispanic population, they ain't too happy about having troops in Latin America. 'Support our troops' has run its' course. Best not to remind people that there's a war on. At best, some supportive generals, or veterans caps in the background for photo-ops." Chip restated the party plan. "Maybe Shared-care. We promote day care co-ops on military bases. It don't cost us anything, and sells like supporting military families."

"Make military wives our foot soldiers, huh?" Dodge agreed, "I like it."

Chip turned back to the subject of winning demographics. "Maybe crime. People are still scared. But the 22nd... police statistics show most the crime is in decline. Embarrassing if the opposition calls our bluff... and they would."

The Senator resumed, "We'll get some military just on tradition, but we don't need to cater to them. Just wave the flag once in a while, talk about how brave they are, and how the opposition cheapens their sacrifice; emboldens our enemies."

"Go for churchgoers. That's the growth demographic." Chip summed up the statistics, "People get desperate, they pray."

"At least prayer don't cost anything." The Senator was not convinced. "Give moral support to church schools then bad-mouthing public education? It's cheap... changing sides is political suicide. We won't pay a price for ignoring the ones that don't vote."

"But Sir," Michael added, "The teachers unions are powerful and students tend to back their teachers rather than their penny-pinching parents in these things. We can't beat the kids-talkin-on-TV appeal."

"Okay, Okay," Chip conceded, "Write off the teachers; hope they sit it out. We can go with corrupt labor bosses and religion at best..." He thought for a moment, then added, "aversion to the fag factor plays well everywhere."

"And we can talk about the gays for the redneck vote," Dodge added.

The Ultras talked incessantly about the 'Gay agenda'. Focus groups had shown that macho thinking men just didn't want to hear about it; called 'the ick factor'. The Ultras used this aversion to proclaim, far too often, that they were on the side of the Ick. For some reason the same macho men didn't blame the Ultras for constantly bringing up the subject that made them so uncomfortable.

Michael didn't care how people decided to form families. He was surprised it was even an issue. The opposition could have easily brought up the fact that, if the Ultras were truly interested in the sanctity of the family, they might suggest outlawing divorce.

That would not have set well with a number of Ultras who were on to their second or third trophy wives.

Chip added an afterthought, "and as always, No New Taxes."

"So Be It!" Dodge pronounced. It was the closest thing Michael had ever heard to an imperial pronouncement; even among the conceded third-world autocrats during his Foreign Service days. Dodge loved to use it. It struck a chord with his devote core supporters; and made him sound infallible. But Michael came to hear those words associated with less noble motives; actually quite sinister motives, and it had lost its' mystical appeal.

Even at his most self-serving, Michael had not used such cold political factionalism. His attitude was changing and he realized for the first time that this was not his party. They would cut him loose in a heartbeat if it served their purpose. Chip and the Senator seemed to interpret his thoughtful silence, his lack of enthusiasm, as noncompliance. He felt the burden of suspicion descending on his head.

He continued to put in his time, escaping whenever possible to the Homestead on Black Lake. The money was good and it was more than Michael and Suzanne needed. They were content with each other and their rustic get-away. Michael was still called away as lead data analyst to attend policy and strategy sessions for the party.

With the proper investments he figured on semi-retirement to teach at a local school, or write about past history. The Ultras were a means to an end. He could live by modest means and leave it behind after a few hectic, high-pressure years. The chance would never come.

His new job gave him access to the hierarchy of the Ultra organization. He would finally make a presentation to the powerful Clay Raven; the Ultra party's powerful behind the scene guru. Michael hoped he didn't remember the impertinent upstart that had intruded on a conversation at the Governors' gala.

"The data indicates that we should settle." Michael had the actuarial tables in hand. This was his chance to present his research in a real dollars and cents solution to an annoying law suit. The Ultras had legally assaulted a local family business that was impeding one of their pet projects. The Ultras' attempt to evict the small business for a massive development was stalled by a court ruling against a party contributor. 'Legislating from the bench' or 'Activist Judges," is what the Ultras called it. That is how they charged any judge that ruled against them. Appeal would be expensive but the developers could afford it. The small businessman would be driven to bankruptcy before the claim could wind its' way through the legal system.

The cold hard facts indicated that the mom-n-pop operation had reduced their demands to a modest $40,000; just lost business and legal fees. And the law was in their favor. The unacceptable element was that they would be able to keep their business. The location was astride the location selected by the developer for a grand retail conglomerate. "Forty grand is small change compared to the costs of...," Michael hesitated. It had suddenly occurred to him that what he was saying may be interpreted as insulting to the legal staff. "... of continuing our legal challenge." He glanced at Clay Raven at the end of the table. Raven seemed a little amused but not offended. This was his first confidential meeting with the legendary power broker and Michael had hoped to make a strong impression.

"You see this man?" Senator Dodge asked indicating Raven. "He is feared by half the civilized world... And the other half have him on retainer. Paying him seven figures to demolish some petty storefront business means we don't have to face ten more in court. Hell ! A hundred more. They just drop their suit and bow out with some shred of their investment rather than risk a showdown. They want to fight; we'll keep 'em tied up in court for the rest of their lives. The big picture, boy. It's power." Dodge spoke low and firm, "And Mikey, just the numbers. No editorial."

Michael felt suddenly small. He had the numbers; cold hard facts. And that led him to a conclusion, an 'opinion', that they should settle. Mom-n-Pop were within their legal rights; but now he realized, that didn't matter. He had stepped beyond his role as a mere number-cruncher. In the future he would stick to the facts and leave the opinions to others.

Michaels' research assistant, Chip Libby, was next to take the stage.

Talking with cold blooded efficiency, Chip bluntly outlined his voter suppression strategy. If high enemy votes, don't antagonize. Let 'em sit home. Most don't pay attention to national; most are locally complacent unless provoked. Use abortion and gays in the Bible belt, flag burning in military communities, gun control in the rural West, immigration in the border areas, crime in the suburbs. It was a potent collection of anti-causes. Let urban areas rest in peace. Rule out labor, environment, civil rights. His game plan for voter suppression had become the Ultras' play book. Opposition elements were referred to as 'enemies'. Those disagreeable voters were jokingly called 'enemy' footsoldiers or lieutenants, depending on their status. The joke appeared in the Ultras' internal play books and soon the joke lost its' humor but the label remained. It made Michael uncomfortable, but Chip was entirely onboard. Michael had the sneaking suspicion that his ambitious assistant was being groomed for his job. They either had something in mind for Michael; or planned to cut him loose. A former worker that was no longer needed could also serve a purpose, even if it was just a head for the chopping block. With the Ultras it was hard to tell.

Chip continued his presentation with a status report on the Commando Project. Chip coordinated this strategy with the radio star, Russ Limpaw, to form what they called rally squads. The shock jock presented himself as a man of the people; an everyday Joe with solid gold bathroom fixtures. Limpaw gave his listeners the impressive sounding name 'Ultra Commandos'. Limpaw and Chip devised a grass roots organization of the frustrated and misinformed. Unofficial radio fans, at first, identified themselves as Limpaws' Commandos. Chip made it official by launching a sign-up campaign to collect names. Fan clubs became chapters of the national organization. The commandos were encouraged to apply for jobs at all levels of police organizations where they could do the party some good. Fans in the armed services were enthusiastically recruited. It all sounded too militant for Michaels' taste. He couldn't imagine an army that someone didn't intend to use.

The Ultra Commandos were flattered with uniforms, badges of rank, mass produced certificates, unit flags and citations and a feeling of belonging. Social events were staged to build the bond of friendship and commitment. They fancied themselves soldiers of a sort and boasted membership in an elite organization. They adopted the term 'commandos' as an indication of military proficiency; and Ultra meant the best of the best. Actually, they were just being used; but it made them feel useful.

Recruiting went on across the country, with efforts in the deep south and rural west the most successful. In military style summer camps, they met and trained in camouflaged fatigues. Prominent Ultra guest speakers congratulated the troops, condemned the government and courted their votes. Whenever a show of support was needed, Limpaw could summon a devoted crowd to intimidate the opposition.

Chip instituted an intelligence division that could stage events and track opposition leaders. A more militant wing could be called on to disrupt opposition events. Supposedly, the Ultras did not condone violence, but some of the devotees, as expected, went beyond their instructions. The Ultras actually counted on these renegades to intimidate the enemy. The official party could wash their hands and avoid responsibility.

Chips' methods provided much more satisfying results for the Ultras. Precincts with high percentage of enemy votes were left to simmer or pelted with negative ads about the opposition. 'Don't talk issues when your stand is contrary to the majority; talk dirt,' was one of Ravens' tenants. 'In the Bible belt show disgust with intellectuals. Contest all counts in enemy precincts to create the illusion of fraud, even if there is none. Decry criminal records of enemy voters. Tell the military they are being left out. Obstruct enemy get-out-the-vote efforts. Hijack their computers and jam their phone banks.' The whole process was targeted to divide and conquer; picking up that extra few percentage points from each interest group to get to 50.1% and screw the rest.

The prevailing Ultra attitude was, 'Everyone wants what I got, and there ain't enough to go around'. Those that hoped to join the ranks of the Fortunate Fraction nurtured an appropriately cold-blooded attitude; until they found themselves on the enemies list.

Michael could see the unwelcome warning signs of a backlash. Danger signs were building. The safety net was in shreds. People were prepared to turn to crime to feed their kids. A families net worth included depreciating home values that were heavily in debt through home equity scams. It would come back to haunt the Ultra speculators if home prices took a dive. Chip saw it as an opportunity to buy cheap from overextended widows. Ultras asked, in more diplomatically acceptable terms, "are there no poorhouses, are there no workhouses?" Then they would propose cutting the programs that provided any relief. Should a critical mass of voters uncover the game, the perpetrators would be in serious trouble. And Corbett couldn't profess complete innocence.

THE 13 STATES RIGHTS

Gravity, cloud condensation, evolution, rainbows and other such scientific phenomena are explained in theory and are proven fact by the test of time and the weight of evidence. The Ultras financed some targeted science, intending to prove a particular point. Usually, the inevitable unknown element in any scientific experiment was enough for the Ultras to exploit. They had some scientists on the staff; in their pocket. Though peer review found them flawed, it gave them an egg-head to send on the talk shows to sow doubt and give the illusion of two sided debate that could stall inconvenient legislation.

The warped logic could contend that it was just a theory that the earth revolves around the sun. To anyone standing on the earth, the sun appears to revolve. Even that generally trustworthy human sense of sight, might be deceived. Science-wise, it was as though for every round-earth, liberal, radical the media had to provide a chair to an Ultra flat-earther or be accused of bias. Ultras usually avoided science. You couldn't as easily refute physics. A policy could be twisted to sound reasonable; debatable. If one of those reasons is 'the good book says so' than faith could inoculate many to logic.

A generation had evolved that was raised on TV plot twists that presented illogical thinking as scientific fact to establish the premise for some movie setting. Modern Sci-Fi, originally the extrapolation of scientific truths, no longer followed the logical scientific method that was drummed into Michaels' head in his research career. The fantasies fell apart under real scientific scrutiny. Science fiction and fantasy were treated as synonymous. When he pointed this out, he was viewed as a spoiled sport or unimaginative by those that wanted, so badly, to believe. The miracle of flight was invented by realists who knew science, not mystics who knew the right incantation. Unassisted human flight was impossible, no matter how hard you flapped your arms. Physics proved it.

Fear of nukes was fostered by a sci-fi educated public that did not understand real science. Maybe the Ultras believed it themselves. Maybe they just took advantage of the misperception. They did nothing to clarify it. In any case it worked. Fearful people voted for them in droves. Nuclear power continued to be perceived as the mushroom cloud of cold-war days. A nuclear accident might have made a few acres unlivable for the foreseeable future, but it didn't mean tens of thousands of dead in a flash. It meant limited evacuation and decontamination. Three Mile Island; not Hiroshima.

The science debate for the Ultras centered around the financial. In effect, delaying the cost of countering global warming so that the fortunate fraction could afford respirators. They would have made their money before the general public knew the cost of doing nothing.

The medical debate followed the same flawed logic. Senator Dodge chaired the hearing on a proposal to inoculate the nations' children against a particularly virulent form of flu. The program would divert the pharmaceutical industry from producing more profitable drugs. The Ultras intended to shoot down the proposal, or at least get it suspended in endless debate. Doctor VonDaniken, representing the Association of Pediatricians, had the evidence and was making a shambles of the Ultra pseudo-science. This was near treason in the eyes of Dodge and the Ultras. They had supported VonDaniken with funding and prestige to sing their sheet of music. And he was conceding that the opposition was credible.

Dodge attempted to end the discussion in the senate hearing with the cliché comment that usually provided the end note of an impasse, "I guess reasonable people can disagree on that point." That tactic would usually end policy discussions; a roadblock that indicated an impasse. This was a signal to Ultra allies that the subject was to be presented as debatable; whether it was or not.

The Doctor looked perplexed and slowly said through his bewilderment, "No... "Michael had to stifle a laugh. Dodge was speechless.

The Doctor had guts; and the facts on his side. It was indisputable. If the Senator wished to spin a story that was not supported by the science, the Doctor was not going to allow it equal weight with the truth. Dodge looked surprised that the Doctor did not take the bait. It was as though he was being told he could have an opinion. He was entitled to an opinion; he was not entitled to disregard the facts. The Doctor didn't let it drop as so many of Dodges colleagues did on policy issues that were not as scientifically black-n-white. The Senator was wrong. His line of reasoning was not logical and the scientific community was not going to accept a political rationale that was blatantly wrong.

"Instead of a few minor fevers, we would have hundreds of children go blind," the Doctor stuck to his guns. Dodge cut off discussion and the panel was adjourned. This issue was a loser. The bill passed, though the Ultras continued to complain about big-government and medical experiments (not to mention spending 6-cents per child). The pharmaceutical industry was left feeling that Dodge had not earned his campaign contribution.

Senator Dodge confronted his expert scientist outside the hearing room. The Doctor had tried to regain his integrity in the public eye and the Senator was furious. Sometimes the experts were pushed too far; embarrassed by the premise they were told to promote. Scientists were in the unfortunate position of seeing the flawed science argued to an under-educated public. They could spot the fraud in the flawed logic while others depended on blind faith in the Ultra cause.

"I don't' have to take this," VonDanikin said. The scientist had sold his integrity to the Ultras to give a scientific veneer to their proposals.

"Yes you do," Dodge shot back angrily, "No reputable institution in the world is going to fund you. You're our party hack. You make what we want sound scientific and we pay you well for it. You don't have to convince scientists; just science drop-outs. You're prominent 'cause we say you are. You know as well as I, that you no longer have any credibility in the scientific community. No school will hire you; no lab will trust you. You belong to us."

VonDanikin had come up with a logical sounding reason to refute childhood immunization. Though any scientist knew that statistics proved the benefits. "All you have to do is testify that some healthy kid had not been immunized," Dodge was screaming, "That some immunized kid got sick…"

The line of thought was what Michael and his research colleagues had called 'UFO-type proof'. By definition, everything that was a UFO was unidentified. Once something was identified, it was no longer a UFO and could be disregarded. The Ultras used this logic as faith based-research when there was no proof. Data always had an element of the unknown. If a hundred aircraft flew overhead and ninety-nine were identified as airplanes and one was unknown, the Ultras bogus science could say that proves that one must have been a flying saucer. If this was subsequently disproved, they could move their argument to the next unknown. They could claim any unknown as proof of their conviction. Or at least to cast doubt and give the believers speaking points. In effect, the absence of information proving the opposite interpretation when it just proved incomplete knowledge. When science was against the proposal, the standard tactic was to express concern and form a fact finding panel that was never intended to find any facts. The egg-heads would cherry pick the data for any circumstantial item that could be passed around as a speaking point to imply uncertainty.

Michael had seen absence of information used as a distraction in his military service. When an SR-71 blackbird was flying spy missions in the Middle East, they required refueling after their transatlantic flights. Portuguese air traffic controls saw a blip on their screens; then two blips converge & separate (the Blackbird and an aerial tanker). The U.S. denied that they had seen anything. The incident was recorded as a UFO incident. Michael and the analysts laughed it off. The UFOlogists, as they called themselves, would have a field day with that. UFO over a generation had become synonymous with alien spacecraft, though this was not the government definition. True, it was a government cover-up; but not a flying saucer cover-up. This obstruction of science and non-disclosure was no laughing matter. It was being used as a tactic to subvert public health.

Michael knew just how the scientist felt. To his shame he had helped write the 13-States Rights. His part was to read the wording so that it was factually true. Misleading; but just accurate enough to avoid embarrassing holes in their logic that the opposition might exploit.

A researcher, generally, accepts the results. When a rival finds the answer first, he may be pissed. Like when a person screams out the answer to a line in a crossword puzzle. An investigator likes to be first. But a reputable analyst doesn't attack a legitimate response in order to discredit a correct answer. If the word in the cross-word puzzle is undoubtedly the correct answer; a solution with a different number of letters, or one that contradicts several other known words is not a legitimate way to discredit the screamer. But that is just what the Ultras wanted in their researchers. Either qualifying the result or seeking error in the method worked for them. "Liberals; tree-huggers; Bible denialists," Dodge would proclaim to avoid the science; then talk up the one case that doesn't fit the mold. Scientifically proven theories could be discounted in such ways.

The power struggle had begun after the second Bush presidency. The Ultra-right felt that they were the faction brought to power to fend off the liberal assault in the popular media. (No liberal media, just the Ultra right hearing what they wish wasn't true and not wanting others to give it any credibility.) The more conciliatory Republican factions where portrayed as elitist, willing to make deals with the devil. Mentioning the devil, even in a cliché was always good to bring out fear in the under educated devote. The 'devils in the detail' was a label often used to describe complicated opposition proposals. The more centrist senators and representatives had to buy into the party line or find themselves under assault as being soft on crime, or drugs, or promiscuity or any other issues the Ultras called cultural. Bring the Do-good Republicans into line with the Ultras, or label them liberal. Discredit the moderates as elitists. The Ultras, generally, disregarded the far left. True liberals were often irritating enough to be out of the main stream. The left never seemed to understand the process of incremental change. They often argued for all or nothing, and got nothing. Most people feared radical change and tended to prefer no change to unknown consequences.

The 13-States Rights were intended to be a symbolic rallying point for the simple masses. Actually an addendum to the constitution, it was disastrous. People flocked to the slogan of "Constitutional reform". Focus groups had told the Ultras that 'Mandate' had a sinister feel to average folks. People don't like being told that they are 'required' to do something. The label was used instead of 'law' to keep the negative emotions boiling. After all, law and order was a good thing.

Then the Ultras pushed through a series of 'Reforms'. 'A grand design to return us to our conservative roots,' is what the people were told. The question of balance of power, if congress could amend the constitution by simple vote rather than ratification by two-thirds of the states passed review of the Supreme Court. A dissenting justice was impeached and removed on a trumped up obstruction of justice charge and the remaining justices were muted.

The crown jewel of the package was the *Balanced Budget Amendment*. Michael and the folks with money loved it and it was an easy sell to a misguided electorate. Everyone to pay their share of the deficit; NOW. A ten percent flat tax meant everybody paid the same rate to maintain current programs. It was referred to as a tithe to add the weight of a spiritual commitment. To poor families that might mean going hungry; but to the Ultras it meant a measly ten percent rather than a 28% tax rate. It was a windfall. Even at 28% there was no chance that they would go hungry. Millions of workers were denied the benefit of their earned income. Capital gains were overlooked. Unearned income was left in the hands of the already absurdly rich. Most people didn't know the difference.

Deficit reduction was sold to the public as a patriotic and fair way to draw down the debt; equal cost to all. The amount was kept foggy, and low-ball estimates were circulated for public consumption. When the Act took effect and the nature of the beast was revealed, the social fabric tore. How few composed the fortunate fraction was exposed and vast numbers, who thought they were among the privileged, found out that they were less than middle class; used for their votes. They had their pockets picked.

Those who could, paid off their share of the deficit, and went on with their lives. Those who had a little to spare, made payments and become indentured to the government. Those who had no means became a cheap labor source for any public project that happened to be in progress. The reasonable sounding formula of 'Hours Worked times Minimum Wage' produced the amount of credit a citizen could apply toward their share of the deficit. The single parent with a couple of kids had three times as many credits to work off as the individual; until the child turned fifteen and they were expected to take a sub-minimum wage job. The deficit share was calculated on total population.

It sounded fair; but that meant kids, grandma and disabled family members were the responsibility of the working family members. And since the work was community service it was in addition of any job they already worked. It didn't go to pay the bills. Those who had no job, showed up for the lunches. Military MREs, Meals Ready to Eat, were served to the work crews. For many this became their only nutrition. Working for subsistence sounded like slave labor. Michael had never thought of it that way before, but he did not associate with anyone in those circumstances and didn't see the suffering; until the house of cards collapsed. It was economic warfare at its most cutthroat. In his selfish days Michael thought of it as good business.

Private bidders appealed to the government, in the interest of the work ethic, to put those in debt to America to work on private projects. The government contracted out the labor of its' citizens.

States reneged on the Lotto payments, supposedly on grounds of morality. In truth, LOTTO payments had become an unsustainable burden on the government. Debt had accumulated paying for public services and education, while excusing those with money from shouldering their share of the social costs. People became disenchanted with government gambling enterprises and stopped playing. LOTTO income dropped dramatically. Over the years, payments to the few winners had mounted until it exceeded the governments' gaming income.

The Lotto Stiffs had never, and would never, really be accepted in the Fortunate Fraction, though their money was. Lotto Stiffs were sucked into land deals, losing stock offerings and other rich-man schemes the winners didn't understand. They paid management fees and were flattered into political donations. Many were broke within weeks and got only cynical sympathy from the Ultras. 'Stocks rise and fall. Land deals fall through', they were told, 'the damn Government torpedoed your gravy train.' Some of the fleeced even bought the spin and remained Ultra activist against their own best interest; as foot soldiers only, of course.

Those lucky few who had retired on their Lotto winning were shocked to find their unearned retirement cut off. Those lucky, suddenly unlucky, few were dubbed the 'Lotto Stiffs' when their stories hit the media. They found no sympathy from the many who had gambled on the government 'Games' religiously for years with no gain.

The *Flag Burning* piece was for show. It brought along some veterans. The politically correct thing to do. Michael had seen flag burning overseas during his diplomatic days, hated it, and thought U.S. protesters were wimps, or at least harmless, by comparison. Calling them terrorists by law gave the government the legal grounds to better control descent. Michael didn't see them as that dangerous. Besides, they had the right to burn their own property. 'Anyone tried to burn my property, I'd hand him his ass,' Michael felt. To the Ultras, though, this was serious business. It meant another percentage point to victory.

With the tough on crime *No Plea, No Parole* guidelines, deadly resistance to arrest had skyrocketed. Each incident further fueled the police rational for preemptive force and better weaponry. Escapes from overcrowded prisons and jails increased and, curiously, the conviction rate across the country dropped. It seems when juries were presented with the circumstances of an individual case they would reach not guilty verdicts rather than be forced to impose an obviously unfair mandatory sentence. It was nearly impossible to seat a jury that did not have a father, child or sibling in custody or under supervision for real or imagined crimes.

Good behavior in prisons was nonexistent. With nothing to lose the prison gangs cut loose and virtually ran the institutions unchecked. Never the less, in a short time a large portion of the population had cycled through the system. Everything from public urination to rude language, that could be construed as immoral, was labeled a sex offense, warranting lifelong monitoring. A life sentence of surveillance at taxpayer expense.

Public and political crimes drew a 'Terrorist' label that suspended due process. The new category of crimes was impossible to beat. If a person pleaded guilty; they were accepting the label. If they pleaded not guilty; they were lying. Refusing to plea constituted obstruction of justice. The Supreme Court was asleep or humbled. Many cases seemed to be brought against people to hang a felony conviction on the 'wrong kind of people' restricting their right to vote; to diminish the Ultras' competition. It was voter suppression using Justice Department resources. Over a quarter of the adult, male, black population had a disqualifying felony over their head.

The *First Responders* Provision authorized police use of automatic weapons to insure they wouldn't be outgunned by criminals. It didn't seem to matter that a policemans' job was targeting criminals when a weapon was used. For special circumstances SWAT teams could supplement street cops' firepower. Spraying the landscape with bullets did not insure public safety, but it sounded good and the public felt safer.

Military weaponry was transferred from Federal to State control. Federal arsenals became a valuable political payback with government stockpiles that could be shuttled around for free. Minds began to change when friendly fire incidents took a sharp increase. Police humvees became a common sight that urban populations interpreted as an occupation force.

Cloaked in the aura of Americanism the *Official American Language* passed. Michael knew this was symbolic and expected it would cause no harm. English classes were implied as a benefit to those in needed. This allowed the Ultras to hold on to the few Latino voters that they had. Implied by not promised, it was promptly forgotten. Speaking points did not have to be honored in law. But what was marketed as patriotic, had the side effect, some say the intended effect, of savings in multi-lingual publications and government translators. Hispanics, Chinese and other groups showed their displeasure by declaring neighborhoods and business districts as traditional language zones.

Symbolic issues that play well in the press and didn't cost anything. That was the criteria for the Veto Proof Congress. An *End of Foreign Handouts* law appealed to a population that felt they had to settle for less. When people were asked if we should help poor countries almost three quarters, about 70%, of the population agreed. When asked if they approve of 'Foreign Aid', only about 25% approved. Another Ultra word game had succeeded and a demon phase was born.

Leeching by foreigners seemed a logical explanation for declining living standards. Most Americans didn't realize how dependent they were on products from foreign sources until protective tariffs put the cost out of reach. A 'don't buy Chinese campaign' fell flat when people discovered there were entire categories of products in the American market that were only produced in China. Outsourcing had taken its' toll.

The rise of homegrown industries, that the Ultras predicted would develop to supply the wanted products, did not happen. The costs of initiating a highly technical business from scratch wasn't a money maker, so business had no incentive to spend the time and money in development. Many technologies, developed by Americans, had been transferred overseas for cheap labor. Americans never expected the day would come when they would be in need of aid from foreigners. The Chinese retaliated by refusing export permits for missile components for U.S. fighter jets, hampering fleet maintenance.

The *Streamline Government* provision took a back door approach to blindly dismantling government agencies that business saw as meddlesome or expensive. Regulators were dismissed en mass. Data collection and analysis was severely curtailed as the eyes that offended were plucked out and the messengers were defamed.

The Ultras had Michael on staff under a strict vow of confidentiality. The numbers he crunched informed those who needed to know the truth, without the inconvenience of telling the general public. His work for state and federal agencies was funded with public money and was, generally, public information. The Ultras inside circle was more like a secret society.

If only three percent of the population benefits and they are the ones with the information, it's in their interest that the other 97% don't know or don't understand. Michael had seen the transition of 'Important information to our customers' disclaimers and warnings required by consumer protection laws designed so that people wouldn't read it; in four point micro type. Pharmaceutical disclaimers were negotiated and softened behind closed doors. Michael was bound to secrecy; besides, he was one of the three percent.

"Government should be run like a business" was a rallying call of the reformers. The *Streamline government Provision* set about a plan to do just that. Of course, Government is not a business. It is not in place to produce profit and reward the productive. A number of non-productive persons had be considered, or consciously ignored. The blind, disabled and orphans were left out; but they didn't vote in great numbers.

Victims of natural disasters found that they had to fend for themselves. 'Act of God' provisions excused government agencies from spending relief funds. Taxpayers could not be expected to reimburse people for an act of God. Insurance companies stalled or sent out teams of lawyers to run interference. Michael was often tasked with finding the glaring fraud case that would be publicized as the norm. The fact that these cases were exposed and prosecuted proved that fraud was not a huge problem. But fear easily replaced conscience with Ultra prompting. All the Federal authorities could offer were soup kitchens and prisons.

Embassy staff and U.S. Government employees overseas were left without pay as the debate raged about whether sending dollars overseas was an appropriate use of taxpayers' money. Senior Diplomatic personnel could usually afford families, if they choose, and often signed on the wife as a State Department secretary for the dual income and government subsidy.

Even with a suddenly unemployed wife and no salary, diplomats were, generally, affluent enough to support themselves; for a while. Staff just got a military plane ride home.

The *Keep Our Troops out of Harms' Way* piece of the manifesto spoke highly of the military and proceeded to dismantle the infrastructure in glowing patriotic terms. American families should not be at risk in a foreign land; therefore, no dependents were authorized to accompany troops to foreign posts at government expense. That mostly impacted the regular G.I.s. Senior officers could afford to bring family.

The Post Exchange system, known as the PX, was originally intended to provide U.S. products at reasonable prices to troops at remote old West outposts. It had grown into a worldwide business; and not just at remote outposts. The PX was seen as unfair competition to domestic business located near military posts. The argument ran that the military PX system was not in business to sell baby clothes in Beverly Hills. The Post PX returned to selling basic military essentials like boots and uniforms. Bases in cities where products were readily available shrank to military knick-knack shops. Thousands of military dependents were laid off and military retirees, accustomed to being subsidized by cheap PX products saw their standard of living slide. Pay at the lower ranks was never intended to be sufficient to support a family. Young couples that thought the military was a safe career found themselves living in poverty. Often family and friends were thousands of miles away.

A poster villain for the 'professionalize the military' budget cutters appeared in the person of Nelson Krause; a PFC with a wife and two small children. For two and a half years Nelson was the picture of the perfect soldier. Well paid, his housing and rations subsidized for his family. He made use of every educational opportunity the Army could provide. When the war in the South America heated up, Nelsons' unit was alerted for deployment. He talked to the local media about hardship for his family, his family's poverty, his sacrifice. "I just wanted to go to college, I never wanted to go to war," he had said expecting understanding and a hardship exemption. When the day came for departure, Krause was nowhere to be found. It seemed at a gut level, people realized that going into harms' way was exactly what an army was expected to do. The public was outraged.

The media, following up on the story, interviewed Mrs. Krause. She was a young girl taken from friends and family to this far off base and quickly becoming the mother of two. She didn't know where Nelson was. She bemoaned being deserted because the government wanted to separate them. Her hard luck story found no sympathy. She was suspected, or tarred by the military, as an accomplice. But Krause was a deserter and his wife was not cooperating. The Army denied any responsibility for the young family.

The public reaction was venomous. They had collected for over two years on public funds for just this occasion and now he was shirking his duty. There was no sympathy, as Mrs. Krause seemed to expect; just a disgust that drove her and her children from base housing. She incurred more public wrath when applying for social aide to feed her kids. The attitude seemed to be, 'Let her kids go hungry. That will get her to cooperate'. Mrs. Krause and the kids were reluctantly given C-130 transport back to her parents' hometown. Krause became the symbol of a breed of lazy garrison troops using the system for all it was worth.

A cynical twist on a famous quote emerged as, "soldiers hate war the most, because without it, they get paid for nothing." The military axiom that 'during times of peace soldiers should train for war' was lost. In times of peace, soldiers were employed as police, social workers, construction workers and peacekeepers. The fact that a soldiers job was to kill was conveniently forgotten in the verbose hero worship of 'Our Youngsters in Uniform'. Mom didn't want to hear that the nation was teaching her kids to kill.

The *Health Care Enhancement* plank of the plan proposed to limit costs by providing block grants to meet peoples' health needs. The compassionate sounding sound bite was 'health care needs would be met equally for all'. It sounded all inclusive but people soon found a block grant with set dollars would spread thinner and thinner as more services were needed by more people. Health plans paid less and less of the cost of even the more common procedures. It was sold to the public as a way to include all family doctors, even "your family doctor". Unfortunately family doctors could not afford to provide service when reimbursement covered only 30% of most procedures; if they were covered at all. With the small percentage paid by the plans, people found themselves unable to afford their family doctor. Many people, who thought that they were fully covered, found out otherwise; rejected on a technicality. Lawyers, not doctors, determined what procedures were needed. And the more procedures denied, the greater the profits to the corporate providers.

Mental Health Surveillance was presented as a victim benefit with the unspoken idea that the public would be better protected (though psychologists expressly said that 99 out of 100 people with mental health problems are not a threat to themselves or society.) The threat was rarely recognized until they snapped, and many never snapped. Nine out of ten who snapped were suicides. The fear of the one who would snap played on public paranoia. Fewer people would seek mental health assistance. Public funding would decrease, which was, of course, the Ultras' intention in the first place. That would also allow them to expand the surveillance of those mental defects who opposed their policies. Monitoring bracelets took the place of institutional commitment. If they opposed the Ultras' policies, they must be mental defects.

Pharmaceutical companies defended outrageous drug prices by pleading that research outlays were necessary to continue to keep Americans alive and healthy. When a drug lost its' patent, over time, a new slight variant was marketed as the latest magic bullet. The twenty-five cent pill was sold for six bucks. The 'Ask your doctor' ads kept just enough hypochondriacs hooked to keep the profits rolling in. The Ultras weren't concerned, as long as the new drug was not subsidized by government health plans. Pharmacies were given the right to prescribe the new wonders and the advertising changed from 'Ask your doctor' to 'Ask your prescriber'.

Marketing research had shown that people were more willing to spend money if a common condition was redefined as a 'syndrome'. Many catchy acronyms entered the language to profit the health care industry. There was PGS (persistent glandular secretion), or sweating. The treatment was actually just a deodorant in pill form. Deficient Muscle Syndrome (DMS) was treated with a medicine (a vitamin) to a population that didn't like to exercise.

It was easy enough to make people self-conscious in a thirty second ad. They could not list all the disclaimers that consumer protection advocates suggested. Lobbyist placed the responsibility to inform the patient on the doctor, though most people did not have a doctor. Everything from sleepwalking and suicide risk were mentioned quietly in a sweet syrupy voice-over to downplay disclaimers. Under the pleasant visuals a casual notice that the miracle drug may 'rarely result in fatal stroke' scrolled across TV screens. There were drugs for dry-eye, blotchy skin, restless legs and, of course, impotence.

Months, sometimes years, after they were introduced, some drugs deadly effects were exposed and the manufacturers just pleaded ignorance. The courts had decided that companies could had the same rights as people and criminal responsibility could be attributed to a company, rather than a decision maker. Criminal corporate deciders were given a loophole. It was always 'the company' that was responsible, never a person. Companies couldn't go to jail. Decision makers, who belong in jail, walked free; often with a sizeable bonus.

The *National Nutrition Act* was born. Food Stamp horror stories were used to discredit the entire system. Not to reform the system that fed hundreds of thousands of people over decades, but to squeeze more money from the bureaucrats. Studies showed about 3% fraud and 5% administration, so the manipulators cut 20% and state and local governments were instructed to eliminate fraud and reduce administration. The reduced budget was stated in big dollars to mask the scale of the drawdown. They could point to the figure that by everyones' standard was a huge outlay. But at a National level the funds was woefully insufficient. The framers knew that fraud and administration could not be entirely eliminated. But the grant levels set by this action allowed the elected to wash their hands of the pain. Besides it was known that this was a large group of people that tended not to vote; minimal damage control. Those cut adrift didn't have a soap-box.

The appropriate story of program abuse was found. Government assistance squandered on cigarettes and alcohol was discovered and talked up as the norm. Direct food service was presented as the compassionate solution. Soup kitchens were put forward as a low cost solution called "Uncle Sams' Restaurants". To end hunger, a government mealticket was implemented in lieu of food stamps. It amounted to a place in line at the soup kitchens or lunch on a Government work project. Military MREs became the standard diet; with an appropriate civilian contractors' mark-up, of course.

The *Family School Act* gave official status to home and church schools anywhere that they could be established. Churches responded by the hundreds to get a share of the education pie. 'Caesar rendering unto God' was the cute tag that the victors delighted in using. This undercut local public schools, who had to pay for certified staff, healthy conditions and students with disabilities, with a greatly reduced share of public money. The Department of Education was disbanded as bureaucratic pork. Standardized testing below college level was discontinued. Again, the eyes were plucked out.

The *Victims Rights* provision had provided for the right to speak in courtrooms. Victims and victims' families wanted a podium and the courts seemed a good place. The public was told the accused had all the rights. These accused rights included the right to mace, warrants, lock-up, courts, and prosecutors.

A few horror stories were passed around to prove the point. Little was said of the victims right to the police that investigate and arrest, patrol cars and handcuffs, the jail and staff where the suspect is held, the court were the case was heard, guards, the jury, and the court recorder and janitor. Law abiding citizens had a right to have this kind of structure in place in a civilized society.

The right to a soapbox was emotionally appealing, but amounted to tax money being diverted from the proper role of criminal justice. Media paid for some slack. It was dramatic, cheap programming. Victims wanted their fifteen minutes of recognition. What they had to say was not evidence. 'Speak Out' was the term used when an irrelevant family member or friend wanted court time to vent. Justice was not served when a weeping victim of burglary sobbed that she would never feel safe again; Ergo the perpetrator should never see freedom again. The teenager who stole her TV did not find justice in a fifteen year sentence.

There is good reason that an unbiased jury, and not the victim, sits in judgment. It is just not in society's best interest to pay for life imprisonment for petty crimes. The Ultras played up crime to claim their tough-on-crime mantle. Anyone guilty of any crime was portrayed as being capable of any crime. Thus, a shoplifter could be treated as harshly as a murderer. Society became more and more paranoid. Schools went into lockdown whenever a car was stolen in a neighborhood. After all, by Ultra standards, a car thief was just as much a criminal as a child molester.

Court time was allocated, sentences lengthened and the slow wheels of justice moved more slowly. Eventually, 40% of court time was taken up with angry, emotional testimonials from people who had suffered some injustice. It made for entertaining television and the networks loved the cheap, reality footage. Some judges with political ambitions turned their courts into Court TV that ignored the rules of order in favor of good TV.

The *Self Defense Act* was a bone thrown to the NRA; authorizing almost any kind of weaponry in any quantity.

Family by family the 13-points alienated and lost supporters as the injustice of each element struck home. People began to walk away from their own government. In a moral sense it was understandable. Most people felt alienated. They didn't benefit. They didn't vote. This wasn't their government. The purse strings and the enforcement capabilities of the government were left vulnerable to the control of a determined, organized minority.

The Army, Navy, Air Force and Marines as well as the Reserve forces were under the command of the fortunate fraction. The CIA, FBI, DEA, INS and Coast Guard took their orders. At the state level, the National Guard and state police were in their power; beholden for a pay check. Counties controlled the Sheriffs and jails. City police in the urban areas were on the government payroll at the lowest level. These forces were arrayed as enforcers against those who had no stake in their government. When it was for the common good, they served the country well. When used politically to secure the status of the fortunate fraction, it was grounds for revolt.

Most didn't want to hear bad news, much less to act on it. Most of the world hated American policies and most Americans didn't know why, so they simply disregarded their critics or accepted that foreigners were jealous of their way of life. They were told, 'they hate us for our freedom' and they bought it. Most were not privy to the abusive international policies of the Ultra hierarchy that fueled such hatred.

Divide and conquer had set different levels of Government at odds. State workers laughed when the Federal workers were furloughed and went unpaid. More money 'In our pockets', they concluded. County workers got nervous when it trickled down to the state worker defaults, while the average Joe continued to laugh. Then business seemed to dry up. Business owners in state capitols saw declines of more than half as state belts tightened. Day care centers, dry cleaners and restaurants went bankrupt.

Immigration reform alienated the Latin community as they were continually required to prove their citizenship. Blacks had a long history of oppression and saw a retrenching of the white communities in the Ultra policies. Asians felt a renewed suspicion as stories of jobs sent overseas inevitably blamed foreign workers in Asia. Increasingly harsh trade restrictions severely impacted many Asian family import businesses.

Martin Mathias emerged as a peacemaker in the black community. All races and creeds were welcome in his movement. Most people had become an enemy of Ultra self-righteousness by being part of a demonized faction; delegated to the enemy ranks by nature of smoking, drinking, illegally cutting down trees, foreign birth, obstructing business or skipping Ultra taxes.

Many Ultra favored companies began to feel the pain of Martins' boycott of abusive businesses. Many companies that supposedly were worth hundreds of millions actually had no assets. Computer fortunes built on $12 a share dropped to 12 cents a share; if you could find a buyer. Many traders held on to the illusion, hoping for the turnaround that never came. One morning they would just find their pet stock delisted. Those who had prior knowledge of trouble had cashed out.

Buy American campaigns failed as people would only buy what was essential. The Ultra policies began trying to reflag American business. Cruise ships operating exclusively in American waters were required to fly the American flag. Rather than adhere to new American legal requirements, the cruise lines deserted the coast and plied the Mediterranean as ferry boats. Foreign subsidiaries of U.S. companies declared their independence, often aided by foreign governments.

Immigration, both south and north, are condemned. On the northern border, the problem was the greater number of Americans attempting to flee to the tolerance of Canada. The Ultras instituted measures to stop the outflow. Most rejected deadly force against border crossers to Canada. Deserters, the Ultras called them, though they were careful not to condemn or condone militia activities. Mexico was more of an open and shut case, as if it were open season on invaders. It legalized summary execution by any Joe with a gun that thought his country was threatened by 'Foreign Criminals and Terrorists'.

Private interests and factions in the United States distorted American foreign policy. The Cubans in Florida constituted an important voting bloc, important to the party in Florida; Florida was important to the party nationally, so the bias was sold as Party doctrine. Most Americans would just as soon forget the antagonism if asked. Cubas' anti-American stance hardened. Trainers and recruits flooded into Columbia and Venezuela in support of their brother Latinos. Similar suspicion of Arabs, Asians, Africans and Europeans created a closed U.S. society. The unity of the American public, that had proved essential to survival during the Great Depression, was lost in factionalism and fear.

Those that yelled wag-the-dog when President Clinton had sent cruise missiles into Afghan accepted such tail wagging when George II attacked Iraq. After years of disillusionment and many lost sons, common folks broke with the deceivers' power base.

A fundamentalist group called the End-Times sect emerged. The Dead-enders, as they were parodied, after the disastrous reign of George the Second, had concluded that Dubya had actually been the anti-Christ. All the pieces fit. He rose through the world of politics. He was the leader of the most powerful country in the world. He presented a likeable everyman image. Displaying the sin of pride, he promised peace, safety and prosperity. He delivered none of it. He was indeed the despotic prince (George the firsts' son). He loudly proclaimed his devote credentials while conducting disastrous war. Most damning to many was that his strong leadership was endorsed by the Jews. He initiated holy war against a convenient hated heretic. The new world order ushering in the destruction of the old world cradle of civilization. He subverted the trust of peaceful Americans with lies that exploited fear and patriotism. It was prophesized that the beast would be popular among the devote. Many otherwise devout people were led astray by his spying, prisons and bombs for the good of mankind. The perfect definition of the 'False Prophet'.

His military avoidance was rationalized and his drunk driving excused, his cocaine use suppressed. He had seen the light; and America discovered it was shock and awe. As more and more Christians lost crusading sons and husbands in the Middle East abyss, they saw Dubya in devilish denial. Veterans and service members saw him as the one who abused the institution. Some saw his actions as human failings. The Dead-enders saw a malevolent evil and concluded they were experiencing the end-times and the political leadership was, indeed, in league with the Anti-Christ.

The more creative cryptics of the cult even discovered the fact that George, six letters; Walker, six letters; and, Bush II, six characters must be the 666 of the beast. It all seemed so clear; after the fact.

The Dead-enders lived the most austere life-style and pooled their resources, like the followers of Jesus, giving their leaders sufficient means to spread their doctrine of separatism for simple room and board. However, this left the flock with no personal reserves. Seniors' communes shared expenses and projected political power. Stridently anti-UN, anti-immigrant, even anti-government in a way contrary to the cozy arrangement that fundamentalists had cultivated with the right kind of officials a few years before.

When the collapse came, they found the church felt no responsibility for them and the country very uncharitable to their separatist communities. Leisure Acres, at the far end of Black Lake, was one such community. Residents were required to be over 55 years old in the walled community and most were retired. The necessities that were taken for granted were the apparatus of an organized society. They could forego TV, radio, elections and such. They didn't considered losing utilities, water, electronic banking, postal service, trash pick-up, and the pharmaceutical industry that were provided by the outside world. There was no longer a safety net or even common social decency.

The Dead-enders austerity had generally proved fatal to the most vulnerable in a matter of weeks when the logistical system broke down. Urban dwellers saw no other way than scavenging for their daily bread. Rural folks fared better with cultivation. Under populated work farms, surprisingly enough, were beginning to produce a surplus. The haves became the have-nots and the have-nots of earlier times became their saviors.

When the systems collapsed, they found themselves incapable of restoring the trust in the miracle of self government that was built up over the years from the founding fathers' model. As though a complex timepiece was scattered into its' many parts and no one knew how to put it back together again. The watchmakers were long gone.

A return to consumer driven demand and supply came into play. Advertising made little difference. If it wasn't useful, durable and/ or worth the cost it was generally avoided by consumers. Consumer confidence really did matter. McFrys cost a couple of bucks for a few ounces. A ten pound bag of potatoes cost about as much. Advertising revenues shrink. Movie and sports stars were willing to promote items for cheap. But they didn't generate enough sales to make even modest salaries worthwhile.

On the other side of the coin, supply and demand doesn't work if the supply falls far short of demand. The product can't be had at any price. First came inflation, then widespread shortages. The dominos collapsed more quickly than anyone imagined possible. Small towns business, dependent on big city jobs, lost commuters spending. Retailers lost business, property values dropped, the local tax base dried up. Medical facilities, owned by multinational interests, deserted unprofitable communities. Payroll deposits for goods and services vanished. At each turn, more layoffs.

Farming was the only occupation that seemed self-sustaining. Ignored for decades, doomed to artificial prices and subsidized not to grow anything, farmers were unsympathetic to the city folks' plight. They may have helped, if they could. But they couldn't, so they didn't.

Service industries discovered that they were viewed as optional spending. Travel declined in spite of Airline prices reduced below the cost of operation. Airlines were bailed out before and they expected a repeat performance. This time, however, the average taxpayer, who made little use of their service, refused to finance a business which failed by sucking up to business travelers. Travel had changed fundamentally from choice to necessity. Airline and rail travel was severely contracted as many losing routes were abandon. Bus travel was dangerous and only attempted when absolutely necessary. Travel agencies and rental car agencies collapse. Delivery companies refused to deliver to remote or dangerous areas, further factionalizing the country. Taxis had routinely avoided high crime and remote regions. Buses and airlines followed suit, shrinking their service area and stranding large numbers of unprofitable people.

Theaters continued to entertain, but cut costs by showing older, cheaper movies. Hollywoods' outrageous price and percentage resulted in reduced circulation. Theater owners were no longer willing to pay the big bucks for blockbusters. Movies could be made much cheaper and stars were forced to accept whatever jobs were offered. Even the lower rates were far more expensive than the classic stock that drew profitable audiences. The studios were forced to cut costs further in a bid to the bottom for talent.

People had been encouraged to engage in creative financing schemes that made huge commissions for the mortgage industry middlemen. The creative mortgages, referred to as 'home equity loans', sounded more acceptable than calling it what it was; a second mortgage. With weak labor unions, people did not get the raises they expected. Instead of cost of living increases diluted purchasing power. When the balloon payments came due, many lost their homes to the housing speculators. Even some of the 'get rich with real estate' speculators lost big, as they couldn't make payments on homes that sat unoccupied or were commandeered by squatters. The legal system, paid for by taxes, that handled evictions was overwhelmed and could not help. Some speculators tried hiring local muscle to expedite evictions but the squatters had more to lose and met strong arm tactics with a united front. Communities pulled together when large numbers of friends and neighbors faced the same circumstances.

Home values plummeted. Many, who were taken in by the promise of easy home equity money, lost their homes. The dangers of the home equity line of credit and Adjustable Rate Mortgages were exposed. Flippers caught in the decline had become the motivated sellers that they had taken advantage of in the boom times of the housing bubble. Most people just laughed at their misfortune. The flippers tried in vain to rescue a portion of the 'million dollar property portfolios'. They found that paper equity did not translate into money you could live on; until you sold. And if there were no buyers, equity vanished. Paper equity evaporated.

Those that had bragged about their 'million dollar portfolio' on pay TV found themselves foreclosed and broke.

Freddie Mac and Fannie Mae were the vehicles that provided and supported the dream of home ownership. Half the mortgages in the country were covered by their provisions. Risky lending put them at risk, and taxpayers were unwilling to bail them out. Banks and landlords wanted their money. The occupants of the foreclosed houses just wanted a place to live.

And America found that the world had walked away. America was a violent culture; fractious and well armed. No one made a serious effort to come to the aid of America; or to invade either. The world at large was content to let the United States sort out their own problems. A bonus was that America, at least for the near future, was not a threat to the world community. Super powers tend to flex their muscles. Americas' introspection seemed an international reprieve.

The Ultras had declared war so nonchalantly on different factions of society that almost everyone could be described as an enemy in some aspect. Like the Drug-War and the Sex-Wars, conducted for the benefit of politicians. The war on homelessness created another whole block of the population who were suddenly criminals. For the Ultra elite to thrive they had to have bad guys; and control of cheap labor.

Confiscation of criminal property was sold as being the best way to finance police operations. Property taken as the result of criminal behavior proved insufficient and the Drug Enforcement Administration began to confiscate all of the suspects' property. Even when a conviction was not forthcoming, which was rare, the property was not returned. More money 'In Your Pocket', the Ultras crowed.

The Drug war painted users and sellers as the bad guys, unless, of course, the drugs were prescription. Legal drugs were, generally, not available to the poorer elements. And besides, the pharmaceutical industry paid the Ultras heavily not to target their profits. They enjoyed bullet-proof political protection.

The Sex wars targeted the desperate and the lonely. The tobacco war portrayed smokers as the villains, recklessly exposing non-smokers to inevitable cancer. The war on alcohol was supported by groups that epitomized the nature of the struggle; those who did not indulge hoping to finance government programs from the resources of the demonized group. Mothers Against Drunk Drivers saw the problem as people to be controlled and punished. Their own children showed them the error in their philosophy when they created the Students Against Driving Drunk. The younger people correctly perceived that the problem was with the abuse and the drunks were as much victims as society. They properly focused on the activity rather than criminalizing their peers. The quick-to-criminalize adults quietly make the change in their name, though they continued to fear and criminalize the demon-drunks. 'Hate the sin; love the sinner' was the cliché that allowed the devote to impose harsh justice on the enemy. The attitude was carried over to the children. 'Love the children. Unless they do something wrong. Then try them as adults.'

Business had destroyed the Unions by labeling them, and anyone who dared defend workers rights, as socialist. They moved to take advantage of the suddenly available labor pool with wages insufficient to maintain a consumer class. Old folks, whose pensions were cut, used what little remained of their aged energy to make ends meet. Retirement was unheard of; demonized as freeloading to those in the workforce. The Ultras saw the retirees as experienced, reliable and desperate. Quick food restaurants advertised using senior citizens going off to work with a warm upbeat jingle. It seemed young yuppie marketing executives had no idea how most people thought and lived. The commercials disgusted Michael and terrified older folks. Working for minimum wage wasn't how the baby boomers imagined their golden years. Then the minimum wage was cut in half to 'create twice the jobs'. The Ultras had promoted the idea as pocket change for school kids, though the jobs were generally filled by seniors with insufficient resources.

Michael knew better. He began to question the motives of his Ultra associates. From then on he was a marked man. His defense of improved wages found suspicious side glances by the Ultras. He had succumbed to the liberal lies in their view. Reputable social scientists countered that it would create a consumer class that would buy products and benefit everyone. That was met with cries of 'It Will Cost Jobs'. This just wasn't true, but it was accepted by the masses as a reasonable line of thought; and fear for their own jobs created a cold blooded disregard for their fellow workers. The Ultras excelled at divide and conquer.

Politicians, however, still needed a bad guy; a threat that would get them votes. So periodically they would trot out some new and intrusive measure to label and punish the current demons. The Tobacco War, the War on Alcohol, War on Illegal Immigrants, even a War on just plain Immigrants. Good God how the Ultras liked to make war on people.

Michael had been a foot-soldier in many of these wars. He knew from the inside that they were never really a threat. They were a distraction and a fund raising vehicle. He knew, yet he went along, arguing the party line. He was more than a foot soldier; maybe a lower level lieutenant. Only now did he wonder what ever happened with the pursuit of happiness granted in the constitution.

It always sounded noble, but just below the surface a brooding class bigotry was the driving force. And the Ultra class at the top seemed to continue to shrink until very few could claim membership. An elaboration of Pastor Niemollers' famous quote seemed to apply. When they declared war on the smokers, I was not a smoker, so I did not complain. When they declared war on the drunks, I was not a drunk, so I did not complain. When they declared war on drugs, I didn't use drugs, so I did not complain. War on juveniles, war on abortionists, war on gays, war on premarital sex, war on the homeless. Then they declared war on me, and there was no one left to complain.

STRATEGY SESSION

"I think we can get started," Senator Dodge, the chairman of the Ultras' planning committee, brought the meeting to order. Representatives from Government, business, media outlets friendly to the cause and faith based groups participated.

The Ultras like to use a slick junction of unrelated things to lead in the philosophically right direction. Michael routinely provided the charts and graphs of deception for the puppet masters. That's how it felt. They asked for the most bizarre selective data to prove some point or other. For his effort he was promoted. As Chief of the Research Section, Michael was assigned a Research Assistant and Administrative Support.

Routine number crunching was left to Chip Libby, the ambitious new analyst. He had one foot in the fortunate fraction and intended to become one of the insiders.

Robert Patson was in attendance to represent the religious community. His prosperity gospel gave rich Christians the right to be rich, or wish to be rich, with a clear conscious. Evidently, Jesus wanted him to drive a Mercedes. Patson was the poster boy of the Christian Soldiers of America (CSA). He could spin the twisted logic of the Ultras if it served his purpose. When he spoke, he spoke as though his views were the only acceptable Christian view. Anyone who disagreed was a liberal or a humanist. Actually, the only ones benefiting from his brand of 'enjoy your rewards in this life' Christianity were well off Christians. His religious retreat, actually an entertainment theme part, boasted a huge oversized needle. For a nominal donation a person could walk a camel through the eye of the needle. It was meant to be tongue-in-cheek but expressed the obvious desire to avoid condemnation by exploiting a Biblical loophole. In the mean time they could enjoy the fruits of the earth with a clear conscious.

The theme park was his biggest money-maker; more lucrative than the fabric swatch, that they called a prayer rug. It was given away as a faith gift for a donation of so-many-dollars. As a gift for a donation it was not a sale and was, therefore, not a retail transaction and their tax exempt status was protected. The faith based community skirted the law and collected piles of money tax-free.

Henry R. Parrot spoke for business; big business anyway. His Urban-Shop-All stores provided urban areas with a full range of products, made by Asian sweatshops. His stateside employees worked for minimum wage with no benefits to keep costs down. The people in the cities detested his methods, but had no recourse but to shop at his USA stores. He had succeeded in driving most of his competitors into bankruptcy and absorbing them.

Other interested parties that could serve the Ultras purpose were in attendance. Small business seemed conspicuously absent. They hoped one day to be big business. Most would be lead along, even though their interests were very different from the big business-big government contractors that claimed to speak for them.

Troy Benedict, the talk show superstar, represented television and Ross Limpaw represented radio. Limpaw, claiming to be a friend to the military, broadcast from a base-side location not far from Black Lake.

Colonel Orville South spoke for the military. He had a reasonably distinguished war record and had served as military attaché to the White House. He could act as go-between with military circles. A number of Lawyers and Lobbyists lined second tier seats representing different interests.

Michael filled the number-cruncher role as the Research Investigator for the Ultra organization. Chip conducted opposition research and targeted research for desired results. Research for Ultras means cherry-picking data. The Ultras provide the result and bits and pieces were collected to support the view. Massive amounts of counter information was ignored or suppressed. Those not schooled in research, saw no fault in the logic. Michael hoped they just didn't understand proper research, but he knew that wasn't true. Their misuse was intentional. They were encouraging, even requiring, a discipline adherence to structured lies.

Clay Raven the political advisor sat mute. He rarely spoke in public forums and even with this select group of people he kept his stoic silence. His advice was for, not just the select, but the highest echelons of the Ultra organization.

And last, and certainly least in the eyes of the participants, was Martha, the widow of an Ultra functionary that was given the job for work that her husband had done for the organization. Martha, the matronly confidential secretary, provided administrative support. Martha was the widow of an Ultra bigwig and Michael quickly found out that, in all but name, she worked for Senator Dodge. On paper, she was Ultra paid staff on Michaels' team. She could be counted on to keep secrets, even from her supposed boss; Michael. She would keep the minutes and keep her mouth shut; it was assumed.

The same wave of paranoia over suspected leaks that ensnared Michael would reach Martha. Unfounded accusations drummed her out of the Ultra Womens' auxiliary and cost her job. But the Ultras didn't settle for just protecting their privilege. They practiced revenge as policy. For Michael that meant prosecution; for Martha it meant pulling her pension. Those suspected of disloyalty had to suffer to send a signal to others inside and outside the organization.

The agenda item was listed as an assessment of party strategy. The first item on the agenda was the military situation in South America. Michael was shocked to find that it was not military experts discussing the nuts-n-bolts of the military situation; but political and media types discussing spin. There was no plan of any sort; only media spin. The disruption of Arab oil was replaced, temporarily by Venezuela and Mexico. But a drug lord coup in the Venezuela, backed by Elian Sanchez, called for military intervention on behalf of an unpopular ousted dictator in exile.

Mistrust in Mexico brought a halt to business from that sector. The Ultras would spin the situation rather than resolve it.

Ultra diversions were well rehearsed media feeds. Military operations were, at this time, an embarrassing distraction. There were other issues. There was Season of the Shark, Summer of Abductions, the explosion of ID theft. Unsafe tires, unsanitary restaurants, convicts in daycare, infections in hospitals all enjoyed their frightening fifteen minutes as news. And the old reliable, sex offenders in neighborhoods. Every few weeks they could trot that one out. There were always sex offenders somewhere. It didn't have to be local to energize local party activists; and votes.

Michaels' research shop had a sign on the wall, only half in jest, that read, 'Don't screw up on a slow news day'. The Ultras preferred an Act of God as theme of the week; tsunami scares, tornado alley, hurricane seasons. Their response was inevitably cost free; prayer. This season, though, they needed something big. As big as war. Not a low intensity Latin American involvement.

It was obvious that the U.S. could not be militarily threatened, so the threat would have to be personal and emotional to the average Joe. Bio-weapons, chemical clouds and mushroom clouds. Bio was settled on as the most obscure and threatening. A Chinese threat or something big and frightening. They could not imagine that the people would not buy the fear.

First the enemy was accused of seeking dual use technology. The Hydro parts for irrigation projects could be interpreted as equipment to disseminating bio weapons. And the people had a right to be protected from bio-weapons. Evidence? Point to a crop duster; appoint yourself guardian of our children. An added benefit was the ability to label any domestic opponent/critic as less than patriotic and unconcerned with the eminent threat, giving aid and comfort to the enemy. Michael played along. He had seen that there was a need for strong-arm diplomacy during his foreign service.

It was amazing how easy it was; how paranoid the American public had become. Once the war had served its' purpose, the U.S. could declare victory, pull out and gear up for the next crusade. Afghan was left to the warlords. The three Iraqi republics had emerged on their own after US neglect. The Venezuelan campaign was wrapped up quickly when it became apparent the Ultras' favorite lacked any popular support. The killing went on as a black operation, but it was no longer called a war. Columbia was conducted as a peace keeping commitment in the name of the U.S. puppet.

The discussion began with concerns with the increased loss of helicopters to insurgent forces in South America. The press had noticed and the Ultras policy was coming under review. The talk centered around, not how to protect the troops, but how to talk around the problem. Real solutions would look like an admission of prior neglect and a failed policy; which it was. The solution was not more armor or better intelligence but to hand out a few medals to survivors in lavish public relations photo-ops and painting any critics as un-American defeatists.

They had not learned or had dismissed lessons learned from history. It is no surprise that helicopters were being brought down with conventional means available to local insurgent forces. Iraq showed that it was possible by aiming at the rear rotor. This avoided the heavy armor that protected the crew but left the craft unmanageable. Then stake out the crash site and ambush the troops sent to the rescue. A hundred men might be put at risk to secure two pilots, who were probably already dead. But that is what happens when political considerations drive military tactics. This was known from lessons in Iraq, in Mogadishu, in Vietnam; from as early as 1954 when the FLN used such tactics in Algeria.

During the Iraqi War, political considerations had ordered an attack on Fallujah after a few contractors were publicly killed. The military was negotiating for surrender of the city and were frustrated by the short sighted civilian interference. They knew such an attack was unadvisable; if not a loser from the start. Many American soldiers were killed and wounded unnecessarily and the political leadership declared victory. Even though those on the spot knew it wasn't true, it sold well. Michael was well aware of this from his military service. He seemed to be the only one that was. But he wasn't there as a military liaison, so he kept his peace.

"We begin by lamenting the vulnerability of the helicopters' rear rotor... Our soldiers at risk... and lead into increase funding for the war effort," Raven studied the page that had been prepared by some inner circle think tank.

"That information is classified. Won't that point out the vulnerability to anybody that watches CNN?" Colonel South asked.

"The insurgents already know," Raven said casually.

"Not all of them," South yelled, "We'll make it common knowledge. Any malcontent with an AK47 can shoot up our ships. Some will be brought down."

Raven looked perturbed, "We may lose a couple. That will give us justification to ramp up our response. Pilots at risk... No man left behind."

"The whole world don't know. Do we want to make it common knowledge? Will the President consent to declassify it?" Colonel South was concerned.

"He will... or we will leak it. Accuse him of a cover-up... of being negligent in defending our troops."

"Whether he agrees or not... can we still accuse him of a cover-up?" Limpaw asked jokingly. Michael wondered why Limpaw was even there. A media insider at a military briefing?

Another odd participant, Robert Patson, the religious guru was on to his pet project. Elian Sanchez, the Venezuelan nationalist, was interfering with his missionary work; actually, political indoctrination with food, medicine and Bibles as bait. "So, where are our teams to take out Elian?" He asked South. "If your boys can't handle it, I have connections that can." Most of the gathering ignored his ranting. In spite of his interference, Sanchez was a convenient fall guy and only the religious capitalists seemed to be thinking of assassination. Political murder in the name of the Lord.

He then resurrected his idea of having the IRS act as the collection agent for his tithes. Too many of his flock had made pledges and neglected to follow through. He felt the IRS would add the intimidation factor that would keep the money flowing.

He intended to set up tithe booths at local malls to sign up payroll deductions collected at government expense and deposited to his ministry tax-free.

Colonel South, the Security Czar, then spoke briefly on WMDs. Michael had worked with Colonel South in the Latin War. He was a competent enough soldier, but a Lieutenant-Colonel in a military hierarchy, that included hundreds of generals and admirals was a rather modest rank. Michael wondered if this was an indication of how far down the food chain the Ultras had to reach to find a kindred military player. Generals and Admirals followed orders, but they hated playing politics. South could at least give the gathering a military assessment. Michael, at least, hoped to finally hear an honest military analysis. He didn't get it.

South noted that chemical and biological weapons are just terror weapons if the population doesn't understand them. "The body count would be low; the effects localized. You would get a larger body count just by yelling 'Anthrax' in a crowded terminal, or yelling fire in a crowded theatre for that matter. Nukes we can disregarded altogether. Non-state groups could no more build a nuke than a bushman could build a jet fighter, or a typical small town could build an aircraft carrier. Those nations that might be able to build a crude model do not have delivery capabilities." The gist of the talk was 'don't worry. It's just to rattle the public... keep 'em on the team'.

Raven added, "Just keep saying how 'eloquent' our guy is. It makes the speaker seem knowledgeable regardless of substance. Or flatter the opposition by saying he's eloquent. It can be a two edged sword. Positive applied to our guy, negative when applied to the opposition if said with the right inflection; meaning shallow, full of himself, elitist. It keeps you from having to address what he says. It keeps the focus on the words rather than what the words mean. The impact will be virtually ignored. And say our guy asks the 'tough questions'. It makes him sound informed and involved. But never say what those questions are. Make whatever predictions you want, but avoid science. If you predict that anything is possible, when anything happens you can claim you were right", Raven declared dryly.

"Researchers can't test 'anything' as a premise", Michael countered. The partisan crowd, ill informed in the use of logic, understood Raven. Michaels' outburst was met with blank stares.

Raven scowled, "And if you find yourself on the losing side of a debate, just say 'he just doesn't get it'. The viewer feels superior because he DOES get it. Because they have defined IT as whatever they want in their own minds. The opposition is left describing how they DO get it." Raven concluded, "And as always, national security."

Next they tackled the public relations aspect of the Thirteen Points."The thirteen points have been ironed out and the public relations element must be handled." Senator Dodge knew that they could sell the elements of the plan to the public using the right spin, but he was concerned that local pressure at the grassroots level may cause some senators to waiver. The proper way of serving up the diverse points would have to be stage managed just right.

"We need to revisit the numbers." Senator Dodge was studying the tables that Michael had prepared. "What if we change the definitions? You know like they did in the school debate in Texas. Change the 'D' meaning Dropout to a 'D' meaning Departed. This one quit to take a job; that one quit to join the army. Present these as the norm. The Liberals ask how many dropouts there are; and we say, we don't know. Absence of news, isn't news. We just take credit. Can we do that Mikey?"

"It's called a Series Break, Senator," Michael responded glumly. He didn't like these numbers games. "Once it is done, the information is can no longer be compiled. We won't be able to restore history if the information isn't kept or collection criteria changes."

"That will work," Raven said slowly. "We need to reduce the rolls; fragment and confuse resistance. Cover the confusion, calling it 'Choice'. After the fact when the program is made clear, it will seem like there had been a debate when actually the discussion was just to dig out the details of the 'new improved' program statistics.

The revealed details can be presented as though it is the results of negotiated debate. We can claim that the opposition had their say."

Senator Dodge returned to his agenda, checking off a number of previously agreed speaking points. "Enemy issues: Elderly rights proponents were greedy geezers, immigration equates with illegal aliens, foreign criminals and terrorists. Lesbian and gay issues; recruiting our children. Organized labor; commies in the workplace. Druggies," Dodge looked up and smiled, "not the prescription kind. Those are our people. We make a lot of money off them. We want them on our side. And the all purpose generic use of the 'Liberal' label for anyone who doesn't agree or presents alternatives to the plan. Support the right to Life, to satisfy the anti-abortionists, God-fearing to bring along the devote, Family oriented to include the anti-gays without stirring up the opposition. Claim support for family farms," Dodge said, "And, avoid talk of the earmarks to industrial agriculture. Talk 'friend of the farmer'. Support gun rights and claim the tough-on-crime mantle. Advocate capital punishment to clear overcrowding... And of course terrorism for anything foreign. Break and defame opposition groups, abortion 'on demand'. People reacted negatively when they were told that someone was making 'demands'. Legislating from the bench... Lip service to the religious crowd. Who else would they vote for? And the Federal Tithe idea."

Wealthy tele-preachers saw the advantage of dollars over principles and rationalize their stand. Patson finally got his federal tithe idea considered as a suggestion that payroll deductions be included in the federal tax collection process. Collected by the government and forwarded to Patsons' coffers. With payroll deductions, he would not have to spend as much of his media empires' time asking for money. His 'Operation Rescue" had brought in tens of millions of dollars, a few thousand of which actually went to rescue operations.

Michael knew that a number of the proposals were just window dressing. There were only a few in prison with a death sentence. Not enough to ease prison overcrowding; even if they were all executed tomorrow. But this crowd wasn't interested. He kept his peace. Their expedient would just be to sentence more 'criminals' to the final solution, suspension of legal rights and increased use of the 'T' label. Always terrorists. There were always terrorists. Just like there would always be drunks. But that wasn't something you could play for gain.

Next Michael had been asked to prepare an explanation of the suggested change of the payroll taxes for the unemployment system. Business had targeted the withholdings as a possible source of income. If they could find a way to dodge the cost without alarming the public. The Ultras had their eye on the unemployment trust fund; the piggy bank.

"The system is supported by a two tiered tax system to make it fair." The audience winced at the word of 'fair'. "First, a company is rated by its' hiring and firing patterns. A second pool of funds, called the socialized costs, is collected that cannot be attributed to a specific employer. Like companies going out of business or reaching their rate cap. Lower cap, higher social tax."

"Each company has a tax rate established by the first condition and all employers share the cost of the second condition according to an employee head count. Unattributed costs are spread out among all employers. So even if business is taxed at a 5%, rate rather than 4%, reduced social tax more than makes up for the higher rate. 'Cause so many other employers, small employers, are sharing the load."

"Say BigBoys Company has a 4% rate and millions in shared social costs. We capped the rate at 5%. They pay another $100,000 in fixed costs and avoid $10 million in a per capita social tax. The $10 million is socialized and divided system-wide among 200,000 small businesses. Small business sees an increase; big business don't."

"Executives and lobbyists are entitled to a 12% bonus on savings, so they take $1.2 million to divide among themselves. Small business decries government deception when they see a tax increase." Michael could see eyes glaze over at the series of numbers that most couldn't comprehend.

"How's that put money In Our Pocket," a nameless lobbyist asked.

"And how does that give us access to the Trust Fund," Dodge added.

"It doesn't, directly. That would be illegal." Michael glanced at the stone faced legal team. "What it does is pay benefits and costs from the trust fund, while reducing contributions from business. The fund will drop and business will keep money they would have been required to contribute."

The ultras lobbied for tax deductions with large numbers of small businessmen acting as their foot soldiers. Small business expected that the brotherhood of businessmen will carry them along. All small business owners fantasize about one day being Big Business. Actually, the big business deductions would be passed along in social tax and increase the share of the burden on small business.

Raven understood. "When the hammer falls the small businessmen will continue to blame the government since they would be the bill collector. We feel their pain, sympathize and do nothing."

The Ultras were very forward in explaining the tax distribution to big business lobbyists. They did not have to hide the fact that the tax burden did not decrease but was shifting to small businessmen. No one in the room had any sympathy for the pawns they would use as foot soldiers in the tax reform campaign. "Every Korean grocer in the country will fall in behind us as fellow businessmen. A few will do the math and may complain but they don't have a voice. Or rather their complaints will fall on the government as typical tax complaints."

Most Ultras didn't follow the math but knew the organization was stacking the odds in their favor. Their accountant would explain it to them in terms of dollars saved. Boards of Directors were so detached from the numbers that they couldn't recognize the real winners as the big business lobbyists. Government bureaucrats, like Michael, could have told them the impact of slanted legislation, if they cared to ask. But they didn't even know the right questions to ask. Michael would have liked to set the record straight, but divulging information without being asked constituted lobbying and he was prohibited while in party employment, unless registered to do so.

"Now, about the Training Wage," Henry R. Parrots' pet project was intended to secure cheap labor. The public rationale was to allow U.S. businesses to compete; the actual effect was to reduce the cost of labor. Parrots' business analyst covered sub-wage jobs. Research showed that it was not the kids in summer jobs earning a little spending money. Most were adult wage-earners in the household and those kids who did hold the jobs, held them throughout the year and were a significant portion of the household income. Ultras recognized it as a losing argument unless they can find an example of abuse to present as the norm. 'The American worker can compete with anybody overseas', they would boast, 'if they had a level playing field'. A level playing field was virtually impossible while corporations used foreign sweat shops that ignored environmental and safety laws required in the United States.

"We'll have to table that for now," Dodge answered, "We need to sound green, and wages have been stagnant. It wouldn't be the right time to talk about Training Wage. After the elections."

Next the lawyers tackled the tricky problem of the various legal complications facing the party. Michael found himself nodding off during their presentation.

"Continue to put out the cliché that 'the little guy can't win'." Actually, the little guy could win and did so pretty regularly, especially with juries; thus the push for judicial reform. "Call any challenges frivolous lawsuits," even though the frivolous cases were most often rejected. "If that doesn't work, waive a jury trial and push for a judicial finding. Judges are easier to influence than juries." The Ultra philosophy dictated that if the case was judged against you, you changed the judge. It was the winning cases that worried the Ultra lawyers. "Talk of Judges 'Legislating from the Bench'…" That meant that the judge often saw the justice of small claimants as oppose to the Ultra lawyers. If the truism that 'the little guy can't win' was accepted by most of the little people, they would give up and the company would win by default.

"If you don't have the law on your side, attack the legitimacy of the charge and defame the organizations motives. Don't argue their evidence. Bean-counters and their data can be too convincing." The lawyer turned to Michael with a cheesy smile, "No offense, Corbett."

Michael just smiled. He was offended, but this was not the place for a display.

The Ultra Lawyers moved on to the legal considerations. They began by pointing out the distinction between the public platform and the strategic plan. The lawyers were interested in whether the proposals were clearly legal, clearly illegal or something with which they can maneuver. "If we can develop a reasonable sounding rational for the action, we can defend any court setback by claiming judges are 'Legislating from the Bench'," the lawyers reasoned. "At least it keeps us out of jail."

The word jail snapped Michael out of his boredom. The lawyers continued, "Convicting someone who is guilty is easy," Michael couldn't tell if the lawyer was joking or not, "convicting somebody who's innocent is much harder." Frighteningly, he seemed to be speaking from experience. "We can always put the judge on the defense by initiating impeachment. He would be removed from the case while the action is pending, and his successor would learn the consequences of not playing ball. We get the headlines and any retractions aren't news. The newspapers will bury any corrections and retractions away on page twelve."

Jail hadn't occurred to Michael. That was something that happened to the lower classes; those that couldn't afford a decent lawyer. What they did was good business. If something was not allowed, they simply passed a law allowing it. Illegal was not something they acknowledged; wrong-doing was the term to use for what they had not yet passed a law to allow. Wrong-doing was not criminally liable.

"Drop it!" Raven insisted, "That's not for this venue." He looked around at the lower level players, including Michael, that should not be privy to such discussion. The lawyers went mute.

"About requalifying for programs as required by the 13-points...?" Dodge changed the subject. "Many recipients will drop out in the face of legal challenges. Lawyers are cheaper than authorizing benefits for everybody. No offense Clay," Dodge smiled at Raven. Raven just continued with his note taking, ignoring the comment.

Michael could see the intent was to confuse enrollees.

Chip spoke up, "Statistically as many will choose the right route as will choose the wrong route, so expect a 50% decrease in those you need to serve." He seemed to relish the power and manipulation of the game. The young research assistant took the lead on this one. The procedure just embarrassed Michael.

Chip took his turn at the podium. His presentation covered how to package data to media outlets. He began with a parable that epitomized the difference between representing an informed electorate and using them for your own ends. "Suppose that you discovered that shifting the working time for city workers as the seasons changed would result in lower energy usage. Call it Daylight Savings Time. It is opposed by the light bulb lobby. An elected representative of a rural district, a district whose residents worked by the rising and setting of the sun, is contacted by panicking farmers who complain that the extra hour of sunlight will burn their crops." A splattering of laughter rippled through the assembled power brokers. "You could ease their fears, or..." he paused for effect, "...if you were elected with large contributions from the light bulb manufacturers and lamp makers, you might turn this misunderstanding to your advantage. Your energy industry supporters will lose money if the cities use thousands of hours less energy and demand goes down, along with the price that they can charge."

"Though the official knows damn well that the farmers are misunderstanding the concept, he may join the fight against those city-slicker politicians trying to fool with Mother Nature. The argument that it would hurt energy company shareholders is harder to make than letting them stew in their misunderstanding while supporting him as their hero. The farmers are not involved enough in the energy industry to know that with the defeat of such a law their energy costs will go up. Most logic arguments aren't as easy to detect and others will rely on the 'Some say' to put out information. But be warned, this is not proof. Don't get sucked in by somebody who says 'prove it'."

Michael felt uncomfortable that his assistant was advising this crowd on how to sidestep his research colleagues' legitimate demand for proof.

Chip continued with his tactics of subversion. "Don't neglect the effectiveness of push-polling. People just love to be asked their opinion. Pay some slob minimum wage to read a script. Asking, 'Would be more likely to vote for Joe Blow if you knew that he was a Moslem?' or "Would you vote for him if he says he's going to take away your social security?' They think they are being consulted when, in fact, they are being converted. And we aren't spreading lies. We're just asking questions."

Michael next explained qualifiers to the planning group. He felt a bit guilty as he explained the 'How to Lie with Statistics' methods to people he knew would intentionally misuse it. "I am the most important man in the meeting..." several scowls greeted Michaels' inflammatory announcement that was blatantly not true. He continued, "...that is from the west coast ...under fifty years old..." scowls turned to smiles as each of those at the table saw themselves excluded from the basic comment by the qualifiers. "...and married to a gorgeous woman..." some attendees looked offended as if he had said that their trophy wives weren't all that pretty. "... whose father was a gardener." That cinched it. No one else had a wife of such humble origins. The group, even those not very good at statistics, recognized how to manipulate qualifiers. "Say whatever you want and qualify it until it's true. If you are quoted in a sound bite, without the qualifiers, you're not liable. Michael Corbett was the highest ranking man in that Ultra meeting... minus the qualifiers. You can all act real humble, if you'd like."

Michael concluded, "And finally, if you want to get information out there that is demonstrably false or unconfirmed, just precede it with 'Some say… or put it in the form of a question. It keeps you from being quoted but gets the buzz going. For example, 'Is it true that you were caught with your hands in a little boys pants at a rest stop south of town last Saturday morning… that it was witnessed by an off duty deputy sheriff and a preacher… that you paid the childs' mother $10,000 not to press charges?' You give a lot of detail and the press thinks they have a story. Would you believe the guy if the answer is simply No? Or would you ask 'where were you last Saturday'? Would the press rush to check the police blotter? Look for money transfers? Suspicion will linger. And with all that scrutiny; who knows? They may even find something. From there the story has its' own legs, and you didn't commit liable. All you did was ask a question."

"Talk percentages. That can make a small difference seem dramatic," Michael concluded. The Ultras were impressed by the young Research investigator that seems to have a grasp of the truth versus the story that could be spun from the same information.

"We need to know where we may run into hurdles…," Dodge continued, "Who will object to which points and what can we do to nullify their complaints before they can do us any damage."

"We can strike out some of them right off the bat," Patson jumped in. "Those that won't have opposition… those that have been talked to death for years."

"The No Parole-No Plea element will have no organized support," Raven added briefly. "Tell people that they are likely to be the next victim, and you get their vote. Hell, you can lock up their mother and they'll thank you."

"Next, Streamline Government… who would argue against that?" When Raven spoke people listened. "Who can argue against the Flag burning initiative?"

Michael joked that they might also criminalize burning apple pie… or Mom. "Maybe we can require them to make Flags out of inflammable material," he joked. "Not that we can control that. Most flags are made in China."

Martha wasn't sure how to note the course of this discussion. She wanted to be thorough. It nearly derailed the meeting when she innocently asked, "what is the proper way to dispose of a flag?" Raven flew into a rage. "This is not a joking matter," he evidently assumed the startled woman was playing off Michaels' cynical comment. "We are talking about radical... destabilizing, " he trailed off still fuming. Only later did to go into the record that the proper way to dispose of a flag was...burning. The difference between reverent burning and protest burning was the issue. It was a respect thing. It was the wrong attitude that was criminal.

"This may be the opportunity to fill the ranks." Colonel South injected. "Recruiting is down with the overseas efforts stalled. Kids just aren't joining up for college anymore, if it means they may be deployed. We can call it National Service. Offer teaching... travel... old Peace Corps kind of stuff... "

"Good," Dodge picked up the theme, "Whatever they are qualified for... "

"And most will be qualified for nothing but military; mostly infantry. We can promote it while avoiding the appearance of a draft," South concluded.

"We don't want a military man to spearhead this," Raven said thoughtfully. "Limpaw, Patson, Benedict... you're the ones who should start the media buzz. Present it as national credits toward their share of the deficit. Something that translates into three years service. Patriotism... It might be a good idea to get some of your media commandos some real military experience."

"The real fight will come with the money issues," Parrot said. "The Balanced Budget provision can be equated with family budgets. That's worked in the past. The state organizations shot down the amendment, but most people don't know enough about the detail to feel threatened. We just have to present it as a tax and spend thing. Something that is costing families... a majority of people will go along. Go with the tried 'n true 'In Your Pocket' argument."

"But the deficit...?" Dodge asked. "Liberals will say we are taxing our grandchildren. Welfare for the rich... that angle."

"How about shared pain?" Patson suggested. "How much does each person owe?"

"He may have something there," Raven seemed inspired, "Total population divided by the deficit... share the burden... pay your share."

"How does that help?" Dodge was trying to fathom how telling every citizen that they owe so-n-so amount would help.

"Think about it," Raven continued. "Each and every person owes this much," he waved his hand indicating a hypothetical amount. "Pay your share and you're off the hook for your piece of the deficit. It could short circuit bickering about health, nutrition, foreign aid... any other money issues. Fair across the board. And at what cost?"

"I see... "Parrot cut in, "Those who can... pay; some make payments... we don't call it tax; fair share or something... those who don't pay can be put to work... community service... military... whatever. How much could it be?"

"About seventeen thousand seventy-five bucks." Michael did some quick math; approximate deficit divided by total population.

"Seventeen-seventy-five? Is that taxpayers? Voters?" Dodge wanted to know.

Michael had not thought that far ahead. "Just total population. A six point eight trillion deficit divided by four hundred million citizens. So, each man, women and child in the country."

"A lousy seventeen thousand bucks?" Patson seemed irritated. "How does that help? How does that put money 'In our Pockets'?" he used the cliché speaking point that had become the mantra of the Ultras to a few insider laughs.

"Think about it," Dodge was a little frustrated with the short sighted selfishness. "How much did you save with the tax rebate? Three, Four hundred thousand? Wouldn't you pay seventeen grand to steer clear of the graduated tax scheme that the liberals suggest? We can come off sounding like the level-playing-field, fair-all-around party, while the opposition sounds like they want big government... tax-n-spend."

"Yes," Parrot had seen the light, "If we call it 1776 it can sound awful patriotic. We can accept home equity, assets, inventory… take the focus off business."

"Excellent." Dodge resumed, "Michael, prepare a situation paper. Figure the cost per person to erase the deficit."

"Everybody?" Michael asked, "Children, disabled, incarcerated…
"

"Of course," Raven said without hesitation.

"We can appear compassionate by issuing exemptions," Limpaw spoke up. "Play up the compassion while demonizing the deadbeats."

"So be it," Dodge was ready to move on to the next issue. "About crime."

"Crime rates are dropping. Have been for some time," Michael announced.

"That won't do," Benedict said, "people want to hear about the threat. We in the media can't play up non-crime."

"A few prominent horror stories and the public will climb aboard," Dodge said. "That should also give us cover for the no parole-no plea provision; the upgrade police equipment and victims' rights provisions. That should buy us every city, county and state police organization; most anyway. The local communities will buy in as a means of getting a share of the funds."

"How about the morale issues?" Patson wanted to know. "Unborn rights?"

"We have a pretty blond woman who survived an attempt to abort," Benedict said, "She is a media magnet. She should be able to bring in enough support to supplement the hardcore anti-abortionists to get a quorum."

"You mean 'Pro-life'." Patson joked. "And just what do you mean 'Hard-core'?"

"Excuse me," Benedict smiled, "Those dedicated to life," as the new speaking point dictated.

"We got to frame it right," Raven, the political mastermind said thoughtfully, "Words matter. We don't need to use the word 'Abortion' or 'Fetus'. 'Child' buys us the moral high ground. Can we find a foreign doctor who performs abortions? That could tie into the fear of foreign involvement."

"The more inept the better," Limpaw said, "With a heavy accent. Why we need an official language… end foreign aid… military home defense… Those kind of protect the homeland and heritage provisions."

"Michael, can you scan the data for a doctor with a foreign sounding name? Maybe find a criminal record," Dodge instructed. Michael thought to himself, 'that's illegal; I'll have Chip do it'.

"The tough ones will be the health, nutrition, education issues," Raven tossed out. "These are things people think they deserve and we have to make cuts."

"We can be intolerant." Chip interrupted, "But don't call it intolerant; call it Zero-Tolerance." Raven looked impatient. As if the comment was a little too blatant. "It sounds cool," Chip continued sheepishly. He was learning the game from his new bosses. Raven looked pleased and took a quick note.

"If we talk Block Grants… Big dollars… we can sound generous while the per capita spending is drawn down," Parrot added. "but who looks at that?"

"Yes," Dodge agreed, "Cost of living increases three percent, population increases three percent and spending increases a dollar. We just make sure that we keep present budgets plus a dollar and we can claim we increased the budget and avoid the charge of cutting programs. Use soundbite quotes, with some of Corbetts' qualifiers. Let the opposition bean-counters try to explain the numbers. They'll put everybody to sleep," he turned to Michael with a smile. "No offense, Mikey."

"Just use the Patson approach…" Benedict said half joking, "We are spending so-n-so Mmmmmilllllllllion dollars. More than any previous administration." The group chuckled at the suggestion, but also took it to heart. They knew it would work.

Martha was scribbling fiercely with a furrowed brow. The minutes of the meeting would go to only a select group and every nuance had to be captured to keep the Ultra organization playing from the same sheet of music.

BEHIND CLOSED DOORS

Rising through the ranks of the party meant the inevitable social hours after the work day. These after work get-togethers were a quit different kind of event than Michael was familiar with in the military or academic world. These were not the mentally stimulating events that Michael enjoyed. His associates were not the well versed intellectuals of the University, or the Embassy staff; or even the well informed warriors of the Special Weapons cadre. The discussion turned to 'What ifs'; time travel as expressed by one of Michaels' heroes, H.G.Wells.

"Think of what a killing I could make on the market. I wouldn't have to bust my ass; or kiss ass to get to the top," Chip complained

"I'd go back to before I got married. No alimony, a trophy wife and a mistress too," Limpaw bragged. "The high school sweetheart looks good when you're in high school, but thirty-five years later all you got is an 'ol lady."

"I could have shredded those papers and saved myself years in court and all those lawyers' fees," a nameless lawyer mused.

"I think you all missed the point," Michael said. He was use to the college discussions and diplomatic debate of the Foreign Service professionals. Educated people bound to reality. Men whose future wasn't based on fantasy. "The point H.G. was making," Michael continued, "was that when people are not challenged, unambitious, lack curiosity, society can become mindless Elois. Or could become bestial, merciless Morlocks, living in darkness." His colleagues gave him only blank stares.

It occurred to Michael that they had never really read *The Time Machine*. They didn't know Eloi or Morlock. At best they had seen a movie. More likely some TV Sci-Fi rip-off that used time travel as a fantasy trip. People, or course, prefer the pure flights of fantasy. The down side is that they fail to learn the human truths and cultural lessons that the masters teach. They would rather engage in the escapism of sex, money and power. Michael found it vulgar and ignorant. He was among Morlocks.

Michael was surprised to find that he was invited to the closed door session. Second tier players were, generally, excluded from the closed door sessions.

"Off the record, Martha," Raven cautioned the note taker. "Why assume we have to pay anything? People have heard of the gold-plated health care for congressmen. Use it." Raven proposed a line of argument, "Why should congressmen, who make an average of so-n-so hundred thousand dollars, be subsidized by taxpayers? Let them pay their own way. Government health care costs are so-n-so million dollars..." he stopped and explained to the insiders. "Government, as oppose to Congress, will include Medicare, state and federal pensioners, police, firemen, governors to groundskeepers... Most people won't distinguish between Congressional gold plated versus government workers. It's all government. Rather than defend a slight increase or decrease, we let the opposition defend tax payer subsidized government plans. Unions will ask for something more. We argue something in lieu of nothing... and the unions will sound greedy by asking for more government spending. They'll have to settle for status quo; maybe less."

"How do we play this situation?" Bennett had to have the question framed correctly to maintain popular support. Social Security to too popular to oppose it directly. The SSI recipient that got a large award from the courts was the current heart-warming media star. "Do we cheer the average guy or condemn the out of control courts?"

"Call it a flexible response," Raven suggested. "On a case by case basis we can avoid endorsing the system while appearing flexible and compassionate. We can continue to condemn 'legislating from the bench'. Labor Union Bosses mean a socialist agenda. Unemployed were lazy. Single mothers were sluts."

"Though we don't use that word," Limpaw added. "We question her moral choices," Limpaws' plump face beamed at his own cleverness. "Everybody knows what that means; Slut."

"Self questioning can be effective; and evasive," Raven was giving directives and all went quiet. "Self questioning allows absolute answers in lieu of 'Maybe' answers to an original question. For example, if asked 'Are funding levels sufficient to achieve your stated goals in public education?' you respond, 'Are we making unprecedented efforts to bring in private contributions? DEFINITELY! Has the educational system failed us? UNQUESTIONABLY! That puts the argument in terms of them and us. If you don't agree, your one of the forces of failure... 'Have they failed us? ABSOLUTELY!' Then steer toward unions or illegal immigrants or violent teens, opinions that are not quantifiable; whatever, rather than dollar commitments. Further, using Absolutely and Definitely signals strength and self-assurance. Unquestionably, derails follow up questions."

"Disclosure," Raven continued. "If asked for 3 pages, give 'em 30,000. Empty your files on them. If the three pages in question get overlooked in transmission. So Be It! They look unreasonable. We look forthcoming... so-n-so pounds of paper. Call it a fishing expedition. And, don't shoot your mouth off on a slow news day."

Dodge continued, addressing the distasteful necessity of congressional testimony, "Draw out your answers from enemy questioners. It leaves 'em little time for follow-up, or other questions. If they interrupt you, they look rude. Meanwhile, short concise answers to many questions from friendly sources make you look honest and responsive."

Next he addressed the growing campaign contributions scandal. Contributors greased the wheels with huge amounts. Unattributed attack and advocacy ads had finally drawn unpopular attention. "Buy access with contributions to both sides. If one side exposed or criticized their actions, we could say that everybody does it. Give a token amount to the opposition, just in case. If the opposition can't be painted, call it a partisan attack. The opposition is left defending their attack tactics rather than talking about so called impropriety."

In a moment of candor Senator Dodge enthusiastically declared that they could "Govern as they please and tell the people what they want to hear... distract 'em with sex offenders loose in neighborhoods, scare farmers that the government will take their guns. Publish in TV and Gossip magazines were the burden of truth is not so great and the audience is not that well informed..." The mild mannered Martha looked appalled at her heros' irreverence.

The discussion continued with the mealticket program. The actuaries noted that they would save $116 million on child nutrition, while paying out just $73 million in spin advertising and gag order settlements for those denied. Serious malnutrition was forecast by the experts. "There should only be a few dead kids," Chip coldly declared, "The families will settle and court record will be sealed."

Martha left the planning session looking pale and hurt. She had just heard the people she thought were the tough-love protectors of the social order plan the overthrow of a loaves and fishes programs that had served the country well for nearly a century. The motive; greed. Michael suspected that she didn't like it any more than he, but she wouldn't speak. As far as she knew, Michael was the same brand of Ultra as the planners. Michael felt her pain and wished he could console her, but that might just mark him as uncommitted to the program.

People expect a dollar back for every dollar sent to Washington. Money allocated to projects was not spread out equally at the state level. Most poor neighborhoods didn't get back in service even a fraction of the taxes they submitted; they didn't have lobbyists.

Supply and demand had been the cornerstone of American industry. Marketing campaigns had evolved that created demand to fit supply. In tough times, this strategy fell apart. The automobile industry was suffering a severe drop in demand for their products. American society had no need for the vast number of cars produced. Furthermore, American manufacturers had played on the customers' ego by pushing muscle cars and oversized trucks; trucks for the workin' man. Though few were ever used to actually do any work.

With the recurring gas crisis, even the macho had discovered common sense and passed on the great deals that were being offered. Dealers found that people could drive less and stretch cars to their useful life; ten years plus.

The solution offered by the leadership was to save on labor costs; break unions. Labor Unions were formed to study and promote issues in the best interest of their members. The Ultras tactic was to turn members against the union leaderships' 'Liberal' agenda. The term 'Labor Bosses' conjured up the vision of the gangland days of criminal corruption. Members were targeted in the media and in mailouts that claimed their Union was giving money to unpopular candidates and self serving causes. The members were encouraged to complain to the Union and withdraw support. Ms. Colt proposed union membership vote on every donation, knowing that would slow the funding to enemy candidates. Never mind that the Unions had taken the time and effort to analyze the Ultra policies and found that they were not in the interest of working families; in spite of the grand sounding worker-friendly titles.

Business leadership had assumed that everyone would want more money. When people began refusing overtime to spend time with family, business found that the carrot was not enough; they needed a stick and the Ultras gave it to them.

Mandatory overtime had been defeated. Employers resorted to the twenty-nine hour week. Fewer hours per worker meant more per worker costs; withholdings and benefits. With workers unions defanged and on the defense by Ultra legislation, employers began a race to the bottom to eliminate the benefits of full time workers by reducing hours, or making them independent contractors.

The push was revived to require overtime; or else. The 13 states rights included the *Right to Work* Act. The *Right to Work* Act sounded good but it gave business the right to require overtime, overworking current employees rather than hire additional people that would mean higher per-employee costs. A worker would work the extra time or be replaced from the waiting pool of unemployed. Companies could freely fire workers close to retirement. The public reason was to bring new blood into the organization, to give the next generation a chance to enter the labor market. The Ultra insiders knew the unspoken reason was to shed expensive workers. Instances of inter-generational conflict abounded. But the older workers were the expensive ones, and cutting off pensioners was just a sound business decision. Thirty hours per week became the new full-time job, though it rarely provided enough for a family's needs.

Many, forced into overtime, were relabeled as 'Independent Contractors' rather than employees. Thus, no withholding, no benefits, no job security. This was sold to workers as 'Be Your Own Boss' independence.

Right to Work meant do as your told or your fired. Legal challenges went nowhere. It was all legal under the 13 States Rights doctrine. Workers were resigned to accepting whatever conditions employers enforced. The competition was 'business friendly' third world countries like Guatemala. They could use twelve year olds in unhealthy conditions for twenty-five cents per hour. The Ultras intended to make U.S. 'businesses friendly'. The policy didn't consider that American workers out of a job could not continue to buy stuff. Even the filthy rich only need so many washing machines.

The assault on Christmas was a God send to the Ultras' religious fundraising. At least, when they created the controversy, it seemed like a God given inspiration. When they saw the incredible windfall, they created an entire 'War on the Faithful'. The Ultras appointed themselves the guardians of the faith. After the holiday it was reworked into a War on Christians so that the fundraising could go on year round. They combed the country for any appearance of unchristian sounding events or court rulings. Patson encouraged the Ultra Commandos to cluster around Tithe Booths that were set up outside factories and other workplaces. People were encouraged, some said intimidated into pledging ten percent of their paycheck to the cause. Calling it a tithe added a spiritual component to the fund raising. Collection on the pledges was left to the not-too-delicate Ultra Commandos. Crosses were burned. Harassment at home and work became common.

The Ultras needed some interim funding. They intended to find an indefensible element of the population to target for more confiscation. Michael refused the assignment. They wanted data to show drug offenders were the equivalent of death peddlers; terrorists. Michael knew that drug users were everywhere in society and most users were guilty of nothing more than self-abuse. The Ultras needed more property to confiscate. He knew that his data would be construed to inspire another round of panic, imprisonment, life sentence labor, confiscation and even executions. They would pick and choose little unrelated bits of data to tell a dark story that wasn't true. He felt there were better things to investigate; more constructive things but his reservations made his commitment to the Ultra game plan suspect.

At some point the decisions turned Machiavellian; irrationally self-serving. Beyond survival, beyond prosperity, even beyond obscene opulence to the point of ludicrous. Dollars were points in some sort of perverted game. Nothing was produced; nothing was invested; it was a shell game. Pension plans, small businesses and public funds were converted to poker chips. Finally, even peoples' private possessions were confiscated to pay the police, when society shirked its responsibility. Most ultras considered it a stroke of genius. Make the criminals pay for the cost of law enforcement. More and more people were classified as criminals to meet the costs. Stiffer and stiffer penalties were levied for lesser and lesser offenses. Unless, of course, you were in the protected Ultra fold.

Michael came to a decision. He could no longer watch people deprived of their property and livelihood for the sake of a status game among the wealthy. He would have to lift the curtain; but anonymously. Just give some reputable reporter a peek under the curtain. He knew the embarrassing bits of information; the data that would disprove their cliché premises. He knew the questions that would unlock the floodgates of public information; that would deflate the Ultra misleading arguments.

The man to handle the story, a man with access and credibility was Frank Murrow. The prominent reporter had given up his high salary at the Network to work for the Public Broadcast System; a job he felt dealt more with people problems rather than info-tainment, fluff journalism or administration speaking points. He was still eagerly sought after as a freelance journalist by the print media.

Anonymous sources aren't worth much, but Michael knew things. He established his credentials with Murrow by leaving clues about what was coming in the culture war. When he called back after several reliable tips, Murrow was anxious to talk. Michael explained his position and some of the relevant data that he could provide without violating confidentiality. Murrow immediately saw the value and accuracy of the information and Michael knew that he could count on Murrows' discretion. He wouldn't be exposed by the newsman as a source. Michael planted the questions that would reveal the lies of the numbers games. When they misstate the plain facts with speaking points, Michael would queue Murrow.

To his shame he had helped write the 13 States Rights Provisions of the veto proof congress; brought to life by combining the many one issue factions. The time had come to face the music; to unmask the beast. Rumors leaked into the newsrooms of an insider, a member of the Ultra team, who had been pushed too far and refused to cooperate. Typical media over dramatization. He had not refused to cooperate. It was an honest assessment that some project was a wasteful diversion of time and money; that some demonized group was actually harmless; that some pending evil was benign. When asked, he made the mistake of venting his frustration with more than 'No Comment'.

"The speaking points will include 'Welfare guarantees that people would never look for a job'. Ask how many leave welfare to take jobs, Frank," Corbett suggested. "It's tens-of-thousands per month. It was all public information. Ask the average duration on assistance."

This was something that the Ultras didn't highlight and that they hoped wouldn't be noticed. The Ultra mouthpiece would conveniently neglect to ask for information, unless the facts were in public discussion. That would avoid the necessity of a lie. They often avoided asking the answers to questions they didn't want answered, if it contradicted their policy proposal. Michael had seen it before in everything from food assistant to veterans' benefits. The Ultras preferred to float the myth of multi-generational claims. The public information that their spin machine could not disguise was '...duration on average was less than a year...' When they proclaim that '...welfare was expensive...and...half of government money is going to assistance programs...' it sounded as though a huge portion of federal funds went to the undeserving. More tax cuts... more program cuts. Michael suggests that Murrow ask, 'Does 'Assistance Programs' include SSI, Medical assistance for the elderly, blind, disabled and war veterans?' The public information said, 'yes'.

These were things that people believed in and were willing to pay for. 'Welfare alone?' 'Single digits,' the Ultras would have to answer sheepishly, exposing their attempt to mislead. The politically softer sounding term for what they did was 'spin', not deception. But people were intentionally deceived. They were being dishonest and those that tried to sound the alarm were accused of 'just playing politics'.

He felt like a traitor. But wasn't a traitor to a devious cause actually a hero? Whistle-blower laws were circumvented by tricky legal non-disclosure agreements so that business had the legal grounds to punish whistle-blowers without denying allegations. The story became the integrity of the informer rather that the truth of the revelation. And any informer faced well financed character assassins.

Michael wouldn't violate his security oath. But the Ultras found themselves facing something that they had tried to conceal in bureaucratic doubletalk. They were forced to reveal the selection process that deflated their claims of public support at some orchestrated rally. Just the right polling data was revealed to counter some outrageous claim. An Ultra mouthpiece, in a run-on sentence, had qualified some issue to the point of nonsense and the ploy was exposed by the awkward question.

The Ultra elite were suspicious. The questions had become too pointed; the most embarrassing piece of data, and all public information. The question that the Ultra watchdogs asked themselves was, 'Who would know such specialized data? Data collected at taxpayer expense by the Department of Labor? Selective sorts that most people ignored? And all public information. The hierarchy concluded that there had to be an inside source that knew where they were vulnerable.

Michael had access to the data and could not avoid suspicion. He knew the noose was tightening when they asked about Chips' loyalty. He couldn't lie. Chip was trustworthy; in their sense of the word. He would spin their perverse logic to earn his place in the fortunate fraction. Chip wasn't the leak. Michael knew they were asking others as well and he had narrowed down the list of suspects, maybe to an individual; maybe to himself.

The next money saving/skimming plan was the Ultras' campaign to gut the food stamp program; just more poker chips. They intended some kind of loaves and fishes symbolism to shift responsibility to faith based organizations. They had Michael find a family meeting their criteria. The showboat fraud that would generate public outrage and justify the hard hearted denial of funding.

Senator Dodge had put his blessing on the food stamp replacement program that the Ultras called mealtickets. The Lawyers had calculated that the savings in food assistance would be greater than the outflow to fully justified lawsuits. The cost/benefit analysis came down against the common good and common decency for the needy.

National Nutrition established the Mealticket program to replace food stamps. The program came under fire from advocates for the needy. Ultras perverse logic promoted the idea that people would be shamed into fending for themselves. The embarrassment would save the cost of service to those who would be humiliated; thus money would be saved.

The request for data came down from the party hierarchy. Run queries against the food stamp databases for the following conditions: Family size four or more, one adult, two of the children born in the last three years, one while drawing assistance, criminal record.

Michael could see it coming. This was not the first time he had witnessed the deck being stacked against some unsuspecting victims. Indeed, he had been the dealer in a few of these scams; and was richly rewarded. First the media talking heads would wail against some supposed widespread abuse. Then the Ultra machine would generate the showcase example to prove the point. They would look prophetic and fiscally prudent and thousands of desperate families would be left to fend for themselves. The Ultras would then reward themselves with a bigger slice of the pie.

The campaign began. 'Lazy, immoral, who knows what criminal transgression.' Michael knew the number of abuses were very small. The benefit to the public very substantial, but the Ultras would keep it vague and threatening. And besides they could not release personal data due to confidentiality so the expectation was that no one would know the magnitude of criminal involvement; or lack thereof.

Other information Michael provided on the handful of cases was conveniently left out. One widowed in a workplace accident. The Ultras had drained the funding for safety inspectors that covered that industry. She was found with an obsolete company laptop in her home. The crime was theft. Another was a single parent because her Military husband abandon her. Four months in dental technician school, not long term. She had lived in base housing when she gave birth. Military housing was categorized as housing assistance. Criminal record? Her husband was AWOL for the birth of her child, which was a crime attributed to the household. Confidentiality meant that this relevant information could not be made public. So Michael did the only thing he could think of.

The venerated Frank Murrow took his seat at the Ultra press conference. He rarely attended, but a seat was always available to him. He was equipped with a bundle of questions. Questions that would shock and disorient the Ultra mouthpiece. They smiled and prepared the speaking points, not knowing that they had just stumbled into Murrows' ambush. And Michael had provided the snare.

'Ask, 'how many cases like that are there? What's typical?' Michael suggested some questions to Murrow. 'Summary data is not confidential. How many military families?' Hidden among the officers, retirees, single soldiers, Guard and Reserve was an unbelievable statistic. Michael did a query to test the scale of the problem. Married, active duty, enlisted, with children. He was floored; nearly all would qualify for assistance and a large number were already enrolled in various programs.

The Ultra press conference was again abuzz with the much repeated speaking points, 'Lazy, criminals, loose morals... people taking handouts generation to generation...' Then the round of questions.

Taking a page from the Ultras' playbook, Murrow primed his colleagues with some interesting questions. The Ultra mouthpiece could avoid Murrow, but they couldn't avoid Murrows' questions.

"How much is spent per family on food?" Shockingly little.

"Are widows, orphans, disabled veterans and the elderly included?" Yes.

"How many kids are kept out of malnutrition on the program?" Millions.

"How many supposed criminals?" Maybe a few dozen.

"How long is the average family on assistance?" A couple of months.

Then the venerable Frank Murrow rose. A hush came over the room and that the Ultra press agent couldn't ignore. "Mr. Murrow," he was recognized to ask his question.

Then the final cut that doomed the Ultras' charade, "How many active, enlisted military families depend on assistance to feed their children?" That was too specific. Just military they could have fudged. Include officers, retirees, National Guard and Reserve and they could present an acceptable smallish slice. But specifically 'Active' and 'Enlisted'. The number was shocking. The admitted thousands of military families put into perspective the insignificant few dozen that the Ultras were trying to paint as the norm.

It had happened before when pay scales did not keep up with the cost of living. National Guard and Reserve troops were pulled from well paid civilian jobs and forced into lower active duty pay scales. Stop-loss insured that many could not return to an adequate civilian job. No longer was the military a weekend supplement; but an insufficient family income. Military families had turned to the social programs to supplement their income and provide for their families. Michael was surprised by the numbers that the computer had spit out. He felt an obligation to his military brothers.

He made sure that the Ultras knew the figure and couldn't dodge the question. Murrow had even provided some answers to the attending press. The Ultras attempt to divvy up food stamp savings through luxury tax relief (their 'what will you have to leave to your kids' campaign) went nowhere. None of the elected representatives would vote to kill a program that helped so many military families.

The event fell flat as follow-up stories in the press painted the typical recipient as the struggling Warrior and his family rather than the Ultra slut myth. The outcry of the public against such a cold hearted provision flooded the congressional mail service and electronic facilities. President White promised another irrelevant veto. The national media, finally finding their courage, roundly condemned the National Nutrition Act as a fraud. In spite of the outcry, the Veto-proof congress felt untouchable. The money was there for the taking, and they had gotten away with similar larcenies so often that they felt invincible. They dismantled the food stamp program before it could be challenged in court. Records were destroyed so that it could not be quickly re-implemented. But Murrow had laid the truth before the American public, and the Ultras suspected that he had help from the inside.

Ultra organization investigated the trail of who would have known. Though nothing was provable, or criminal, suspicion was on Michael. They had not asked for the little details provided as background. They found it suspicious that it had been provided as non-speaking points at a particularly awkward time.

As suspicions grew the Ultra security team took steps to root out the leak. Phones were bugged, Michaels' among them. It wasn't legal, but it was never intended to be used as evidence in court, so that didn't matter.

BLACK LAKE

Michael referred to it as 'The Homestead'. He had kept it apart during his high powered days of rushing around the country putting out political fires for the Party. He expected that when he was ready to settle down, this would be his retreat. He had searched out just the right place with just the right features. He found it at Black Lake in the wooded area just outside the state capitol. It was Michaels' wedding present to Suzanne; their special hide-a-way.

A development had grown up around the once secluded lodge. Black Lake was prime development property in commuting range of the city. A quite modest community settled in between the lake shore and the vast public forest. So out of the way that the street plan had not even been completed. The main drag followed the shoreline along the lake. Just back from the lake was the slope of a gentle hill and another row of houses with a lake view. On a second tier of hills just beyond, an additional band of lots was laid out.

The newer additions on the fringe were as yet, and would remain, dead ends. They were planned, during the optimism of the housing bubble. Each of the neighbors, to discourage overbuilding and to insure a green belt, bought the lot behind their home. The uncleared lots formed a band around the eight houses sharing Walden Court. These would have been building sites for the next street. But that next street was never completed and the neighborhood had a splendid isolation even from the larger community of the housing development. It wasn't even on the county maps. The new development, on the far side of Black Lake, was outside the city limits and still just a crossroad on the map. It seemed only the residents even knew it was there. The single access road led only to the homes within. This insured that there was no through traffic.

The planned link to the highway beyond was never completed, and that was fine with the inhabitants of Black Lake.

The land around the lake was bought up by developers so that the entire shoreline was private property. Community action groups tried to sue to get public access but Michael and the neighbors fought them in court and kept them at bay indefinitely so the lake stayed pristine and private.

In the down-time between campaigns and legislative sessions, Michael and Suzanne retreated to the Homestead and slowly, quietly built their retreat. The large lot, double in size to start with, was expanded with the greenbelt behind. The large wooded addition was crisscrossed with trails and surrounded with a solid six foot fence. The nature trails were accentuated with tall evergreen trees that insured cool summers and a windbreak during the stormy months. A thick, thorny hedge of blackberry bushes lined the front and sides, providing privacy. It also gave the neighborhood kids, walking to the bus-stop, a light snack.

A small orchard was his first project; just a few dozen trees. Cherry trees, apple, plum, walnut, peach and pear trees were planted. At the time they were too young to produce fruit, but it was a long range plan. A plot was laid out for strawberries; Michaels' favorite. They began to produce in abundance almost immediately. Suzanne insisted on a vegetable garden. Michael was complacent about that. He had never much cared for his veggies. But the garden produced carrots, radishes, tomatoes, potatoes with smaller installments of other edibles and exotic spices.

Another season saw the addition of grape vines. Michael thought he might dabble in wine-making; though he liked grapes more than he liked wine. His pioneer spirit originally focused on useful, edible plants. Suzannes' sense of beauty, though, inspired the rose garden and a profusion of colorful flowers with pleasant scents that Michael had grown to appreciate; even though you couldn't eat them. During vacations, he would play at self-sufficiency by attempting to go for a week without a trip to town. If something was wanting, he would try to fill the need for the next visit. Running short of gas for the pairs' jet skis during one getaway, Michael installed a 500 gallon gas tank. Another season saw the addition of a couple of mountain bikes.

There was a small outer building in the fenced back yard that Michael had converted to dry storage. He assumed that, with inflation, prices would only increase. The little building was stacked from floor to ceiling with food and supplies that had a shelf life; bulk foods bought for storage to save on future spending.

The adventures of the old sailing ships had fascinated Michael. He was amazed and thrilled by the fact that men would go to sea and remain out of touch with civilization for months. He modeled his hideaway on the self sufficiency of the old time sailors.

Supplies were saved for a time when the value of paper money and the debase silver-colored coinage was worth less; inflation. Or deflation; goods produced in vast quantities while there is less money in circulation. It could happen. China, Korea and Japan were increasingly leery of the United States' deficit. They had already suspended exports of some products until the Americans settled outstanding debts. That left only enough supply to satisfy those with the ability to pay. That's the business community he knew. In any event, his supplies would only become more valuable.

For cereal, he had stacked Wheaties, Rice Krispies and Corn Flakes. Wheat, corn and rice, he figured, for long term use. The several cases of each were some of the last available when the production and distribution systems broke down. Large airtight bins of salt, sugar and flour that he hoped would save him a trip to town became the stuff of survival. There were also crackers, pudding and various other common things that he never would have thought of as staples.

Routine items like jelly, peanut butter and dehydrated milk were stashed away. If it didn't need to be refrigerated, it was stocked in bulk in the storehouse. Suzanne had made fun of his juvenile passion for the plain shortbread animal crackers, but he had a number of the clown shaped kegs of the cookies to last as long as he thought he would need. He packed away a few luxuries like cigars, incense and such.

They had the basic medical supplies; vitamins, aspirin, antiseptic, gauze and band-aids. Bleach, soap and some non-consumables. Also, bulk pocket lighters. Boy Scouts had taught Michael that every adult should be able to make fire.

In addition to his hobby orchard, he had cases of peaches, pears, pineapple, applesauce and some mandarin oranges. Lemonade, soap, soup, cocoa and coffee were stacked by the crate. A self-charging flashlight and radio were stored away for any power outages. It would only get more expensive, he reasoned. At the time he didn't imagine how vital these supplies would be. Money of any denomination could not buy what was not available.

Subsequent seasons saw the addition of a Kennel and a pair of Huskies; Caesar and Cleopatra. A few sheep were brought in to act as lawn mowers in the orchard. The neighborhood kids earned barter credit as caretakers. Suzannes' Easter chicks matured into plump hens. Though Michael would joke about fried chicken, she would have none of it. Michael ended up building them a chicken coop instead. He even provided a rooster to keep the hens happy. A salt lick was added to attract the, almost domesticated, deer that roamed the nearby woodlands. Caesar and Cleo became competent herders and seemed to enjoy the exercise. With Suzannes' gentle care and guidance the animals all seemed to get along.

In another season, the sloped roof of the house at Black Lake sported a coating of solar panels that provided enough power for the house and the out buildings. An aid organizations efforts to bring clean water to Africa, introduced Michael to the idea of a private well powered by a kind of merry-go-round. To pump water all that was needed was a few turns of the platform; or a brisk run by Caesar and Cleo.

The neighbors were initially amused, then sold on the idea, and before long several of the houses in the community also had solar power and a private water supply. In addition, a large water tank was installed to catch rain water for irrigation and an occasional swim by the Homesteads' animals.

The neighbors seemed to share his rustic views. Jonathan, the neighbor to the right, fancied himself a gentleman of property and built a stable with fenced areas where he raised several horses. Being a retired rancher, he knew the ropes. His sons had taken over the family business. Mosey and Lois, the retired couple of the left had what appeared to be a farm in miniature. They tended their property with a miniature lawn tractor complete with snowplow and tiller; even 'ol Bossy, the cow. Furrowed rows of corn and other crops stretched in straight, well cared for rows. Mosey even plowed the dead end street when the snows came. The county never got around to serving the out of the way streets of Black Lake. The newer areas, Walden Court among them, did not even appear on the regional maps.

The residents, collectively, insured that the development would have everything they needed. A twenty-three acre park was set aside for wildlife and community activity. Deer and ducks frequented the park seasonally. The community built a club house on the lakeside with a boat launch and recreational equipment to be shared by the Lakers.

As a reaction to the high cost of everything, the Black Lake residents instituted the Service Exchange. In effect, a barter system among the locals. The Plumber earned service credits to apply toward having his roofing done; the carpenter received credit to have his kids vaccinated; the local mechanic found a tutor for his failing child. Black Lake barter clubs provided day care. Suzannes' needlepoint bought them landscaping. Classes were conducted as fireside chats regarding financial planning, gardening and a range of other subjects. No money changed hands. No taxes were paid.

Coming from a working class background, Suzanne had learned sewing and had become an excellent seamstress. Her sewing was a personal hobby where she found relaxation in a creative outlet. Michael felt rather useless at the organizational meetings. As a Statistical Analyst he had little to offer in exchange for services. His skill was not considered particularly useful. Suzanne, on the other hand, was in demand for her incredible needlework; both the finished work and her informal classes. The proliferation of such clubs eventually drew the attention of the State and Federal authorities. They saw their revenue sources circumvented and sought a way to bring the renegades back into the fold; or more accurately, return them to a paying basis.

The Legislators responded to their business contacts by passing a law requiring barter clubs to declare the fair-market-value of the exchanged services for tax purposes. The clubs were outraged, but they had little political power and were generally ignored. In response the clubs generally ignored the law; declaring only when it was unavoidable. Another group of ordinarily law abiding people became part of the criminal class in the eyes of the governing authorities. These authorities, like Michael, had few marketable skills and did not benefit from such arrangements. Their job was to allocate tax revenue and the barter system undercut their source of funds. The goods and services were not on the table and subject to electronic measuring and manipulation.

The Internal Revenue Service, well aware of the routine avoidance of the law, used the courts to demand records of service credits from community groups. Many groups resisted as best they could, but faced with the overwhelming power of State and Federal government, they didn't have a choice. Michael found that Suzannes' skills were assessed at several thousand dollars for tax purposes. That translated to a couple of hundred dollars more in taxes.

Many people dropped out; others shorted the hours and credits with a cooked set of books. Most went underground. Michael wondered about his culpability if it were revealed that he knew of the secret set of books that the Black Lake Barter Club began to keep.

The Black Lake residents benefited from each others' expertise. Michael was able to give some tips on financial planning. His neighbors, Mosie and Lois, had already done some planning. They did not own their home. They had retired and signed over the business to his three sons, as had his rancher neighbor. His house was also signed off and he was renting at the cost of his Social Security payments. Food and clothing become the responsibility of his sons and the retired couple became dependents on their childrens' taxes. It was the Hamilton system gone mainstream.

Michael continued to receive his hefty paychecks but it counted for much less. The Ultra organization was still able to raise the big bucks from its' satisfied fat cats. People would not put up with this unequal distribution indefinitely. He saw his job as rearranging deck chairs on the Titanic. He felt he didn't need to worry much as long as a place on the lifeboat was saved for him.

Without government money, not only government workers, but contracts to private industry dried up. Highways deteriorated. Construction and maintenance work evaporated. Construction workers who had cursed government intrusion were out of a job. Local small business felt the pain of an unemployed community. Gift shops went first; then flower shops. Name brands were passed over for subsistence spending. Large ticket stores full of things people didn't need saw sales plummet. Products that depended on fitness, toys or glamour struggled. Marketing firms saw no effect of their services and lost their client base. Impulse buying was rejected. Products used for their entire useful life meant factories needed far less production. Downsizing was back in vogue. Real need was being satisfied rather than need manufactured by marketing firms. These firms, many newspapers and radio and TV stations failed. Many who had misunderstood and damned the social safety net found themselves destitute and in need of just those kinds of services.

Martin had also received a lot of attention from the entertainment-cloaked-in-news industry. First as a somewhat comical but charismatic self-proclaimed prophet. His crusade to boycott cards for all occasions was covered as a joke filler piece. 'Don't get your kids a card, get them fresh fruit' sounded comical to those who never had to worry about the next meal. His urban garden sermon was adopted in many areas, as was his 'don't give flowers, give seeds' campaign. He started a 'reprieve a chicken' program with the slogan 'eat chicken once, or have eggs for life for chicken-feed'.

Some of his other teachings such as, 'divine or not, the JC story shows religious and civil authorities can kill an innocent man' struck home with poor white Christians as well as blacks.

Street gangs, such as the Bloods and Crips, had matured and made peace. Under the guidance of Reverend Mathias and his brother Moses, the urban dwellers resurrected the Black Panther label in the form of community welfare and education for the underserved. A new generation of black youth were educated to the accomplishments of their baby-boomer parents. He encouraged people to cut-out-the-middleman. His 'Talk to a farmer and skip the middleman' put him in serious news. The establishment portrayed him as a tax cheat, but the average viewer cheered him on.

A series of price cut wars started that not only did not restore confidence, but served to show consumers just how low prices could be. Rage of past years of gouging translated into boycotts. Communities bought up local stores and ordered according to their needs rather than to support marketing ploys. Mathias' communal stores idea outraged Parrot and drew away business from his USA stores. Meanwhile, old established institutions like public libraries and the postal service were struggling. A letter cross-country in a couple of days for less than half a buck seemed a distant memory. Books and information free at public libraries were remembered as the good 'ol days.

Asian methods of pooling their savings for community financing gave homeowners reasonable rates. Landlords who had been living on other peoples' earnings were furious. The cash flow and equity seminars that showed people how to maneuver themselves into home ownership, and ownership of other peoples' homes, didn't prepare them for a mass renters' revolt and mortgage default. Their cash flow stopped flowing. Evictions were impossible with most of the legal and police personnel on furlough. With limited staff, courts rejected most cases and police could only handle serious crime calls. Threats and intimidation did not work. Landlords held the paper but banks continued to collect mortgage payments from their accounts whether their tenants made payment or not. Inflow dried up, but outflow continued. The get-rich-from-motivated-sellers schemes collapsed.

Neighborhood watch groups supported and protected people in their communities. Teams of evictors hired by landlords were outnumbered and ejected from apartment complexes. Changed locks were summarily broken and removed. The government ceased to produce rent subsidy checks. Petty slum lords, who had complained about a few dollars in taxes and government regulation, found out what their money had paid for; a stable society with power of enforcement. Without police authority they had no protection and no sympathy from people that saw them as abusers. Investors overseas found that their American citizenship had protected them from extortion and other common third world business tactics. Without an effective diplomatic corps, they fell prey to foreign abuses.

The landlords incomes were drying up and they had no way to stop it. Some recanted their anti-government regulation views; sending in past money, in hopes society and government would right itself and they could resume routine collections from their tenants. But it was too late. Tenants could plainly see how powerless they were without the courts, police and government regulation.

Banks and credit unions with large holdings in mortgages began to fail. People who had proudly boasted on info-mercials that they had over a million dollars in equity found that their resources amounted to a couple of hundred bucks in their checking accounts, if the banks honored the checks. Those with equity worth millions found that paper wealth meant nothing in a squatters market. They were not Ultras and not only 'not Ultras', but the Ultras were more than willing to drain their electronic accounts.

A tenant who refused to be ejected was shot dead by a landlord. For a week the media portrayed landlords as the bad guy. There were cries for a law to protect tenants from landlords. Of course there already was a law called premeditated murder. But the knee jerk legislature responded with a new law against forced evictions by other than authorized civil authorities; just symbolic, costless.

Then a landlord was shot dead by a tenant and suddenly the tenants were the bad guys of the week. The law enacted in response functioned like the widely misunderstood restraining order. It could not prevent someone from making contact but served to provide legal or criminal grounds for an arrest if a violation occurs. But arrest and prosecution still depended on police and courts without the resources to enforce the law. The new laws were good for peace of mind but made no difference to landlord-tenant relations. But that didn't matter. It was just window dressing.

A property owner shot a thief that burglarized his home and the gun lobby rose to his defense. They were a little embarrassed to find that he had shot the man at a bus stop three days after the theft. This changed the situation from a dangerous 'heat of the moment' response to premeditated murder. But the gun groups held their ground.

Human redefined as conception meant that an at-risk woman could be confined till birth. Personal decisions that women had made for thousands of years made American women and doctors criminals. Incrementally, women and their doctors become guilty of child abuse, manslaughter then murder. The Ultra slut myth portrayed women and doctors as sex offenders. Everyone became a criminal of some sort.

A new law was enacted to please the Ultra anti-abortion allies that tracked pregnant women and doctors suspected of providing abortion. There was an unintended result in that stalking laws were used successfully by health care workers and doctors to prosecute conceptionists that tracked workers to their homes. The Conceptionista movement chose to retreat rather than be bunched into the same category as stalkers and sex offenders.

The Ultras were falling out of favor. Many of the worst abuses were becoming public. The unfortunate masses were getting an unflattering picture of what the fortunate fraction had been up to, and they were out for blood. Among the Ultras that could mean only one thing; heads would roll. Not very well placed and expendable heads. Michael suspected that he fit the profile. They would be looking for someone to take the brunt of the anger. They would eat their own.

Michael was vacationing with Suzanne and her folks at Black Lake when the story hit the news. He had hoped to stay out of the spotlight, but the Ultras were throwing him to the wolves.

The major new organizations had the full story from unanimous background leaks; Chip and Raven, Michael suspected.

"Evidence of insider abuse by those in power is, dramatically, coming to light," Limpaw was doing his part to get the story out in a way that suited the party. "Michael Corbett, an intelligence analyst, was caught on tape conspiring with the liberal media, damaging national security." By national security, of course, he meant Ultra privilege. "Chip Libby, speaking for the Ultra organization, informs me that the information is too sensitive for public release. But indications are that this 'Corbett' worked for state and federal government; even a U.S. Senator. Inside sources tell me that Michael Corbett was the most important of the young, west coast researchers in attendance at a number of policy meetings." Michael couldn't argue with that. They had qualified their accusation to the point of truth. "Using his secret security clearance, he evidently passed damaging information to the liberal attack machine and, some say, to foreign enemies."

Michael was speechless. James and Ruth looked at him in disbelief. Citing the leak as national security kept the public from knowing the exact nature of the information that was compromised; actually just public information.

"Homeland security has recordings of Corbett arranging data transfers. Did he seriously damage national security? What did our enemies give him in return for secrets that endanger our children? Some say, his lavish lifestyle was far above the means of a government worker." A not too flattering picture accompanied the story.

It was obvious that they would be coming for him. He could call a lawyer, try to stall, but that would just keep the story in the news. Eventually they would trace him to the Homestead. Better to give himself up in the city and let the search end there rather than risk being portrayed as captured on the lam. He knew his best chance was to keep it low key. No fuss, no publicity, no lawyers. He made the short trip to the house in the city.

The press had the place staked out. There was a news van with a smartly dressed newswoman giving some kind of broadcast as his car pulled up. They, evidently, knew what car to look for as he was instantly besieged by a bank of microphones thrust into his face as he climbed out. A barrage of illegible questions bombarded him as he made his way to the door. Within minutes the police were at the door and the perp walk to the patrol car followed.

'Hopefully,' he thought, 'it ends here'.

SPEAK OUT

"If it costs just one life, it's one too many." The middle-aged women in conservative dress had her chance to be heard; to 'Speak Out'. That was the term used to indicate that a pronouncement didn't have any news value, but the producers wanted to present it to fill air time. After the hour of real news, the 24-hour news channels needed something to fill the remaining 23 hours. So, testimonials and uninformed opinions were broadcast as news. Cheap to produce, and as enticing as spicy gossip. Talk shows were a media moguls' gold mine.

The popular daytime talk show was just such a forum for people to 'Speak Out'. The show presented sensational stories of the way life sometimes is; but seldom is. Rare and outrageous themes were presented as the norm and often resulted in a public demand for new laws; that often had horrific unintended consequences. But it served the Ultra purpose of maintaining the atmosphere of fear that kept them in power.

Troy Benedict, the shows' host, incited anger in an entertaining way and usually provided a few sacrificial lambs on stage for the audience to abuse. The show began as a light theme show with constructive ideas and a panel of experts that spoke of solutions. But education was boring and distasteful facts were dismissed as liberal deception. The episodes lost their serious subjects and took on a pornographic tone. Attention grabbing guests, or rather victims, took the spotlight.

Violent skinheads? Why not? Violence also got a viewing bump. Many people were willing to appear for a minute of fame. They didn't need to be paid like a panel of experts. Curiously the shows descriptions became vague. How to cope with difficult children or home remedies shows had a constructive purpose. Themes became, 'Teenage hookers!' Not 'rescuing teenage hookers' or 'educating violent skinheads', just a daily freak show. Any thought of helping anyone was lost in the cheap media hype for entertainment and abuse by a judgmental audience and host.

Anything could be presented as a disability in the land of plenty. People listen as a man described his struggle from 610 pounds to achieve 180 pounds. He got enthusiastic applause from an audience who had themselves struggled with weight problems. The audience wasn't entirely sympathetic. Many saw this as abuse of the resources of the planet. To call obesity an epidemic when so many people in the world are starving, endeared no one to America. Michael thought it obscene that a country could be self-centered enough to speak of an epidemic of obesity; after the misery of hunger and want he had seen in overseas shit-holes.

The guests were herded up one stage like zoo animals. Come see the human freaks. Laugh at their misfortune. Judge them with only the sketchiest information and verbally abuse and humiliate them for your pleasure. Sexual subjects got the best ratings. Like the frustrated puritans devoutly inspecting the naked bodies of accused witches, the audience felt they were doing something constructive while subconsciously getting their titillation.

"And if I told you a law could have saved little Kristy's life?", Benedict continued. Little Kristy, blond, blue-eyed, had been hit be a Pakistani diplomats' son. The nineteen year old Pakistani youth had lived in the United States since he was ten. His father was an attaché before being appointed ambassador and had raised his son in American culture. The family, however, had retained its' foreign citizenship and as such had diplomatic immunity. A terrible accident had occurred that was being portrayed as negligent homicide; even murder. Actually failed breaks; General Motors brakes. But that didn't stir the emotions and grab ratings. But Benedict had just primed his victim by implying the subject was safety or quality engineering. He had something else in mind.

Senator Dodge, a prominent Ultra political representative, and Robert Patson, the self appointed representative of God and rich

Christians, sat on stage waiting for their queue. Benedict was walking the isles, jabbing the microphone in the face of opinionated viewers.

"We need the law then," the women said confidently. She thought she had her daytime hero on her side.

"So, Cheryl here thinks we need another FEDERAL MANDATE?" He paused as the audience moaned right on queue. Occasionally Benedict would ambush an audience member like this. State all the benefits without the mention of the downside until the unsuspecting person had bought into his superficial proclamation. Poor Cheryl now found herself saddled with the term 'Federal Mandate". Everyone knew that was a bad thing. A law kept the riff-raff in their place. A mandate took money out of your pocket.

This time he had begun talking public safety and in mid discussion, switched from the term 'Law' to 'Mandate'. A codeword of the Ultras' for Government interference. Benedicts' focus groups had told him that people had a negative reaction to the word and he used it, like the showman he was, to surprise and disorient his victims; and to stir up the audience. The unsuspecting audience member found out, too late, that the subject wasn't traffic safety; it was foreigners. "Mandate a 30 mile per hour speed limit everywhere, all the time, and we will save thousands of lives a year," Benedict baited.

The audience roared in objection. The women cowered meekly at the rage directed at her. That was not what she suggested. She considered herself an Ultra. But she was in the crosshairs.

"We don't need more Federal Mandates," Senator Dodge said calmly from the stage. He presented himself as the voice of reason, "We need common sense." Benedict and Dodge were old friends and Benedict was giving him a victim. Dodge was good for ratings and Benedict was more than willing to give the Senator a platform. "For example the *Home Defense Provision* of our thirteen States' Rights petition not only brings our troops home but protects our borders as well. I don't want any more Americans put In Harms' Way by foreign criminals and terrorists... or foreigners driving the roads of our great country with no restraint."

The audience started to applaud but Dodge raided his arms for quiet. He hadn't reached the punch line yet. "Do we need our troops in Columbia, protecting Columbians? Or do we need them here at home protecting our borders? We have foreigners in this country that are putting our children at risk. Here is where the focus should be." The war in South America was not going well and the Ultras were ready to declare victory and pull out.

Patson jumped in, "Little Kristy could have been saved not by another Federal Mandate but by making sure our borders are monitored to keep out the trash that abuses our medical, education, transportation systems and American children."

So that was the direction. Not traffic safety, but using the military to seal the borders; or rather misdirecting the public to a threat at home. The new focus could cover a policy reverse. The Ultras would then announce success and disengage from the Columbian disaster. Dodge and the Ultra cadre played the talk shows and news programs in a coordinated public relations effort. Driving their points home by repeating the same cliché lines loud and often; cranking out sound bites that made simple solutions sound reasonable for complex problems. In an Orwellian way pushing for a decrease in Federal power by tightening Government control. A wink, and nod and a sound bite and thousands of people would support the Ultra cause against the new boogieman.

The audience was applauding with gusto. Save American children. Yah! And keep foreigners off our roads. Sure! Protect our borders! Who could disagree? "Diplomatic immunity was not intended for foreigners to abuse." Benedict said, "Little Kristy's killer... should he be allowed to flee this country?... having his fun but unwilling to pay the price?" The audience was mumbling their disapproval. "Senator Dodge has some solutions and we'll hear more about that after these messages."

The station cut away to a commercial for a home security firm. This show was good for business; frightening people into a home security mentality. Actually the elaborate lights and buzzers were for the buyers' peace of mind. The security service never had the ability or the inclination to get police to the scene of a crime. After dozens, hundreds, of false alarms, the police rarely responded to these calls. The home security folks continued to promise police protection that they could not provide. Home security agencies just relayed the calls to 9-1-1 like everybody else. Paying them as a middleman actually increased the response time for local police and fire departments.

In the statistically deceptive way, crime was up. The tough-on-crime crowd, to carry on their crusade (and continue collecting donations), misstated the threat during the good times. Suburbanites were told that assaults in their neighborhoods had doubled. It meant that one in a thousand last year rose to two adolescent scuffles this year. Two assaults; thus doubled, 100% increase. In urban neighborhoods assaults were up a mere ten percent. It had been 250 per thousand last year and rose to 275 per thousand this year. Michaels' job with number crunching had taught him to read statistics and he did his share of 'lying with statistics' to support the Ultra cause.

The figures not cited by marketers or police, who wanted an increase budget, was that one in 500 suburbanites and one in four urbanites were at risk. Stolen cars were up 200 percent in rural areas (3 per 1,000 had jumped to 9 per 1,000). Inner cities were up only five percent (150 per 1,000 to 165 per 1,000). But the way the Ultras presented the information as percent increases seemed to show that the suburbs needed forty times the funding as the inner cities. Michael had known better, but his community was scheduled to get some of that increase funding so he held his peace; justifying his silence by the Ultras' confidentiality agreements.

Similar rates and contrived threats were used to justify more protection for the relatively safe outer areas. Over time this had created a safe but paranoid belt around most major cities. The use of public funds on Police and ineffective drug and school programs had deprived the cities, where the real threat smoldered, and sent them even deeper into conditions of despair. It was just a matter of time before the criminal elements began looking to the richer areas for targets.

Next a CrimeGuard ad, asking for donations. People were being told their taxes were not sufficient to protect their community. As people become less convinced of CrimeGuard effectiveness, businesses curtailed donations and money was being solicited from citizens, who had the right to expect police protection.

"Have we heard from the Pakistani Embassy?" Benedict was asking his stage manager. "I'm just asking," Dodge stated innocently. Of course, he was not 'just asking'. He was leading the audience to believe that they were at risk from diplomatic personnel. Of course, diplomatic immunity was not intended to protect foreigners in America. It was essential to protect Americans in repressive foreign countries.

"They are still declining comment," she replied.

"I can use that," Benedict said scribbling a note.

"Back from commercial in 5-4-3-2 ..." the stage manager cued Benedict.

"We're here with Senator Dodge and the Reverend Robert Patson," he began, "discussing foreign privileges that even our citizens don't enjoy."

"Senator Dodge," he turned to the stage, "Kristy's story is just one example of abuse. How can we protect ourselves from foreign criminals and terrorists?" The phrase was beginning to sound repetitive. This was one of the Ultras' new tag lines. Anyone not born in the United States, any reference to a non-American was expressed as 'foreign criminals and terrorists'.

"Our generals have performed remarkably, but President White wants us to keep our troops in foreign countries..." Patson gave his view, which coincidentally conformed to the Ultra speaking points. "That will put our borders at risk and cost the American taxpayers in blood and treasure." Actually, President White had proposed increasing the budget for border protection, but the Ultras had interpreted that as a tax increase and they were proposing the military as a free alternative.

"First, why should our tax dollars go to support a liberal organization like the U.N.?" Dodge fanned the fires, "U.S. troops should not be used as a one-world police force." One-World was another buzz-word of the Ultras; used to mean the murky overseas conspiracy to eliminate national borders. Of course, there was no such conspiracy but it worked well on an ill informed public, who feared their standard of living was slipping away. Insiders knew it was being siphoned off by the Ultra elite, and blamed on foreigners. "The Texas Rangers have done a wonderful job of protecting our southern border." The Texas National Guard, deputized and working in a police role, were stationed on the Mexican border with orders to stop the flow of illegals. After a number of deaths and a full scale riot, the border was indeed sealed, but it was expensive. "Our tax dollars already support a bloated Federal Government, an out of control justice department, CIA, overseas trade missions, embassies and staff in every backwater country on earth. Why? What benefit does the American taxpayer get for his money? I can tell you, without hesitation that the money is better off 'In Your Pocket'. Join me in saying, 'we will pay No More Taxes' ", he pointed emphatically at the audience, awaiting their knee jerk approval. The neon 'APPLAUSE' sign, strategically off-camera, blinked on. The audience applauded and cheered.

"No more taxes," they took up the brief chant.

"No new taxes," was Dodges' campaign cry. This was expanding on his theme. Did this mean no additional taxes, or taxes no-more? Dodge didn't seem to appreciate the difference. His rewording, or misstatement, would have far reaching results. "American taxpayers should not be burdened with foreigners' medical bills, education... Christ we even pay to lock up and hold their criminals. All this when we already pay for our own government." A low moan rippled through the audience. Dodge was good at playing one of the hometown folks, even though he was an elected senator; and a millionaire. "Yes," he said smiling "Our congress is expensive. And I want to help with that too. You pay for Social Security, Medicaid, government agencies, staff and layers of government. I wonder if we wouldn't be better off... if government wouldn't be more responsive... if we just stopped paying their bills until the tax-n-spend government becomes more accountable. We hold the purse strings." Loud sheers closed the show. The 'We with the purse strings' he intended was the legislators, but the audience and viewers took the "We" more universal and personal.

The next day, the newspaper headlines read, 'Senator Dodge says, No More Taxes'.

His comments had struck a nerve and the media fed on the excitement. The Department of Treasury reported a sharp decline in taxes collected in the few weeks following. First individual taxpayers refused to pay, in spite of the threat on penalties. The media picked up the Tax Revolt as the story of the day.

Small business cut back on payroll deductions for their employees. The average folks were thrilled with the sudden increase in disposable income. It didn't seem to occur to them that eventually taxes must be paid. The Government threatened collection, but took no action. Even Ultras' in government jobs were amused by the lack of government response. Governments depend on most of the people, obeying most of the laws, most of the time. It lacked the means to force compliance if most people decided not to cooperate. Many of the Ultras had taken Government jobs with the express purpose of starving the beast. Many were independently wealthy, anyway. They didn't need their government paycheck. Tax cuts they devised saved them ten times their annual government salary. With the wave of anti-tax feeling, and the number of enforcement agents drastically cut by the Veto Proof congress, the tax receipts continued to dwindle.

The Ultra budget writers jumped in to take advantage of a popular movement. Budgets were revised to exclude the Education Department, the Drug Enforcement Administration, the Department of Commerce and most congressional staff. Agricultural subsidies were eliminated, highway construction projects were shelved, housing assistance disappeared and the school lunch program vanished in the rhetoric of self-sufficiency. Any program that did not offer tangible benefit to the Ultra hierarchy was deemed nonessential and summarily cut. Smug and satisfied with themselves the super majority passed the new budget expecting a new streamlined government to emerge.

The emotions that they had stirred up ran deeper than any political ploy. The tax revenues continued to drop. Many government workers were furloughed without pay. Unemployment spiked. State and local governments began to feel the pinch as people who had lived paycheck to paycheck found themselves destitute. Unemployment funds were quickly exhausted and the food banks ran dry. Many Congressmen waived their salaries in a show of solidarity with the common man. They pledged to continue serving the people, but that symbolic gesture was not near enough to relieve the burden.

Government pensions were suspended, pending a redetermination under *the Eliminate Abuse of Taxpayer Funded Programs Act*. The Ultras knew that redetermination would buy them several months of withheld payments at the expense of the pensioners and, with more stringent requirements, many people would fail to requalify. 'Tough Love', they called it and people who did not depend on Government funds cheered.

Bennetts' show served as a focus group for Ultra proposals. After broadcast the party decision-makers could gather and discuss strategies for implementing or revising their presentation.

Television had become remarkably free of advertising. The viewers disgusted by the attempted manipulation were watching with a critical eye. Though ratings remained high, the response to advertising declined to near zero. No matter how many celebrities, or how much sex appeal dressed up a broadcast. People were not buying things they didn't need. Marketing firms were at a loss to restore confidence. They had made a good living off slandering the other guy's product and making people feel inadequate without their product. It seemed when the competitors called each other cheats and liars, people believed both claims. Businesses in many cases simply pulled advertising and lowered prices.

TV spot prices fell. TV stations found no advertisers willing to spend for spots on reruns and talk TV. Some of the more popular talk shows survived, masquerading as news. Info-mercials disappeared. The promise of 500 stations made not long before, gave way to a few dozen surviving stations. Stations that survived did so by cutting staff and equipment. The huge glut of post Watergate journalists found no one willing to pay for their over dramatized entertainment style journalism. The fact is there were not that many Watergate scale stories no matter how much drama was attached to insignificant events. Conspiracy reporting sounded silly and paranoid to a society that grew up with TV

When Constance Church, a pretty faced anchorwoman, referred to the 1991 Gulf War as the 'most decisive battle ever fought', she was just dramatizing her broadcast. But in doing so, she had dramatized to the point of blatant inaccuracy. The station was inundated with called. How about Gettysburg, Lexington and Concord, Midway, Waterloo, Hastings, Normandy, Guadalcanal? Any one of which were far more important. Her journalistic license defense did not resolve the fury. She was fired.

Viewers wanted news; not editorial. Overuse of dramatic terms crept into news reporting. The man was said to have 'literally' died of embarrassment. 'Literally' had been overused to a point where it was generally understood to mean 'Really!'. Of course if the man had literally died...then he would be dead. Empathy came into vogue. Where empathy had been used to mean 'I have been through it myself', it came to mean 'I REALLY sympathize' without the negative, condescending connotation that sympathy conveyed. Sympathy was too detached; empathy meant 'I'm one of you'. A man could be said to 'Empathize' with a pregnant woman. The language was diluted just a little bit more.

One of the strengths of English had always been the variety of terms for differing shades of meaning. That made it the international language; a language that the world outside America was astute enough to use for its diversity. Americans sought simplicity and lost the variety and virility of their own speech.

Entertainment as news fell out of favor with bland, factual, uneditorialized broadcasts appealing to most people. The BBC, British Broadcast Corporation, had held on to their integrity. After the brief embarrassment of pro-alley Gulf War reporting, they had resumed the unbiased reporting of facts that made them famous; and trusted.

A year ago Corbett would have cursed the low-life, trash that made a joke of the Ultras' cleverly worded policies. It was political camouflage used to manipulate an unsuspecting public. If stated clearly, over 90% of the people didn't support such lopsided policies.

Interest waned for the bizarre stories that ran under the pretext of increasing 'Awareness'. Kids in Oregon need not be frightened by a kidnapping and murder in Florida. No more, the notion that someone 'speaking out' was news. Speaking out was the term generally used when the journalists realized that their story wasn't news but they wanted to run with it for the ratings that the entertainment aspect would bring. Yes, the stories brought out good ratings at next to no production cost and next to no journalistic effort. The stations swore it was not exploited for monetary reasons but to increase 'Awareness'. Awareness was scaring the children into anti-social cloisters.

People became aware that they didn't get the news that mattered. When a far off crime drama was paraded as news, the switchboards would light up with complaints; people switched stations. Studies had shown that Crime-stoppers and DARE and other school programs were entirely ineffective. Furthermore, the studies of the DARE drug familiarity prevention program showed that DARE increased kids familiarity with drugs to such an extent that by graduation, the kids who had gone through the program were MORE likely to have tried drugs. It was counterproductive feel good for parents.

People found they had more to worry about than whether same sex couples wanted to get married. Defense of marriage laws, that the Ultras had put forth during elections to inspire revulsion in the straight population, fell by the wayside. The campaigns were finally defused when critics began to ask, 'If you want to safeguard the institution of marriage, shouldn't you outlaw divorce?" Most average folks, even self proclaimed conservatives and Christians, didn't want to defend that argument.

Sexy, supposed news stories, met critical parents. Why was this pertinent? My child does not need to look over his shoulder because of a pedophile 2,500 miles away. Keep it regional. News not puerile, voyeuristic entertainment. Awareness no longer served as a reason to broadcast tabloid style stories. Parents refused to pay for the 'Grief Counselors' in the schools when a classmate died from whatever cause. They refused to be held responsible for 'the Healing Process'. Without unlimited media sensationalism, crime reporting, for the sake of entertainment, was out of fashion. A crime in one state was not automatically news hundreds of miles away. Crime and vigilance programs broadcast bulletins less often and appealed for money more often. Media outlets no longer granted time as a community service. The air time was more valuable than cops & robbers programming yielded. Crime stories still commanded an audience, but the publics' tastes had shifted from street crime to the public policy criminals; politics gone soap opera.

The ultras had an internal matter to attend to. Their staff research director had been arrested for unauthorized contact with the media. He had evidently engaged in conspiracy and fraud. The party had to show appropriate outrage, while limiting possible disclosures which might expose complicity.

Michael Corbett had conspired with the media to defraud a government agency. He had implied that the Party was being deceptive; that their motives were dubious. The security officer implied that he had violated confidentiality; which he had not, but that was irrelevant. They wouldn't charge him with being an unregistered lobbyist. After the damning innuendo, that charge was dropped. He had enough unclassified facts to embarrass the Party in open court and they wouldn't risk that.

A call to the prosecutor outlined the course of the investigation; drop conspiracy and feed the prosecutor evidence of fraud and possible housing irregularities. Put the prosecution far from Washington DC on the west coast. The bait to get the state on board was the west coast house that they could seize to defray their costs. But the charges he faced would have nothing to do with his Ultra work. They didn't want that on display in a televised courtroom. The charges were brought in state court out west to keep it low profile. Some vague personal financial transgression was concocted.

He had not declared the shares of some shady shell company that he had accepted and flipped for the Washington townhouse. That was a common enough Ultra payoff that didn't show on the books. He hadn't thought about the under-the-table deal at the time, but it left the stock issuers blameless and made him look like a pension pillager and tax dodge; which he could not deny, he was. The transaction never would have come to light if he had played ball.

The million dollar Washington D.C. townhouse was confiscated. 'Chip would probably get the townhouse', Michael mused to himself. His home of record on the west coast was also confiscated. That one he had paid for fair and square with years of state service. That had been legitimate pre-Ultra work, but it was the States' piece of the take. The rustic Homestead in the foothills outside the city was overlooked; or was considered insignificant.

Suzanne had moved out of the spotlight to their getaway at Black Lake. The neighbors at Black Lake were regular folks. The well connected Ultra insiders, that shared the posh upscale D.C. condos, were always rubbed elbows in full view. The people at Black Lake, on the other hand, knew that Michael did some kind of Government work but didn't associate him with the ruling elite. He had never been a poster boy for the party. He was no talking head; his work in the shadows.

His neighbors around the Homestead were a lawyer, a hardware store owner, a rancher, a few retirees and a garage owner. Nobody knew or cared about each others' politics. As far as they were concerned, Michael and Suzanne were just regular folks too. There would be no media; no guilt by association. Michaels' mother had a house on the second tier and Suzannes' folks left the city to be with their daughter. He knew with friends and family, she would be okay there. Her name would not appear on the public assistance rolls for the labor pools or public works projects.

URBAN UNREST

The Arabic Peoples' Army used a surplus Stinger missiles to disable a tanker ship navigating the Straits of Hormos. The President asked that fuel consumption be kept to an absolute minimum. The strategic reserve was nearly depleted and negotiations to resume the flow of oil had broken down. South American sources were unstable. The Alaskan pipeline was continually attacked and remained vulnerable. Arab blackmail resulted in fewer Mideast convoys. Americas' economic engine was starving.

The taxes paid, though in the hundreds of millions, was still far too little and too late to stop the deterioration of the economic system. Like most citizens living paycheck to paycheck the government was paying out nearly as fast as the funds were. Debt piled up faster than an unwilling congress could raise the debt ceiling.

The Social Security Trust Fund was carried as an asset loaned to the Government on the assumption that the credit of the U.S. Government could always be trusted. Now over committed and with little or nothing coming in, the Government could not make good the 'Loan'. The fund was, in effect, broke.

Most people were law abiding and observed the niceties of the legal system. The urban squatters, though, were a different matter. They didn't listen to lawyers, didn't respond to summons and would be moved only by force. When the USA Stores drove the people they served to desperation, they killed the goose that laid the golden egg. UrbanShopAll Stores were the one-stop shopping brainchild of H.R.Parrot. He designed a company patch with a cursive U.S.A. armband that looked like slithering snakes. Parrots' USA stores with lawyers, politicians and Chinese labor offered cheaper goods than competitors. The competition were driven into bankruptcy and absorbed, or held indefinitely in court.

The Reverend Martin Mathias, a black community leader emerged. Martin organized for tough times that he expected. His urban rally was widely covered. Pro-Mathias organizations estimated the crowd at a hundred thousand; anti-Mathias outlets said there were just a few thousand. With attendance somewhere in the middle, both elements exaggerated. Each side called the others liars, and both sides were right. The end result was that nobody believed anybody. Both sides looked deceptive.

Martin Mathias' name became national news. Media outlets ceased to see him as an amusing clown. The new seriousness was real news that couldn't be ignored. His odyssey with inner city school children to the posh suburban schools was intended to expose the farce of the 'No Child Denied' cliché. School choice vouchers denied ALL children, except those who could afford to relocate their children with the modest Government supplement; and they were few. The vouchers did not give parents a choice of schools. They only served as an additional tax deduction for those wealthy enough to already have their kids in better schools.

Martin organized the march and made sure all the media outlets knew about it. He prepared to lead the march, with urban parents and children, to the more affluent suburban area schools to enroll. The cost of the schools far exceeded the voucher amounts and the rejection of the poor childrens' enrollment would dramatize the inherent injustice in the school voucher program. Suburban parents were outraged at the invasion. They preferred to quietly collect the subsidy.

There was a huge crowd to send off the marchers. Traffic jams, real and orchestrated kept many from reaching the approved parade route. In spite of the likelihood of interference, no police protection was ordered; just security points to keep out any weapons. There was widespread sabotage of vehicles and roadways by Ultra commandos the night before. Though this was subverting democracy, the party foot soldiers relished the role as some sort of military mission.

The motorcade was funneled through a weaving maze of restricted streets to narrow and divert the crowds and slow progress. Martin boldly led the pack, against the advice of his advisors. The motorcade slowed to a crawl.

A confrontation seemed inevitable; the tragedy that occurred was not. If the Ultras were not directly to blame, they provided the perfect environment. Guns were banned as a requirement for the parade permit. The Panthers, organized by Martins' brother Moses, provided security to the marchers. Ultra Commandos lounged around the police checkpoints making sure the weapons searches were thorough. Some elements even harassed marchers on their own authority; which was nonexistent. Ultras, even armed, passed through unmolested. The parade route, originally restricted to two traffic lanes, was reduced to one lane by some unidentified city functionary.

The motorcade snaked its way to the well populated school yard in the exclusive country estates district. Hostile crowds jeered, while bored police looked the other way. The tattered but clean clothes of the marchers contrasted sharply with the well tailored residents who kept a vigil from their doorsteps.

Suddenly a young man lunged toward the open car that carried Mathias. The startled Panthers, walking security, moved quickly, but too late, to keep the intruder from reaching the car. The assailant screamed some defiant threat and pulled open his shirt to reveal a vest of dynamite strapped to his chest. With a self-satisfied grin he pulled a detonating cord and a brilliant orange cloud engulfed the man, Mathias, his driver, the security detail and the nearest of the surrounding crowd.

The concussion knocked the front row of the spectators off their feet. A few were stunned and singed; a number with minor injuries. Two of the Panthers lay motionless. Two more, bleeding profusely, pawed frantically at the twisted panel of the car where Martin lay slumped in the back seat.

Emergency response was immediately dispatched, but had a difficult time getting through the crowd. A number of good Samaritans tried to assist the wounded. The final death toll amounted to nine persons. The bomber, the driver, two Panthers, three small children, one parent and, the target of the attack, Martin Mathias lay dead.

Those who were there offered interviews as survivors and were dramatized in info-tainment type pieces. The irrelevant testimonials were typical lazy journalism. 'I was just two blocks away and ...' ran as news. Invariably survivors always sob 'I never thought it would happen to me' and countrywide, statistically, they are right, but it led to a paranoid population that sat at home in fear. They also thought, 'It could never happen to me,' Viewers reasoned, 'if the guy giving the testimonial thought it wouldn't happen to him, and it happened to him, then, if I think it won't happen to me, it might'.

Survivors' testimonials took focus off the cause of the attack. So why is a survivors' testimony news, except as an emotional horror story? People began to see themselves as the next victim. Frank Murrow, doing a story on media hype, began asking questions that put the story in perspective. "How many survivors were there? Or rather, how many fatalities were there? Nine?" A tragedy for sure, but in a city of fourteen million, that is less than one in a million, so why is a 'Survivors' testimony relevant? Hardly a reason for four hundred million citizens nationwide to suspect and mistrust their neighbors. He went on to ask, "Where did such hate come from? What motivated the bomber? What was Martins' message?" Murrow went on to chastise his peers for their superficial coverage.

The commando that did the deed was conveniently clean; no obvious Ultra affiliation. Most Ultras were just mute. Limpaw, in typical Ultra denial of responsibility, blamed the situation that led to the attack. He stopped just short of blaming Martin for his own assassination, or saying he had it coming. The government investigation decreed that the bomber had acted alone.

The innocent children were the emotional hook, so that is where the media focused. Small bloodied wounded were displayed on the nations TVs. The nation was shocked at the destruction of the innocents. The black community was in mourning over the loss of Martin. Slowly the shock turned to a simmering rage.

The march degenerated into full scale rioting on the fault line between the urban core and the suburban strip malls. To suburbanites, this confirmed their fears of what 'the other' people would bring. Police and military, with live ammunition, cordoned off emerging dividing lines; guns pointed inward. To the urbanites, it highlighted how cheap their lives were valued and the extent to which those in power would stoop to keep them in their place.

Lilly, Martins' ancient mother, speaking in her sons' memory, implored the urban groups not to destroy their environment, as had happened in Watts years before. This was taken by the Ultras, and indeed some of the urban residents, as an implied suggestion, not to stop the rampage, but to express their outrage outside their own neighborhoods.

The Ultras needed an enemy without to refocus the situation. Any threat would do and the urban riots provided it. The militants needed to disown the crime to keep an admiring public on their side. Defenders of the Ultra commandos proudly said, '99% are good, honest, God-fearing heroes'. Critics asked, 'out of their boasted membership of 100,000, didn't that leave 1,000 of questionable values?' Overnight the talking points changed to say 99.99% are honorable. Old soldiers knew that many more than one percent of any military brotherhood were hard drinking, foul-mouthed and sex obsessed. In time of war, foreign or domestic, 'all of our good Christian soldiers are honorable and deserved praise'. The Ultra Commandos stepped forward, presenting themselves as vigilantes in white hats.

The urban centers exploded in protest. The symbol of abuse focused on the USA Stores. The stores themselves came under attack by the communities that they had abused for years. Shoplifting became blatant and security guards were intimidated. The elite corporate governors arranged a military response from a compliant government. Ultra politicians were beholden to the corporate financers. They were the ones whose money greased the wheels of government operations.

The Government proceeded to 'farm out' or contract the response to the urban squatters problem. In league with UrbanShopAll guru

Henry R. Parrot, an assault force was put together; an assault force of Ultra commandos. The recruited militia thought they were fighters because they had studied battlefield tactics and uttered all the right clichés. They would discover that street kids knew less about history, but experience had taught them to be far more proficient in urban tactics.

"Join the Army?" The burly man rubbed his bristly chin. "Why ? We get paid more, we don't have to follow orders and we don't answer to nobody. Bounty huntin'. That's the way to go." The unofficial force of UrbanShopAll security guards was being assembled by the company to end the standoff that commandeered the business center. Payroll was redirected from the army of elderly greeters and shelf stockers to a gang of mercenary security guards. The new staff, recruited by the company brass in Arkansas, carried guns and company issued badges. These were the shock troops that would liberate their urban stores.

"But we ain't deputized," the rookie complained to the old pro. "We can't arrest anybody, or shot anybody…"

"Unless they pick up a brick or throw a punch," his grizzly old companion responded. "Then I'll blow 'em away. You can shot in self-defense."

"The company will back us up?" the rookie asked, "and the party?"

The former bounty hunter turned USA security guard continued, "The Army shots somebody and everybody wants to know how come. The chain of command… who gave the order. We shoot somebody, we just have to say we was threatened. And with all the protesting and pilfering who's to say we ain't threatened. Turns out somebody's innocent, they just got caught in the crossfire. Hell, the Army is actually negotiating with the squatters. They're the criminals; we're the law."

"What I wouldn't give to get my hands on that Moses Mathias," the rookie said unconvincingly.

"Why not," the veteran responded, "He's just a terrorist. This Army truce is crazy. Dealing with terrorists. We have every right to nab him. That's what UrbanShopAll is paying us for… to protect their property."

Colonel South with a battalion of infantry secured the area. The troops manned checkpoints just outside the urban barricades. At Colonel Souths' elbow hovered the USA Store point-man in the person of H.R.Parrot. He spoke for the Chamber of Commerce and business interests. He was the fast-track link to the government. No need to go through the complicated bureaucracy of the military to reach civilian authority.

"Damn contractors," South sounded off to Parrot. "Untrained, undisciplined and they don't follow orders." Parrot didn't agree, but held his peace. This was cheap muscle as far as he was concerned. "How can I keep the lid on with these guys itching for a fight?" South continued.

Then the word came down from Headquarters. Colonel South was ordered pull back several blocks to avoid a confrontation. The order had come after a meeting of the UrbanShopAll management with their government allies. The Government had agreed to withdraw to give the businessmen a chance to peacefully regain their property. Those in the meeting had no illusion what this meant. Negotiate was the excuse they would give the press. What the USA Store hierarchy had in mind was to unleash their newly raised security force to retake the stores by force.

The camouflaged face peaked carefully around the corner across the urban ruin. With intricate hand signals, he sent forward another half dozen men in camouflaged fatigues scurrying to cover a few yards further on. They knew the people were here but they couldn't see them. Their camouflage, though it made them feel like real soldiers, was completely inappropriate for an urban concrete background. It may have made them blend in with a jungle setting, but in the city, it just made them stick out.

The roadblock was unmanned as the militia approached. The Panthers that had stood watch had blended into the urban landscape. A bulldozer roared forward and cleared the street. The burly, well armed men; several hundred all told, were moving in to retake the urban heartland.

Their reward was a family mealticket. Somewhere in the suburban safe zone their families would have something to eat, somewhere to shelter. Many of the militiamen were unconcerned with the mealticket; they were more interested in the chance for loot; pillage and the adrenaline rush that comes from hunting your fellow man. This was a free fire zone. All residents were given the opportunity to surrender, none had.

"Where's my mommy," a small boy of nine or ten sat in the rubble just around the corner.

A militiaman rounded the corner and demanded briefly, "Seen any gangsters, kid?"

"The boy stared blankly at the hulking man. "Ignorant nigger," the man said under his breath as he leaned in a broken window nearby. His look turned to surprise as he pulled back to see the boy with a pistol leveled at his face.

"I AM a gangster," he hissed in a voice far too mature for his age, "and you one dead cracker." The shot tore away half of the mercenaries face. Grabbing the mans' gun, the boy disappeared through a doorway. Three more security men charged around the corner, firing at thin air. They stood in the small courtyard looking around for a target but could find only their dead comrade. In frustration they shot blindly through windows, doors, alleyways.

"Come out and fight!" one yelled. A low grinding sound was heard and an old rusted Buick was pushed across the alley, sealing the entrance. Several heads of boys, old women and men appeared two stories up lobbing bottles with rags burning fiercely plugging the neck. They shattered in the court below, throwing a sheet of flame over the intruders. They fired to no effect and screamed as the flames ignited and spread over their clothes.

Several more Mercenaries vaulted over the blocking Buick and helped the men, now rolling on the ground, to extinguish the flames. The radio man nearby called in to their headquarters. "Kappa six to TriKappa, come in, over."

"TriKappa here, go ahead Kappa Six, over."

"This is Kappa Six. We have contact. One dead, three wounded. We need backup, over."

"... retire to the starting line, over"

"I said we have contact," the radiomans' look turned grim at the response. "Pull out? Run from this trash?"

"Repeat, evacuate your wounded. No backup." The call for backup was an increasingly common plea from the commando squads that assaulted the urban core of the city. They were interested in pillage for pay and no one wanted to be left out of the free-for-all. Consequently there was no reserve to call on.

Martin had foreseen some kind of confrontation. His premonition was shared with his brother Moses. Moses' credentials had given him credibility in the chaos of the city's urban core. He had risen through the ranks as gang-member and escaped the ghetto through military service. With demonstrated aptitude he worked his way into a sergeants' rank. When one of his troopers was convicted of gangster affiliation, the shadow of suspicion clouded his career. Before the charge of conspiracy could be brought, Moses went underground, protected by a downtrodden public that appreciated his former efforts on their behalf. His Panthers became the security arm of Martins' movement. Veterans of his motley group of followers had teamed up with streetwise urban warriors into what the neighbors called a 'neighborhood watch' but the authorities called 'gangs'.

The urban dwellers had taken precautions. 'Preparing the battlefield,' the military would have called it, though the invaders took no note of it. The young, old and helpless were moved to predetermined safe areas. They worked at preparing food and urban cocktails for the fighters. It was their mealticket. Children as young as ten years old, already veterans of an urban combat zone served as runners and often fought as effectively as the full grown street warriors.

The training that Moses instituted for his people lasted only a few days. That was all the notice they had. But for years they had lived in an oppressive environment. Most seemed to know instinctively what had to be done. They set booby traps, prepared firebombs and practiced evasion techniques. Years of conflict with the police had prepared them for a state of war.

Moses had established a command post in the office of a commandeered UrbanShopAll store. Instructions were issued to occupy all grocery stores, gas stations, plus gun shops, hardware stores, and other businesses. Orders were given to collect batteries, fuel, weapons and to safeguard food. Expendable foodstuffs were to be used first, with canned and dry goods to be rationed as needed. Outer bands of stores were cleared to more secure interior locations. Police stations abandon by furloughed cops, were ransacked. Most weapons were gone but some teargas and radios were collected. Restaurants became nutrition centers where food could be most efficiently prepared with a minimum of fuel and waste. Neighborhood street gangs made plans to defend their turf and their people. The cavalry, Panthers mounted on mountain bikes, waited for a call to action. A rudimentary communication system, short wave and CBs and walkie-talkies, were used for longer distances. Roof top signals by hand and voice worked well enough for most purposes.

"Moses," a voice cracked over the radio. "We got 30 or 40 intruders at 78th and Central."

"How many Central Court Bloods you got?"

"Six wit me. Most gone over ta Mickies gettin' fed."

"Listen T-Ball," Moses said, "Draw 'em in. Just a few shots and back off. Head for the courthouse. Help's comin'."

With a few brief comments the cavalry, with assault rifles slung across their backs, moved out to rendezvous at the courthouse. "Get our people to the upper floors. Single shots," Moses called, after them. "Save your ammo."

"Suede," Moses turned to a light skinned girl waiting at his side, "I won't make you do this, but it gotta be done."

"It's okay, Poppy." The young girl had a sweet sincere smile. She had learned to use her slender good looks to get what she wanted from men. "Just another trick, with a screw-you chaser."

"You know what to do." Moses handed her an elaborate jewelry box with a cache of gold chains and bundles of cash. "Them greedy bastards still think this is worth something. When they think they broke you steer 'em to the courthouse."

Rock led the mercenary platoon carefully and under cover into the heart of the city. Several men cursed in frustration as the stores they passed were striped clean.

"Rock, how we gonna get paid?" the Merc asked through green grease paint. "Nothin' left worth taken. Parrots' minimum wage ain't no more than a mealticket."

"Keep your eyes open," Rock countered, "it's here we just need to find it."

A womens' scream froze them all in place. A shot rang out in a side alley and a frail looking women stumbled from between the buildings, clothes torn, clutching a box. "Help me," she panted.

"Watch those windows," Rock warned as he carefully made his way to the women. He grabbed her upper arm and half dragged her to a nearby doorway. The Mercs formed a perimeter and the questioning began. She was running from gangsters. She had found their stash. The Mercs seemed skeptical.

"What you got there?" The commando that called himself Rock snatched the jewelry box.

"Gangsta's. They'll kill me," she protested breaking into sobs. Another commando was tying a noose with a sadistic smile.

"We'll do worse than that," Rock wanted information. This was war. "Where is everybody? Where'd they stash the stuff?" Psycho was pushing and slapping and fondling.

"The Courthouse," she hesitantly blurted out, "the basement. I gotta go now," she screamed as if in a panic.

"You stay right here till we know you ain't lying," Rock said. "Psycho, watch the girl till I get back." As Rock left the room, a shrill scream and cruel laughter erupted from the room. Psycho would have his fun; one of the benefits of free-lance soldiering.

The main party made their way to the huge granite courthouse five blocks away. The streets were eerily silent; just a few shadowy figures who fired a shot then ran.

"That big monument looking thing," Rock pointed to the courthouse, towering above the tenements. "Alpha team left, Delta team right. I'll take Bravo and Charlie up the middle. Converge on the front steps."

The last few black clad skirmishers ducked into the courthouse. Huge wooden doors slammed shut. The commandos followed in hot pursuit. On full automatic, several dozens of rounds sprayed the building and shattered the barred windows. A grenade knocked one door ajar. The Mercs entered cautiously. An unused metal detector was pushed aside and some cash and other loot was scattered about but the place seemed deserted. The men followed the trail to a locked basement door. A few shots and the door was knocked from its hinges. Most of the Mercs were inside scrambling to pick up scattered bills strewn around the floor. Several charged down the wide marble steps to the lower level. Piles of bank bags lined the wall. A loud whoop arose that attracted most of the Mercs to the scene.

"The mother lode!" Rock exclaimed as he tore into the pile.

Meanwhile, the bait was being helped out of a manhole a block away. "Buildings clean of our folks," T-Ball radioed to Moses.

With no eyes on the outside of the building a cordon of men emerged from the surrounding buildings and approached the iron bars on the windows. Four men carried two pressurized tanks to the front door, opened the valves and rolled them into the courthouse.

Rock heard a low hiss coming from the first floor. His expression was at first quizzical, then his eyes flew wide open. "Gas!" he yelled as he made for the stairs. His compatriots, rolling in the piles of bills, had only enough time to look up when an urban cocktail touched off a cloud of natural gas. The screams of the men in the basement were lost in the rubble. The granite shell remained, but the floors of the second and third story collapsed. A few choking refugees crawled from the wreckage, only to be met be a circle of armed cyclists; the cavalry. Two, sensing the danger, tried to run but were shot dead. Half a dozen were taken alive, throwing up their hands in surrender. The others were buried in the courthouse, dead or alive, nobody cared.

"Prisoner of War," one terrified man cried, "We have rights." The bikers roughly relieved the captured men of all their useful equipment.

"Somebody want to shot that bastard?" T-Ball said, "Rights my ass!"

The tough guy, gone weak kneed, was served a prompt click of an empty chamber near his ear. "It would be that easy," T-Ball said. "But you gotta take a message to yo masters." The surviving mercenaries were herded back to the edge of Moses' urban protectorate. Suede waited on the curb cleaning her nails with an ice pick. Her captor lay in a pool of his own blood with his pants around his ankles.

"It takes balls to kill innocent women and children," Moses pronounced.

The Panther band included a number of women warriors as proficient as the men. "Hand 'em their balls and send 'em home," Suede said.

"Them fascists on the outside gonna learn there's worst things than dead," Moses added.

One by one they were castrated with red hot shears that cauterized the wounds. Then the squealing mercenaries were none too gently kicked and pushed them through the barricade.

The Mercs, who had played at soldiering for years, were prepared for a war against government agents or foreign aggressors; conventional, uniformed military forces that they understood. When confronted by common people in desperate circumstances they became confused and often ended up dead. Most found nothing or found themselves outnumbered, outgunned and outmatched.. The street warriors didn't play fair.

DAY IN COURT

"Who would risk to speaking at my hearing?" Michael thought, "No one. This wasn't an issue that could be milked for sympathy, titillation or political advantage. His former bosses were already pissed that he didn't put on more of a show. No viewer appeal. There would be cameras. He had expressly forbidden his wife from attending. Family were often used for entertainment; the dramatic camera cut-away. The prettier, the more distressed, the better. A troublesome or disruptive family member would sometimes end up charged as well. Conspiracy was broad enough to engulf anyone.

The Government borrowed a page from the War on Drugs. When a person was arrested, their spouse was often encouraged to testify against them or risk being charged themselves. 'Testify or we will charge you too, and your kids will end up in foster care.' Many wives, violating the long standing American tradition of family loyalty, felt forced to testify against their husbands, so that their kids didn't end up inmate orphans. Ironically, the government often did not have sufficient evidence for a conviction without the testimony of the spouse. However, most people did not understand the legal proceeding sufficiently, or could not take the risk, and bowed to the prosecutors' pressure. The Ultras' generally dismissed party spouses as empty-headed nurturers adopting the old mafia philosophy of the family being sacrosanct. Michael expected that Suzanne would be safe, if kept out of the public eye.

Michael probably knew better than most of the real results of the legislation that ensnared him. He was backed into the dilemma of having information that average citizens did not. Any mention of that would sound like a bitter accomplice and played by the prosecution as breach of faith; treason. Any attempt at defense would not get him off; but might get him in more serious trouble. He felt lucky that he was being tried at a time when the street rioters were coming to court. The routine public corruption case received little attention when the more violent, more dramatic cases were broadcast.

Justice was not an option. In the case of the veto proof congress how it played in the press mattered more than justice. The hole Michael found himself in would just get deeper, if he tried to fight it. Any attempt at defense might even result in indefinite detention. He would claim to find the Lord, but that didn't work anymore. That ploy had been played too many times to too many juries and parole boards to have any effect. The party wanted to put him on display and shut him up. He doubted if they gave him a second thought once he was conveniently out of the way. There were those of his party who weren't bothered by the moral dilemma. They would make sure any inconvenient testimony would be withheld from the public. Most citizens weren't aware of the short delayed broadcast. An agent from Homeland Security held the mute button. The result of the irrational proceedings was not apparent to the average citizen. Those speaking against the proceedings could be easily discredited with the 'Liberal' label; 'Soft on crime'. Most viewers cheered for the entertainment style TV. Michael found himself in a system he had helped design to disenfranchise and silence critics. Stereotyped groups of people did not deserve consideration. Criminals, immigrants, the gamblers, drug users, smokers all had become non-persons in the vote counts and power blocks that emerged. Once a member of one of the demon groups, there was no redemption.

The tax burden has been shifted to groups that had a hard time defending their choices; smokers, drinkers, gamblers. People who did not indulge agreed that someone else should shoulder the cost of government. Government became dependent on the taxes imposed on alcohol, tobacco and games of chance. When the lockups started the tax base dried up. They had to resume taxing law abiding citizens and the citizens were pissed. First there were the traffic tickets, permits, licenses and fines. Then the property, sales and income taxes. Multinational business dodged the bullet with Ultra protection.

Michaels' back began to ache, perched forward as he was by the handcuffs wedged behind his back. As he waited on the rough bench, another man was brought in and deposited beside him. He was tall, bald and black with a beard that reached down to the middle of his chest. Just the kind who the Ultras stereotyped to strike fear into the meek masses. Their vote could always be bought by appealing to their paranoia. He looked at Michael with a defiant confidence. His left eye was quite swollen and a little blood seeped from the corner of his mouth. He had not come quietly.

"What's a white boy like you doing in them bracelets?" He sneered, "Her daddy catch you with your pants down?"

"Fraud," Michael said blandly. "And conspiracy."

"Conspiracy," the black man roared with what Michael thought sounded like sincere laughter. It made him smiled. "That's what they use when they can't think of anything else. Tougher to beat then a real crime. You S-O-L, whitey..."

"Name's Michael."

"Count yourself lucky, Mikey. If you was a street nigger like me you coulda been shot resisting arrest... threatening an officer... whatever reason they like. A death sentence on the street is cheaper for the man when it's done before arrest... trial... that shit. I jus' lucky I'm one scary nigger. Jus' the kind they want on TV to show white bread they doin' they job. Otherwise, I probably be dead now."

To his discomfort, Michael knew he was right. He had helped craft some of those laws in his 'it couldn't happen to me' days.

The *Defense of Private Property* act had resulted in a rash of shootouts and deaths. Mostly adolescence, mostly black in the act of petty crime and vandalism; rarely the property owner. They sat in wait for a chance at payback and their actions bordered on ambush. When an occasional upstanding citizen was hit, it resulted in renewed cries that this showed that the law as needed; a dead intruder, evidence that the law worked. The crime rate remained unchanged. However, the violence of confrontations escalated.

"Now me… I committed a real crime. I punched a recruiter," he answered, "Mutha come in my neighborhood trying to get girls off the dole and into their family boarding houses."

Michael felt a chill and hoped the man didn't notice. Another one of the veto proof congress' ideas. The boarding homes for young single women on welfare were intended, as it was advertised, so that they could meet men; object matrimony. There were some good ideas; shared day care, shopping and transportation. But they were packaged in a despicable program of warehousing the unfortunate.

The men, though, tended to taste the wares then get on their way. The matrimony part was for public consumption. Actually, it was cheaper to warehouse these poor women and the impression was that they had proved their promiscuity. Twisted logic dictated that they should be open to a proposal from a man with the means to care for them and their children. A few show-case weddings were sold to the public, through the press, to prove that it worked. Some enterprising women even worked their way out of the houses. As should have been expected, the program devolved into government sponsored sexual indentured servants.

Michael knew the statistics. He had researched the reasons people were on public assistance and the best ways to get them off. He knew most women were white in their mid-20's, had two or fewer children and were on assistance for less than a year. Further, they were in this predicament, not because they were promiscuous, but because a man that vowed to love, honor and respect them till death did them part, had deserted them when faced with the pressure of fatherhood.

The Ultras' conservative values were unmoved by the developments because it was cheap. Cheaper than welfare and the women, so the cold-blooded joke went, were doing a community service. Refusing a proposal was tantamount to waiving any assistance. They could be turned out without a troubled social conscience. And was it surprising that a man, after a brief acquaintance, would find that kind of women unacceptable? A womens' fiancé would often find an excuse to call off the ceremony just short of marriage. The public heard the success stories without realizing that ninety-nine out of a hundred did not reach the alter.

Work requirements for assistance forced people to take any job offered at any wage or lose subsistence for themselves and their children. Recruiters for strip clubs and date club pimps sat outside welfare offices waiting for young mothers; giving them an offer they couldn't refuse. Like cigarettes, alcohol and gambling, the government got hooked on the money that they could divert from social programs to pet projects.

"So, I punched one of their booty hunters. They say I torched cop cars, stole cars, run guns, recruit gangs, played in the uprising. Some 'ol stuff they always hang on you when they don't know. Gets white folks scared and sure to convict. My crime was I stepped outside the city. A nigger steps outside the city and they haul him away. One less nigger on the street. With me all they can prove is I was in a fight months ago. They don't know one black man from another."

"Pssst," he leaned close and whispered, "they right, but they don't know." He straightened up and spoke out loud, in spite of several officers in earshot. "They don't know who they got. Brother Martin says use the system. Peace is the way. I find a fist gets more respect. It's boot camp for me," he continued, "for you too, I expect. I'm Moses."

"Boot camp?" Michael asked.

"Yah," Moses answered blandly, "The man sending us brothers there to organize. White man call it 'networking'. Someday soon you gonna see the Panthers rise up and defend the people. The work farm, jail all the same. Jus' a training camp for the movement. Boot camp."

"I'd make a lousy Panther." Michael said.

"Nonsense, Mikey. Panther ain't about color. You gonna pay your dues. You 'bout to join the down trodden."

"How'd this happen?" Michael said under his breath, "What happened to live and let live?"

"Live and let live?" Moses was amused, "You gotta be a white boy to think anybody ever cared, brother. Nobody cares. Maybe people cared about white folks, once upon a time. But times get tough you blame black folk, people not born here, little folks in other countries that work cheap or starve. Truth is you white trash got too expensive, so old rich white men make a nigger out of you. You white folk jus' go along. Think someday be a old rich white guy. Us brothers never bought that line."

"You call me brother," Michael said. It was refreshing to hear someone being so brutally honest and fearless.

"Any man in chains is my brother." Moses said with a friendly toothy smile.

The proceedings were quick and businesslike. Suspects lined up at the door. One by one they were paraded before the judge. No victim statements. Once it became a common occurrence, the media lost interest and only the big stories got the attention.

Lawyers were often cited for collaboration with a client who was later found guilty and charged with conspiracy laws. Nobody liked lawyers. It was easy to construe their attempts at defense as criminal conspiracy. The Bar Association enacted a new code of conduct that included a pledge to see justice was done. A lawyer was required to enter a guilty plea, if he knew his client was guilty, or even suspected that he could not win. Conducting a losing defense became the equivalent of furthering a criminal conspiracy. Breaking the code meant disbarment and no work. Public defense interviews were brief and irrelevant. Clients refused to talk to informant lawyers and lawyers were afraid to ask for details for fear of becoming part of a conspiracy.

"The Court recognizes, Michael Corbett." Michael shuffled into the courtroom. A stern faced judge sat at the bench with a jury to his right. A boisterous balcony was filled with what appeared to be the typical studio audience. The prosecutor opened his case. "He took government money and betrayed his trust," the prosecutors addressed the jury. The audience booed and hissed on queue. Curiously, the conspiracy charge was dropped. There would be no testimony regarding his work for the Ultras. Michael shuffled front and center in the too tight leg irons that made for a comic perp walk.

Michael didn't mount any defense; it wouldn't have helped and might have hurt. Be respectful. Look contrite. "Your honor, I am prepared to accept the judgment of the court." Pleading the fifth was tantamount to admitting guilt. Viewers and jurors with limited knowledge of the Bill of Rights, interpreted the Fifth Amendment to mean, 'if I testify, I will be giving evidence of my guilt... Ergo, there is guilt, thus the fifth amounts to a confession'.

The verdict was swift. Guilty, of course. Forfeit the house in the city and bank accounts to make restitution plus five years on the work farm. It could have been worse. His status was a double hit to society. One, he would not be paying taxes; and two, he was now a government expense. If his family was not in a position to support themselves during his absence, they would need government support; strike three. They had taken it easy on him. He had assets that they could confiscate to defray costs. Michael was roughly ushered to the holding pen for those destine for confinement.

The next defendant was brought before the court. "The court recognizes Moses Mathias." The bailiff called out.

"The defendant is charged with assaulting a civil official in the performance of his duty," the prosecutor declared.

"How do you plea?" a bored judge asked.

"Not guilty," he proclaimed proudly.

They judge looked up looking aggravated. "Mr. Mathias, We have the testimony of the Job placement officer and two community service workers."

"Your pimps and your thugs have been known to lie. I can call a hundred people who will swear, they was tryin' to recruit a minor for your cat house. They was on my property in the act of committing a crime and according to the Home Defense provision, I could of kilt him."

The judge was use to vulgar language and anger. Good entertainment for the video feed. He wasn't ready for the twisted logic, that the courts used to ambush difficult defendants, to be turned on the court.

The judge looked to the jury. Twelve simpletons that were selected like a game show contestants. The viewers tended to like the whimpering, apologetic type; good entertainment. It made them feel superior; like a vengeful Lord on Judgment Day. Michael knew, his type, the straight faced, boring kind could pass through virtually unnoticed. But Moses wouldn't give them that. He looked directly at the jury. Not as a defendant, but as an accuser.

"These men violated the law," He spoke calmly and forcefully, "Now they want to spend your hard-earned taxpayer money to put me away to cover their crimes. I pay taxes. I support my family. They would have you put me away and put my family on public support just so they can take your daughters to a government barracks." He looked contemptuously at the seedy looking government recruiter. "Pervert."

Michael was amused; silently wishing Moses the best. This was entertainment, but not the kind the system intended. Moses had charisma, or at least a stage presence. Several jury members were squinting at the witness in a manner usually reserved for the defendant. Moses had taken the role of prosecutor. The jury was being diverted to a different scapegoat. "That man is defrauding the taxpayer. Making his fees entrapping innocent girls," Moses continued.

The judge didn't like the way things were going. He cut short the defendants testimony and tried to refocus the jury on Moses by calling the recruiter to testify. It was a disaster. The surprised recruiter tried desperately to explain himself, making him sound like a suspect. This was the kind of performance a jury was use to seeing from the guilty. They were increasingly uncomfortable with his nervous manner.

Moses was found guilty, anyway, but he got only five years rather than the routine seven for assault. A good performance could sometimes save a defendant a little time. The recruiter was denied his civic reward. He probably ended up accused of something. You didn't embarrass the criminal justice system and get away with it.

The next four defendants were arrested during the urban assault and charged with looting. The failure of the commandos was being whitewashed with the prosecution of the few urban residents that the military had detained trying to escape the urban battle zone.

Any non-commando that tried to pass through the military cordon was assumed to be fleeing the scene of a crime. The charge was looting. They all had some property for which they had no receipts. One by one as they left the docket for the accused, they gave Moses the clinched fist salute.

All six of the accused were guilty and destined for the work farm. The farm was typical. A fenced compound surrounded by fields, or rather orchards. With the 'War on Illegal Immigrants', the agricultural work force had dried up. Large agri-businesses pushed through a proposal to give Americans the jobs. It sounded real patriotic but Americans wouldn't accept the work. Inmate labor and deficit debtors were cheap and available; and they didn't have a choice.

NO MORE TAXES

The urban assault had repercussions far beyond the failure of the commandos to retake the USA stores. They could at least be used for entertainment value. Troy Benedict invited family members to 'Speak Out' about the brave Ultra Commandos that had tried to restore order to the nations' cities. Senator Dodge appeared to honor the brave and Sarah Colt was invited as the embedded journalist. Though she had not actually been on the scene of the operation. Reverend Patson was there to give Gods' blessing to their effort. The media circus was intended to present a united front of religion, the arts and government in support of the new minutemen.

"Roy was a good man," a conservatively dressed women wrung her hands and fought back tears. Troy Benedict hosted the families of victims; all white families; Christian families. The news was that the urban posse had kicked ass. But the story was the poor militia families; white, law-n-order kind of folks who had lost a loved one. Good drama. The man they called Roy was the same man Suede encountered as Psycho. "He died trying to bring our country together," his widow was saying.

Reverend Patson was there to speak for American Veterans. Though he meant Christians with guns. His brand of extreme blind faith never appealed to more than a fraction of good Christians, but he made for a lively show. He was out to convert anyone with a dollar or a vote. He spoke of great principles with great authority. The Ultras went looking for an 'Our Youngsters In Uniform' story to maintain morale. "This was a family man who volunteered for God and American values. The Lord has given them dispensation for peacekeeping," Patson declared.

Patson, the founder of the Christian Soldiers of America, was painting the militia volunteers as pious patriots. The group had joined with Chip Libby's Ultra Commandos en masse. They didn't seem to publicly reject blacks or Hispanics and others but there was little reason for the ethnic Americans to join such an organization. In the meantime, the Crusaders portrayed themselves as traditional Americans.

"Roy didn't have to go... but he heard the Lord call..." Patson had picked up the lecture. "He saw America besieged by the dark forces of anarchy. He died protecting a young girl from gangsters... a young black girl... He was murdered. Who knows what the murderers did to the girl." Patson was good at painting sinful mental images in a 'this is what I'm against, folks' style. Then the 'send me money to make it stop' pitch usually followed, but this was a talk show, not his prayer pledge circus, so Patson stopped short of asking for money. The women broke into a muffled sob.

Sarah Colt, on stage to provide her brand of moral outrage shook her head in sympathetic agreement. " Roy's companions were sexually mutilated," Sarah Colt jumped in, "Their wounds terribly burned. Is that right Marge?" The grieving widow nodded. Classic Colt; make the old ladies swoon and the young zealots pray all the harder. Meanwhile, the mental image of depravity was implanted; the damage done.

"More than 20 killed or missing," Benedict added. "Dozens injured."

"Some say, this Mathias, is from Somalia; trained in Afghanistan," Sarah continued. Michael was often haunted by the advice he had given long ago to add 'Some say' to keep from being caught in a lie or being quoted as a source; the legally defensible way to start a rumor. Sarah had perfected the art of citing a few facts with pure fiction in a way to make the whole sound believable. "Heaven knows what terrorist connections this foreign terrorist has."

Patson took up the theme. "This Moses is the brother of Martin Matthias. He preached peace while his brother recruited foreign terrorists. And now this brother has gone underground. Who knows what mischief he is up to? Some say he is in Pakistan training terrorists." The mention of alien involvement would give them a couple of extra percentage points with public opinion. It was a lie, but Patson was sure God would understand. Even if the untruth was corrected, not everyone would hear the half-hearted retraction. The rumor passed on by all those that heard it could not be undone. So the rumor would survive and grow.

Unknowingly, in their quest for ratings the Ultra were serving Moses' purposes. It was more satisfying for the commandos to think they were bested by an individual with some kind of exotic training and background. It boosted the Mathias image and the castrations had dampened the warhawks enthusiasm for the bite of combat and the honorable wound that would get them glory. Their broadcast did not damage Moses for his savagery but discouraged a number of Ultra recruits.

Patson solemnly proclaimed, "And they that do such things will incur retribution. These are forces of Satan." The good versus evil, black and white view of the world suited his purposes, "The Christian Soldiers of America will guard Gods' people and Gods' country. I heard large numbers of illegal aliens are moving in trying to take a piece of America for themselves." Patson was allowed a seat at the Ultras' table because the party was convinced that they couldn't hold on to power without his following. "American families are at risk. Operation rapture is helping these families with over two hundred and fifty thooousand dollars per month... " he drawled out the word thooousand as though it were a sermon. He expected the audience to be impressed by the figure. There was a confused silence. Earlier in the program he had said that they had collected over twenty-seven million in tithes during his monthly telethon.

Troy seemed to do the same quick math as the audience. Twelve months of 250,000 is just three million. What of the other millions collected? Patson noticed his discomfort and lamely finished his sentence, "... as well as other Christian endeavors."

It was unusual for Patson to engage in the unscripted give and take of a talk show. His program from the pulpit was carefully scripted with no guests; no call-in. He spoke as he pleased with no interruptions; no contrary interpretations. His projects kept the money and converts rolling in. His specialty was the three cent 'faith gifts' that brought in the twenty dollar donations. "And to help these families and support out boys, you can call 1-800-GodWork." His area was the political connections and the legislation that protected his multi-million dollar conglomerate, loosely defined as a church. Sitting there with other persons on stage and an audience, he seemed a little disoriented.

"We'll return to our guests after these messages," Troy cut off the segment in his smooth professional manner. Once off camera, "You better get an answer ready about your extra millions." He coarsely spoke to Patson. The live studio audience was shocked. "I guarantee that people out there are doing the math and they'll be calling."

"Call it spreading the word," Patson volunteered, "Gods' blessing."

"Hell, we can't very well trot out your yacht and seven figure salary." Dodge turned sheepishly from Patson to the audience as he remembered that this was no strategy session. He was in front of two hundred citizens; witnesses.

Patson and Dodge spoke quietly together as Troy entertained the audience with a rather distorted description of events. The stage manager signaled that they were returning from break.

"We are discussing the standoff between the Urban Gangsters that have seized several metro areas, and law enforcement." Troy was leading to some kind of pronouncement from Dodge or Patson. " ... And relief efforts by Ultra supporter Senator Dodge and Reverend Patson. Reverend Patson was telling us how the relief effort was going."

"That's right, Troy," Patson started, "and most people don't realize the red tape and bureaucracy involved in trying to help your fellow man. The tax and spend government taxes the stipend paid to our staff as income. That's your donated dollars taken by the government. And the Government reports, we are forced to do, cost us staff time and hamper the relief effort."

"The cost is becoming a big issue," Benedict prompted, "We are joined today by bestselling author, Sarah Colt, who focuses on government waste and the cost to families. What do you see as the moral cost of this urban revolt? Are the morals of these foreign influences creeping into this country?"

Sarah tried, what she thought was her cute chip-monk smile. It looked more like a pinched clown grin. "If government doesn't protect us from foreign criminals and terrorists, what do we owe government? Better to spend OUR money OUR selves. In my book, *Wasted Government*, I list the many expensive ways government fails us. This Corbett case is a perfect example." The Ultras seemed upset that Corbetts' conviction had not received more attention. His head-on-the-block had passed virtually unnoticed. Unless the guilt could be laid at his feet, they would need another head; maybe a higher profile sacrifice. "Taxpayers paid his lavish salary for years, and what did he do? He betrayed us. Why do we pay these government parasites? I'm with Senator Dodge. We hold the purse strings. It's time to slam the purse shut."

"Like a spendthrift child," Dodge chimed in, "we the people, like a parent must pull in the purse strings. Let grass roots people spend the money where it is needed. Why should Washington get a slice of the charity pie? If we all stopped paying the government for their inefficiency, then we would all have more money In Our Pockets." The worn out Ultra cliché received modest, instinctive applause.

"I would like to see every bit of fraud and abuse rooted out before I send the government one more tax dollar," Colt cheered, wagging her finger.

"No More Taxes," Dodge concluded.

"No More Taxes," Colt parroted Dodges comment. "No more taxpayer dollars paid to criminal elements in the government in sweetheart deals."

The comment was taken up as a rallying cry for anyone who already felt their livelihood threatened. It was the Presidents' problem. The President wasn't an Ultra, so it wasn't an Ultra problem.

The Radio, TV, Newspapers and bloggers exploded in righteous indignation against their government. Political operatives had described non-crimes as criminal so often that actual criminal actions could be defended by labeling the reports as spin; at worst wrong-doing. Entirely innocent actions had so often been labeled as criminal that when nothing came of the initial charges, there were always the 'Secret' meetings to cast suspicion. When two people met in the hallway and exchanged greetings, it could be described as a secret meeting. Why wasn't anybody else invited? It must be a cover-up. Politics and advertising endlessly told people 'this is what they don't want you to know'. Though the 'they' always remained vague. Then there were the secrets that everybody knew about. Though how everyone knew there was a secret, seemed to be a secret. But no one seemed to doubt it. Anything could be construed as a crime and anyone a criminal.

Unfortunately the man-on-the-street interviews continued to provide a steady diet of uninformed opinions to pressing questions. But news? People longed for the good 'ol days. The days of no drug war, no sex war, no revenge sentencing for minor offenses, no one-size-fits-all justice. Though many accepted the way things were as inevitable and had given up any chance of change.

Dodges' off the cuff comment built steam. "NO MORE TAXES!" He had intended it to be taken as the standard Ultra line 'no new taxes' or 'no tax increase', but the public took it literally as 'No Taxes'.

People laughed with evil delight at the Ultra induced government shutdown. They had thought it reasonable to say, 'Love my Country, but Fear my Government'. This brand of paranoia suited the Ultras. The Ultra friendly talk shows gloried in the suspension of payments to bureaucrats and freeloaders on government entitlements. It was about time that they were cut off from the government teat. The business community thought they were free of harassment from government intrusion; no regulators, inspectors or mandatory reports.

"The Company pays one point eight billion per year in taxes. That's $451,765,370 per quarter in federal taxes." Thomas

Hamilton, Parrots' Ultra associate, studied his tables. His boss listened intently as the rest of the USA Store board members tried to stay awake.

"So, just under half a billion?" Parrot asked.

"Yes, sir," Hamilton confirmed.

"Damn, speak English Tom," Parrot sighed.

"If we hold those funds in the bank, rather than submit payments to the Government... at three and a half percent interest..." Parrots' eyes glazed over at the array of numbers. He never liked math anyway, except when it came to counting his money. The business analyst continued, "... we will see interest income of $15.8 million..."

Parrot interrupted, "Wait..." he knew what interest income meant. "You're saying if we just keep the money in the bank, we will have an extra fifteen million dollars at the end of the month?"

"Fifteen point eight million, sir," Hamilton confirmed. The other USA Store board members, who were on the verge of nodding off, perked up. In their heads they were calculating the ten percent executive bonus for generating company income.

Parrot said what they were all thinking, "So, the eight of us divide ten percent of that, or about $200,000 each." This kind of math he could handle. It meant money 'In His Pocket'. "... each month?"

"Yes, Sir." Hamilton had earned his salary this month.

"How long could we get away with it?" Parrot asked.

"Well," Hamilton thought, "deposits are due quarterly... that's a few weeks off. It would take about a month before the Feds noticed that the deposits weren't paid. Another month before they notify us and set a drop dead date to respond... our lawyers could stall in court, pleading innocent error or electronic foul up or something... I'd say a fiscal quarter; three months or so."

"The Ultras' 'get the government off our backs' legislation has stripped the IRS of most of their regulators, investigators and lawyers," one of the board members added, "We may be able to keep them tied up in court indefinitely at the cost of a couple of hundred grand in legal fees."

"Finally," Parrot said triumphantly, "those political donations to the Ultras are paying off."

The response at the government offices that processed their quarterly tax payments had slowed considerable. The money just stayed in the banks. The actuaries crunched the numbers and responded that each day would bring big bucks in interest on the collected funds as they sat in the company accounts. This was dutifully reported to the organizations' management. A new and selfish thought took root. "What if we withheld tax payments until the end of the disruption?" Parrot floated the idea. It was obviously 'wrong-doing'. But was it criminal?. Not if you had the right connections and an army of lawyers. The question the board struggled with was, 'would we be prosecuted?' By who? Would the company alone and not the decision maker be held responsible? They had often avoided personal accountability by employing 'The Company Says…' Companies didn't go to jail.

The interest on these funds over a few months, while the Feds sorted out this crisis, amounted to big bucks and executive boards in cynical self interest ignored Government pleading. After all, the Ultras had gutted the government collection agencies. They justified the illegal actions by appealing to the peoples' mistrust in the governments' runaway spending. Management self-righteously declared that they would wait until the Government could insure proper use of the funds before submitting their share. Of course, this was entirely self-serving, but it sounded good to the public.

Many medium and small businesses, seeing the same benefit of holding their payments, supposedly to insure Government accountability, boldly declared that they too would follow suit. What could the Government do? The IRS had been de-fanged and who would prosecute them with the inspectors furloughed?

Payroll officers were instructed to recalculate salaries and wages to distribute SSI, and taxes that had previously been deducted. Some organizations even revised pay checks so that the employees saw a slight increase while the company kept a lions' share of the windfall. Their employees approved of the few more dollars without an overall understanding of the consequences. Their actions were justified as government living within its' means; like families. Lack of Government seemed to be a good thing. They would live to regret it.

The Draw-down required by the Balanced Budget Provision was the new mantra of the Ultras. In earlier times 'Expand or Die' had been the call word as small business were gobbled up into huge concentrated conglomerates. When this became inconvenient the call became 'Down-Size' to justify cutting executives and support staff of the merged companies. Next came the dismissal of senior workers who were proving too expensive; and more likely to be organized into Unions. The call became 'Right-sized'. It sounded reasonable.

The Ultras had passed the new laws knowing that a number of people would simply give up, providing an additional source of savings. The entire social structure was brought down to the poverty level. Applicants for assistance were confronted by a bewildering maze of requirements in order to qualify. Not that the new requirements prevented cheating; they didn't. Analysts, predicting the past with uncanny accuracy, declared that recipients with excessive incomes should have been suspended years ago. There was even talk of confiscating their bank accounts. That they didn't was a sign of their compassion. Fewer and fewer people bought the slogan, 'Compassion is our prime concern'.

The Association of Retired Persons began to mobilize its' membership. Business groups, operating in self interest and in concert with Ultra political strategists, subverted the effort. They had learned in the Health Care debate during the Clinton administration that you could turn the membership against its' own leaders with the right spin. After intense study and analysis, the AARP in that instance favored the bill as being in the best interest of their members. Members, however, were told that their leadership were 'Greedy Geezers' living off the organizations funds and promoted socialist schemes. The arrogant elite leadership would deny their members choice of doctors and use their membership funds for political activities to promote 'diversity'. That was another word that the Ultras had turned into a 'bad thing' buzz-word. Diversity meant Fags and Flag-burners. Every uninformed Ultra in the lower strata who voted against their own best interest, knew that.

The debate became, not the quality of the legislation, but the division within AARP. The organization survived due to the trust of a majority of their members, but the Health Care debate never happened. What had passed for debate was not the quality of the proposal, but whether an organization was acting in the members best interests. Members of trusted non-profit organizations began to doubt their organizations' motives. The Ultras would use the same tactics again with Labor Unions and to suppress dissent in the military. Macho hardhats and patriotic troops were inundated with stories of Ultra enemy's support for socialist ideas and transgender rights.

The private sector, once gleeful over the government predicament, began to feel the ripple effect. Welfare and Social Security offices went unmanned. National Parks went unattended. State Capitols with a high portion of government workers saw business losing over fifty percent of their sales. Consumer societies depend on consumers with income to function. A large part of the economy depended on consumer spending, and consumer confidence was strained. The pool of consumers diminished. Local small businesses found themselves in as dire of circumstances as their laid off neighbors. The interdependence began to unravel.

Businesses en-mass copied the major industries non-compliance with the tax code. Partly motivated by greed with a dose of self-preservation in the face of lost business, people withheld their payments to the Government. Seeing it as an opportunity to make a few months interest on the withheld funds; bigger businesses held on to quarterly government deposits.

The public were told that welfare cheats were a drag on the Federal Government; and Entitlements represented 50% of the Federal outlays. This was an Ultra twist of words that implied that welfare was half of the government costs. The use of the term 'Entitlements' was craftily introduced to give that impression. Actually, welfare was a tiny portion; single digits. But entitlements included the Social Security checks for the elderly, the blind, the disabled, veterans, foster kids and food programs; things that most people saw as compassionate and necessary. Welfare was the hate-word that brought out the emotions and so that is where the Ultras focused to engage the anger. Entitlements were drying up across the board. The blind took to begging on freeway exit ramps and the elderly sought subsistence with minimum wage jobs.

Massive spending bills were hung up in congress. The Ultras were unwilling to spend future income. The balanced budget required an equal draw-down in all government spending; a draw-down of agencies that were not abolished altogether. This gave political cover to the politicians. They did not have to vote to cut popular programs. It was automatic. 'Sharing the burden' it was called. A clever way of shedding blame for the pain that would follow. President White took the heat as head of the government, though he was helpless against the Ultra financed, veto-proof congress.

Lawmakers could tell the folks back home, 'At least I tried'. Projects from dead-end highways to iceboxes for Eskimos went on hold. Joe six-pack dutifully went to work content that government spending was finally under control and he had more money 'In His Pocket'. He would find out how useless this green paper was without the good faith of the U.S. Government.

The transportation and energy bill had over six thousand infrastructure projects; bridges, highways and communications jobs were all in suspense. Portrayed as government spending, these projects, in fact, employed most construction, agricultural workers and financed many other industries. It meant thousands of jobs that went unfunded. The blue collar worker, who had laughed at the government predicament, got a pink slip as his company's contracts went unfunded.

Prison guards and military were still considered necessary. When their payday rolled around, vouchers with the good faith of the United States Government were issued instead of paychecks. Some businesses would accept them, confident of future payment, some would not. Senators and most congressmen were sufficiently well off that they could weather a few months comfortably without pay and, to show solidarity with the common man, they waived their salaries until the crisis had passed.   But the crisis did not pass; it deepened. Eventually, even the Armed Forces were issued vouchers due to the lack of funds

Incremental steps designed by Congress to end the crisis only served to send more people into desperation. Late payment penalties were suspended to encourage payment. Instead, many more people decided on non-payment. Military families were brought on bases to be fed by military kitchens. It was not authorized, but no one could stop the soldiers from caring for their own. Benefits for military families overseas failed and the more compassionate host countries saw to their basic needs. SSI recipients with outside income or families found that they no longer qualified. Under funded pensions of most companies simply stopped processing payments for their retirees.

DOWN ON THE FARM

The perimeter and towers were manned by the State National Guard. Part of the National Guard Community Support Act. Michael remembered the planning meeting that came up with that one too. "Soldiers hate war, because without it they get paid for nothing," Raven had dryly declared. You didn't say that in public, just in Legislative planning sessions. Military duty was expanded to include guarding borders and detainees. Duty had become dangerous and exhausting. Long gone were the lightweights who expected education or family benefits from a military term. What remained were unskilled, barely educated youths, who were drilled into hard core soldiers. They hated this kind of duty and let the detainees know it.

Michaels' sentence to the farm was for five years. Three inmates per room. Michael and Moses were put into a cell with a man named Travis. Travis was a young boom buster. A skinhead, under education, or rather mis-educated, and violent. He hated Moses immediately. Skin color was enough reason.

Michael was surprised to find that Travis had a somewhat privileged upbringing. His parents were 'LOTTO stiffs'. Average citizens did not want to hear that they should pay for a safe and sane society. Mentioning taxes was political suicide. Voters wanted their elected representatives to find another way. Legislators around the country scrambled to find money. They discovered gambling. Over the years several thousand people had won jackpots that supposedly made them millionaires. The Government had made money hand over fist as Americans got use to the idea of a chance to be lazy for life.

Awards were generally paid out at about $50,000 a year for twenty years. As the participation in the gambling schemes tapered off, the few thousand winners became a burden. The moral reformation, actually a cold-blooded effort to cut government costs, was passed suspending payments to increase awareness of the importance of work. Friendly media outlets were enlisted to prepare the way by running stories of winners who spent foolishly and did not contribute to society. Those people who had quit their jobs and went into debt spending their future money were 'stiffed'. Houses and boats were seized and auctioned off. Those who had not alienated family and friends had somewhere to turn, but many became homeless and destitute.

Travis blamed the double-talking government for his parents' predicament and his own; though he had next to no concept of what government was. When you're rich, education was not a priority. In his world the government was a large, sinister force that existed for its own benefit. It needed to be brought down before it cheated anymore people. He had never voted and didn't care to. If someone wanted your vote, they were a politician and politicians could not be trusted, so you don't vote for anyone who wants your vote. It was a circular argument that justified his non-participation. But then Travis had never studied logic. His generic view of government seemed to extend to almost anyone or anything. Government was evil, politicians were crooked, niggers were lazy, wet-backs wanted Americans jobs, Jews controlled the money. It was distressing to see this spoiled two year old mentality in a full grown body capable of extreme violence.

Michael found the philosophical arguments between Moses and Travis quite entertaining. Travis tried to defend the 'old, rich white men' of Moses' pet theory.

Travis was in for two years plus restriction. It seems he took offense with a bumper sticker on a Winnabago. The 'I'm spending my kids inheritance' was meant to be a cute joke. The boom buster generation wasn't amused. They knew with SSI, Medicaid and other programs, the truth was these people WERE spending their childrens' future earnings. The deficit proved that. Travis had never had a credit card but owed $17,076 like everybody else. Someone, not him, was enjoying the goods or services that that money bought. Travis would swear they were welfare frauds and greedy geezers, while Moses asserted that they were 'old, rich white men'. In any care, Travis remained responsible for the $50,000 Winnabago that he had destroyed. It would take an extra three years to make restitution; indentured to an insurance company. Living on his parents' unearned income hurt his case. It was viewed with disgust by regular working folks and restitution was justice; or revenge. Economically speaking, it was Ultra legislation that let insurance companied off the hook.

On the outside, Michael would have agreed with Travis, out of self-interest, but he knew Moses was closer to the truth. Let the wealthy keep more of their money and they will create jobs and pay it out in wages. 'In your Pocket' was the cliché that the Ultras found effective in focus groups and could be used in almost any situation. The new laws let the money lenders keep more of their money, but they didn't pay it out in wages. They bought peoples' houses and raised their rent. Fixed assets; that was the way to wealth.

The work in the orchards was rather peaceful. With no TV or radio, the stresses of the outside world faded away. No visitors, no mail, no talk shows, no news. After all, this was punishment.

The three men occupied themselves in the off hours with discussions, or rather arguments, about their circumstances and the outside world. Michael the Capitalist, Travis the Anarchist and Moses the Socialist. Michael became more uncomfortable with his line of reasoning. Moses was right. When Michael heard himself talk of caring for people, he came to realize that he was only thinking of family, friends and himself. It came out sounding illogical and selfish. It wasn't the same as those backyard barbecues. All the guests were in similar circumstances and nodded their heads in agreement. The twisted logic that made it sound rational, that was used to get people to vote contrary to their own best interest, was coincidentally in the best interest of the select few with the money and a mouthpiece. They all used the same flawed clichés for the same reasons; self-interest.

Moses cut through the semantics, innuendo and went right to the bone of human nature. "Funny folks, you Capitalists, use to be an insult to say someone valued money more than people. That's what the Commies called us. You people use it now like a badge of honor. Membership to the club. Like 'Politically Correct'.

"I remember young white boys like you, hippies, come up with that. People who cared. Our southern good 'ol boys would talk up equal opportunity line then vote against anything give us darkies a chances. They call it 'Politically Correct'. They talk the way that get them all them votes and get themselves reelected. Them Bubbas down south know they just talked the talk, but they don't let them Negros, women, Mexicans get special privilege. Never was about bein' special. Just equal."

"The 'ol hippie label been brought back. Now it mean you been had by liberals." Moses exaggerated his features, acting wild-eyed and suspicious like a boogieman was close at hand. "And if political correct votes are unpopular, like they say, then it ain't politically correct. Politically correct means you get you more votes than you lose." Michael thought of Chips' many percent gained versus lost briefings. "Make people think they stand with the rebels against politicians. Then they hustle votes from ignorant rednecks, like Travis here. How you like that Travis?" Moses jabbed, "You politically correct. Most people would agree with you that the Winnabago needed to be pushed off that cliff."

"Political Correct don't do us black folk any good. Like the way they shafted affirmative action. A quota," Moses said with disgust. "Never was a quota. Tell us about sta...tis...tics, Mikey."

Michael felt like he was giving one of the Ultra seminars; but this seemed more honest. "If the community was 20% black and you had 18% or 23% blacks, no problem. But if you had 2% or no blacks, then you're obviously doing something to keep the black man down. And that could be proved statistically."

Moses turned to Michael with a cynical smile on his face, "like the kind of sleight of hand Mikey here use to play. You ever been asked by your Ultra bosses to show that brown people been slighted?" He knew as well as Michael that that wasn't what number-crunchers were paid to do.

"Reverse discrimination," Travis countered with a defensive tone.

Moses continued, "You can't prove that Whitey's been put down. But dumb crackers bought it. Our 'Special privilege' was that we could prove discrimination and whitey couldn't. Statistically. You know about that Mickey."

He couldn't disagree. It was one of those things that the Ultras misused to aggravate people like Travis into voting for them. Real winners were the white women. Second incomes. Gravy checks for the beach house or the Winnabago."

"You didn't mind when it meant keepin' them niggers in their place." Moses said, "Travis here been told their takin' your jobs; your rightful place on the top of the heap. Funny thing is they ain't getting to the top of the heap any more than a street nigger." Michael had never heard the philosophy of the fortunate fraction states so simply or accurately.

Travis seemed to think that because he was white, he was inherently smarter than Moses. He was wrong. Moses and he still exchanged insults on a daily basis and seemed to have reached an understanding. Both seemed to relish the verbal sparring. The midterm election came with Michael still picking fruit to earn his keep and pay back society. Both major parties racked each other with savage results. Rumors and accusations of 'secret' meetings emerged on every subject. If no damning information came out, there must be a cover-up, because everybody knew the secret evidence existed. Though the source of the secret was always fuzzy. This was the old kangaroo court TV tactic of proving the negative. And it worked for all the major parties. Voter participation reached an all time low.

President White got the blame and most incumbents got reelected. The veto-proof majority remained intact. Citizens were encouraged by radio shows and talk TV to express their dissatisfaction with the purse strings. Some shady businessmen tried to turn it to their advantage, enrolling their employees as independent contractors.

In effect they became self-employed. Their egos stroked by talk of them being businessmen themselves. Businesses stopped collecting SSI and federal tax while cutting salaries, and still paychecks rose slightly. Most workers didn't notice the change until they were out of work and couldn't qualify for unemployment, or tax time came around and they found themselves responsible for the entire years' tax bill. By that time the Government, not their employer, appeared to be the bad guy. The average Joe, like the large corporations, simply refused to pay.

Federal funds dropped off dramatically. In an effort to appease the public, and buy themselves some time, a law was enacted to reestablish the eligibility of everyone getting a government check. Government vouchers, instead of checks, were issued. The intent was to redeem them after the crisis passed. 'Cutting out the deadbeats,' had a good sound to sell to the public. In the interim six months, no funds would be paid out. Of course, the military still could count on room and board and military families would be allowed in government mess halls. The result was savings wrenched from the blind, disabled, pensioners and the elderly.

Public service offices at the state, local and national level began shutting their doors for the duration of the crisis. The government did not have near enough staff, even before the mass furloughs, to do the screening. The Ultras never intended the screenings to be done. That the six month review period was insufficient was, therefore, irrelevant.

Radio and TV programs, which had helped fuel the crisis as entertainment portrayed as news, saw a rise in viewers and listeners, but sponsors were finding a precipitous drop in business. Marketing firms tried every twist, telling folks what they thought they wanted to hear. Still, advertising revenue continued to drop. Even celebrity spokesmen failed to gain support. The audience became very cautious regarding nonessential spending when their very subsistence was in doubt. Families found generations coming together to cut household costs. Consumer confidence, along with discretionary spending, fell to zero.

The Veto Proof Congress passed the *Return Power to the States* Act, supposedly to allow the states to collect delinquent taxes. Actually to wash their hands of the mess while sounding noble. And to leave the cost of collection to the states. Non-essential workers were told to stay home, and then laid off or fired outright. The rational was, if you acknowledged that you were non-essential then you weren't needed. The private sector applauded.

Politicians' six-figure salaries disappeared. The rich public servants that took the job for reasons other than a paltry six figures were able to carry on without the government dollars. They proudly announced that they would decline their salaries to show camaraderie with the little guy. But they made money in other ways. Regular line workers were not as lucky. Then the high stakes players found that their electronic millions were an illusion. They panicked.

The elderly, retired veterans and others who had received government checks were require to prove that they were eligible. But then there was no one to take their depositions. Thousands of people scheduled for eligibility reviews simply went unheard. A great many of these people lived from check to check with nothing to spare or to see them through the reenrollment process. Those with families or friends, who were able to help, held eviction and malnutrition at bay. Those without resources did not. Horror stories began to emerge about the elderly dying from lack of medication and grown children declining help to their seniors.

The destitute with no means and no family were sent to senior centers. Entitled was the euphemism used, as though society was doing them a favor. Warehousing was a more accurate term. The centers were actually a more acceptable form of work farm. The only difference was that there were no guards. Where did the seniors have to go anyway? They did the menial work formerly done by illegal immigrants, but this was cheaper for the owners and the centers claimed a cloak of compassion as they tapped this latest cheap labor force. They could cover room and board but didn't have to pay wages.

The Veto Proof Congress had a solution. As a family was responsible for their children under eighteen, they should also be responsible for their elderly and sick members. The *Respect for the Dignity of Our Elders* bill was pushed through congress. It had nothing to do with dignity. Its main feature was it didn't cost a thing and made the politicians appear responsive. All family members' resources and income were considered when determining eligibility. Of course, this meant that most of the retired and disabled no longer qualified for help.

A woman refused to call her family when facing expulsion from her nursing home, afraid she would be a burden. A heartwarming story. The family scoured the city and she was found and brought into the bosom of her family. Headlines were strangely mute about the other stories of people jumping from bridges, overdosing on their medications, or seeking an end in some other way. Far from being shocked, the families often seemed relieved.

Most of the helpless were taken in by family members in spite of great hardship. What choice did they have? A new law was proposed, the *Protect the Independence of Senior Citizens* Act. A noble sounding title. Children and grandchildren of burdensome elderly family members could be issued an exemption from responsibility. This, however, did not exempt family assets from the eligibility determination. That would have been an expense to the government and as such could not satisfy the cost-benefit-analysis.

The end result was many more elderly homeless. A rash of suicides were at first portrayed as a poignant act to spare the family the burden. The families were the callous ones. As the suicides continued more and more cases of less noble motives emerged. In many cases it was a question as to whether it was suicide. Accident rates soared, and those with serious medical problems or expensive medications simply began to die off. The country was hardening its heart and a savage self-interest dominated.

Many families attempted to liquidate the collectibles that they had horded for years. Online auction sites saw a surge in items described as collectible, as people scrambled to get the extra cash to pay bills. Many discovered that no one was willing to pay for what they thought was their emergency nest egg. Many had been sucked in by marketing schemes that said that these items would be, 'sought after by collectors'. Commemorative coins and the like flooded auction sites and pawn shops. The collectors knew that they were just a slug coated with a thin veneer of silver. People had more silver in the fillings of their teeth than was in those coins. Many people who had felt confident that they had treasure set aside for times of need, found that they had nothing. The glut of such items made even the marginally collectible items virtually worthless. Those that religiously collected the set of fifty state quarters found that they were worth about twenty-five cents each. They weren't precious metal. They were cranked out in the millions and everybody that wanted one had one. Collectors did not seek them out; they shunned them.

Inconvenient souls continued to be sent to the work farms. The farm accepted a new arrival; Michaels' old associate, Thomas Hamilton. He had incurred the wrath of the Ultras when his family wealth scheme came under question. A sacrificial lamb was needed and Hamilton found himself charged with fraud. The prosecutions stopped with his conviction. His Ultra clients continued to enjoy the wealth transfers he had arranged. Putting him away covered the tracks of the party insiders that used his system.

"I got nothing," Hamilton complained, "I had everything I owned in one basket. The house, the car, bank accounts... everything in plain sight. They took it all and sealed the court records so it would end with me. They convicted me for a comma. Sure, it was my software that detected the glitch in their program, but I didn't write the damn bill. Who says Federal, State, County and City has to be a four way split. No comma after County means County and city get one share, right? A three way split. It has legal precedent. I know what they meant, but legally, it didn't say that.

"My code is now public domain and I bet they still use it. I looked like the kingpin. The wife went back to her parents. I never realized how alone I am. Associates, clients, people I wanted something from ... and people that wanted something from me. I

175

was one of the Fortunate Fraction. Know what I mean?" Hamilton was able to conjure up a smile, "Of course you do. I didn't think... Some got art, antiques, off shore bank accounts, boats, gold... I had all my chips in one pile. They took it all. You got anything Mike?"

"Just a little retreat in the country." Michael felt lucky for the first time in months.

THE MELTDOWN

Senator Dodge came to regret his flippant comment. The tax revolt at the Federal level began to trickle down to state and local levels. Delinquent property taxes soared from single digits to over half almost overnight. Dodge and other Ultra heavyweights made the rounds of the Sunday talk shows, trying to repair the damage he had done. He was attempting to reverse his 'No More Taxes' comment, but in a way that didn't betray his stop government spending mantra or admit responsibility. It was too easy to be labeled a 'liberal' to risk a complete about-face. "Our children whether in public or private schools need this funding to make a better world." He continued to say 'Our children' to make it sound like a community responsibility, but his youngest child was 37; hardly a child. The elderly sitting at home with skyrocketing medical costs were not climbing on his bandwagon.

The Ultras talked children when talking to parents and educators; security and health care when talking to the elderly; and opportunity when talking to the Boom-busters. Their research branch put out contrived information to satisfy each group. The laws were in place before the many diverse groups realized that the whole range of laws were not in their best interest; a net loss all around. They may save a dollar here that would cost them ten dollars in lost services and surcharges.

When their guru, Henry R. Parrot had urged the small businessmen to pay in their taxes with Government vouchers, people responded in the thousands. They congratulated each other on sticking it to the government. Proselytizing that they would 'fix the system'; that they could shrink funding until they could 'drown big government in the bath water'. It proved to be a poison pill.

With government receipts drying up, businesses found their suppliers unwilling to provide goods for government paper. Those around military bases, that always applauded 'our boys in uniform', found themselves the victim of a rash of burglary and armed robbery; pillaged by unpaid soldiers. The businessmen didn't seem to have realized how much of their income was dependent on Government money. When it was not forthcoming they suffered as much as the troops. And 'No Money, No Goods' did not satisfy hungry troops in the absence of the restraints of day-to-day law enforcement.

The Veto-proof congress had fixed Social Security. Or rather revised the system from an insurance system into a system of self-savings. The rationale was that the retirement age had been set at 65 because that was the life expectancy at the time. Those having reached that age had beaten the clock and could retire. Since the life expectancy was now 74, age 82 for women, that should be the age at which to qualify for SSI. Supported by the Gen'Xers and the Boom-Busters, along with business interests, the assault on the seniors began. First a particularly hideous example of fraud was used to stereotype the whole group as greedy geezers.

Insurance and pension plan companies, saddled with losses and no income, went into default. Old line life insurance companies sought bankruptcy protection leaving their customers stranded. Retirees who thought they would have legal and government protection found no recourse; no flesh and blood person to talk to. The companies no longer existed. The smiling executives that reassured them, bailed out with sizeable severance packages. That left just a few shady executives in jail or retired offshore. Customers were out of luck and company workers out of a job.

Senator Dodges' 'why educate other peoples' kids' had struck a chord, but not just with the private school supporters that he intended, but with the elderly. Evidence of the demographic shift in the American population had not been considered. A majority of households, elderly and boomers and yuppies, did not have school age children. They did not funnel money into his private schools rather than a public school system but just agreed in principle and kept the change. Most of the unpaid property taxes were not available for public projects, but was to be found 'In the Taxpayers Pocket'.

"How can private schools help?" Reverend Patson asked. "I am proposing a law that would allow schools to issue receipts for money received. In this way people can contribute directly to their local private school. Church schools or even…" he seemed to smell something bad, "public schools. No taxes just local contributions. No bureaucrat, no government involvement. All you need is the receipt showing your care for 'Our Children'." The call for voluntary contributions was widely ignored. The public tended to rally round any child whose face appeared on a tragic news story; but not every student could appear on TV.

The debate, if you could call it that, concerned private schools. The disagreement ran something like… private schools were better because they produced better test scores; versus, private schools are better because they are run by concerned parents; versus private schools are better because…the next speaking point. The Ultras' premise being the undeniable truth that private schools were the solution. The debate was 'in what way are private schools better'. Public education was a forgotten socialist idea. The discussion proceeded from the undeniable truth to different degrees of hair splitting, but no dissenting voices were invited or considered.

The Home Schooling Movement had been fully implemented. Church schools and private schools expanded to accommodate those who could escape the public school system. Those not ready to accept the private philosophy were left behind in a system failing from lack of funding. Starve the beast did not just refer to Government where the Ultras were concerned. The poorest and most difficult to serve children were condemned to a system short of supplies and teachers in crumbling buildings as families that had the means took vouchers and joined the exodus to private providers, or just took the vouchers and kept the kids at home. Home schooling with no standards or monitoring was a secondary source of income for families in tough economic times; not to mention, money withheld from the burden of supporting public education. Many of Reverend Patsons' followers dutifully turned the money over to his education front organization, but many more desperate people just kept the money 'In Their Pocket,' as they had heard the Ultras preach so often.

The better off families, who generally paid for a private school anyway, were more than happy to accept a little more gravy in the form of vouchers; and public education suffered. The illusion of getting their child into a better school bought the support of many poor and hopeful parents. These were mostly the poor white families. Black families had listened and learned from Martin. They knew the short falls and roadblocks of such a system.

When they realized the insufficiency of the vouchers, they knew they had been fooled. A poor family with an exceptionally brilliant child couldn't buy their way in. The voucher only bought into a public school. In wealthier districts the parents could make up the difference; in poorer communities the vouchers bought inadequate supplies and crowded, dilapidated buildings. Well off districts paid the difference and complained; poor families just complained.

School choice was an illusion; one that the Ultras had used before to doom health care. It was not that people could not pick the school of their choice; they could. But the vouchers paid only a fraction of the cost. So, schools routinely rejected those who could not make up the difference. Then the Ultras passed their follow-up piece. The *Parental Educational Responsibility* bill cancelled all school vouchers. The funding was not restored to the educational system; it just went into the pockets of the Fortunate Fraction. School lunches were curtailed. Grocery shopping was not the role of education. The Ultras themselves were surprised with how easy their shallow argument floated. They claimed that 'parents of kids getting school lunches were just too lazy to get up and make breakfast for their kids'. And people chose to believe it in cynical self interest; though subconsciously, they knew it wasn't true. At least parents of kids who did not get free lunches agreed, hoping to save a few bucks. It was as good an explanation as any to support such a cold hearted policy guilt free.

Patson wanted to finance his private school network with public funds and the Veto-proof Congress gave him his wish; per student blocks of money paid out to anyone who ran what was loosely defined as a school. "We owe it to our children to give them a decent education, and the best education is a private education," he declared. By selecting the most promising students, he had rigged a sample test score far above the national average. With Senator Dodge leading the way, the *Freedom of Educational Choice Act* was passed. Though teachers and their unions strongly opposed the measure, they were slandered by labels of Unionists and Government Workers. Surprisingly, the general public bought the Patsons' "why should we pay to educate other peoples kids?" argument. Many supported the plan because of promises of relief from education targeted property taxes. And probably more important to the religion industry was to eliminate the 'Secular Curriculum' that spoke of evolution and honest, if unflattering, American history.

The elderly shocked by the harsh changes in the Social Security System were seeing to their own security. Public schools were failing but the private alternatives could not or would not absorb the mass of unserved children. Many families, even those with children, found themselves responsible for elderly relatives with no means of support and saw withholding property tax as a way to meet the added expense.

Making the problem worse was the fact that food programs for the needy were under assault. The monthly ration had not been increased, even though the purchasing power of the dollar had severely eroded. Food intended for a month gave out in about three weeks. Further the Ultras were spinning this humanitarian pittance into a public abuse issue by claiming that if it weren't for cigarettes and alcohol the ration was sufficient. A popular Senator, to prove the point, vowed to feed his family on the ration for a month. He found they had run out of food in less than three weeks. And even at that, the family complained about inadequate meals of questionable quality. He was quite proud of his theatrics until the press discovered that his children were sneaking candy at school and visiting friends at meal time quite often.

Another women senator tried to trivialize the reduction in benefits by saying that a family could make up the difference by collecting aluminum cans. An advocacy group for the poor exposed the lie of her comment by depositing the difference in benefits, converted into aluminum cans, on her office doorstep. The volume was many garbage bags full of cans that completely blocked the entrance. And this was the amount needed to subsidize one family for one month. Research showed that if applied to all cases for the average duration of a family's assistance. Nationwide, the entire production of aluminum would have been insufficient to make up the difference.

Health care suffered a similar deceptive maneuver in the health care debate. The Ultras, again, scared senior citizens with 'You won't be able to pick your Doctor'. True if your doctor was not a participant (which most were), but at least everyone would have had the chance to see a doctor. With the reimbursement rate cut from 70% to less than 30%, people found that their doctor could not afford to keep them as a patient. The scare tactics worked as effectively as with the school debate.

Never the less, the Ultras program passed. Evidence of the undesirable effects was condemned as liberal theatrics. Drawing down the monthly supplement to an amount sufficient for about two weeks was the actual effect. Most knew, though the Ultras wouldn't admit it, that it was not a supplement. There was nothing to supplement. It was the entire monthly nutritional supply for millions of kids and it now covered only fifty percent of their needs.

"There's no reason a parent can't work at least part-time to make up the difference and feed their children," Dodge again brought out his assumed premise that those in need just didn't want to work even if it meant their kids went hungry.

He conveniently neglected to mention that even working part-time would mean a reduced level of assistance, so the situation didn't improve for the child. Many of the working poor already worked full time. Day care for off school hours ate up much of the extra earnings. Shared care was assaulted by the Ultras as tax evasion. The traditional American attitude that widows (for widows include deserted women) and children deserved some help was rejected as liberal and encouraging laziness. Senator Dodge had come up with an appropriate case of fraud that was presented as typical to enrage the public and justify the Ultras' proposals.

This was just one of the false premises used by the Ultras to demonize the needy. There was the state migration for better benefits that implied people would move to the state with the best benefits. This had triggered a race to the bottom as states slashed benefits so as not to be a welfare destination. Of course, the migration myth wasn't true, as all of the studies showed, but the public bought the myth when told it would keep more money "In Their Pockets." The myth of having babies to increase benefits also played well as people were convinced that the poor women were morally degenerate and as greedy as the Ultras themselves. Also not true as birth rates of those on assistance was actually less than the general population.

The myth of multi-generation dependents was highlighted with a long term case as proof. The long term cases tended to be blind, disabled and mentally handicapped. But the research proved most of those receiving assistance desperately sought employment and were helped for less than a year. The rhetoric, sounding sincere and compassionate, stated that charities and churches should be the point of service for those in need. The average citizen nodded approval, evidently unaware that charities and churches had helped bring about the current system when they pleaded for help because they could not handle all the families that sought their help. Now they were expected to solve the problem; a problem which had increased several fold since the time when they couldn't cope.

Numbers didn't stop the Ultras. In a disturbing, irrational ad they refuted the numbers, citing fuzzy math to a population that didn't like math. The ads asked people, "We don't buy these liberal numbers games, do you?" They were just asking a question. They then went on to explain a particularly vulgar case of fraud as indicative of the system. Whether from fear, or self interest, or lack of logical thought, the Ultras' distorted explanations were accepted by a misinformed public.

In spite of putting Hamilton on the work farm, the Ultras continued to use the Hamilton method of family wealth protection. Retirement and estate planners had perfected the art of transferring family wealth from one generation to the next without government or legal interference.

Insurance companies sought government protection when faced with catastrophic natural disasters. This was perceived by the public as bad faith and those that were still enrolled just cease making payments. Payroll deductions were suspended. Employers and employees applauded the extra money in their pay checks. The authorities couldn't enforce a law when 87% of the public didn't cooperate. Mandatory insurance laws in most states went unpaid. The requirement did not trump family need and the lack of government enforcement gave people a contempt for the laws. Tickets were written, courts dates set and routinely ignored and fines went unpaid. Warrants were issued that police ignored. There was no space in jails to backup the government threats. There was only recognition of the powerlessness of the enforcers.

Federal and state accounts dried up. Government checks suffered a drawdown as the agencies tried to provide at least some assistance. Soon, the only thing to be done was to suspend payment altogether. All the government could do for victims of pension default was to offer a mealticket. The Government handout was presented as generous. When the gravy train of payroll deductions ended, insurance companies avoided the mounting claim costs by declaring bankruptcy. The signal sent to corporate officers was that they would suffer no ill effects of pillaging company assets if they enjoyed the right political affiliation.

The first to get the ax were government workers. IRS staff and Federal park employees were immediately furloughed. Leave without pay was declared to retain seniority while saving the government millions per day. But saving didn't fill the government coffers. It just meant a little less red ink. The Environmental Protection Agency and Department of Education were abolished all together.

Diplomats and their dependents were stranded in foreign lands; living on embassy grounds and fed by the host countries out of compassion. But just as quickly, the Ultras began offering the U.S. Embassy facilities in other countries for sale to the highest bidder. Host countries reclaimed the compounds and in many cases simply gave the diplomats and their families a one-way ticket back to America, just to be rid of them.

Other non-essential costs were withheld. States, loosing federal funding began to tighten their belts. Many state employees' jobs were eliminated. They discovered that Federal business, conducted at the state level, had funded much of the state work with federal money. With the Federal funds drying up the jobs were gone, and so were the workers paychecks.

An argument was crafted to blame families for letting relatives draw assistance. To most, influenced by the distorted rhetoric, this meant Food Stamps and Welfare. This fit nicely with the *Family Responsibility Provision* of the 13 Points. Entitlement checks stopped and those who maintained the system were furloughed. Most people cheered; until grandmas' check did not arrive. Then the grim reality set in. Entitlements were not just welfare. But the law was absolute; it said entitlements. It did not spare support for the old, blind, disabled and orphans. Foster families lost the funding to care for their charges. Failure to adopt was dismissed by the Ultras as another way to defraud the system. Many foster families simply could not afford to care for a child without assistance. Group homes were more impersonal and more expensive, but the only alternative, for the states.

The *Individual Privacy Protection Provision* insured that any personal information maintained by the government was destroyed when no longer used. Those in the Ultras' inner circle knew this meant that when the payments stopped, the recipient lists would be destroyed. When people realized the impact of the end of entitlements, the system could not simply be restarted. It would have to be rebuilt; and by the Ultras' strict eligibility requirements over an extended, cost saving, period of time.

An elderly retired computer analyst enraged by the deception took his revenge on the Government computer system, introducing a destructive worm that disabled virtually the entire Federal automated system. System administrators, attempting corrective action, found a constant barrage of disruptive viruses and worms from numerous sources until the system was corrupted beyond repair. The internet began to fail completely. Ebay livelihoods, online retailers along with private and government electronic financial transactions evaporated. Supporting jobs disappeared. Thousands of computer jocks at all levels were helpless and unemployed; and without useful skills.

Launched as revenge of the disenfranchised, a new and evasive computer virus, dubbed the 'Backlash virus', was spreading through virtually every computer system. Backlash not only corrupted active computer programs and data files, but seeped into backup files whenever a system was restored from other sources. A corrupted program didn't need to be downloaded for the infection to spread. As soon as a machine made contact with another machine or disk, the virus sent an infected feeler. Corruption was transmitted like the old TV signals; through the air. Wireless and plug in models alike were equally at risk. Cell phones became unreliable and text messaging was virtually impossible. Weather and spy satellites began to act peculiar. Media using these facilities suffered periodic failure. Rumor spread that government eavesdropping had inadvertently spread the infection to space based platforms. The public was shocked by the costs estimated for repair and maintenance. They didn't see the cost benefit in their lives. No one was that interested. Satellites malfunctioned; some crashed.

IRS files were corrupted in a similar act of electronic sabotage. The staff tried to restore their files from tapes only to find the renewed files and the backup tapes useless; infected by the simple act of loading the files.

The masses giggled and applauded the confusion. It was a sit-com-like plot-twist that amused the general public. The IRS was generally hated and feared anyway. A TV education had trained them to react to any plot twist. Just something different.

The Backlash virus found its way into the government payroll system and government records of all sorts were purged. Military payroll files and pentagon procurement information just disappeared to the PacMan-like infection that seemed to have a mind of its own. Federal criminal records evaporated, followed by state records. When government checks failed to arrive, people felt the impact. The average citizen realized that the negative effects would reach them. Before long the backlash had worked its way into the stock exchange. Electronic traders found their mountains of electronic wealth gone. Common investors that could bail out did. Most had to settle for a brokers' explanation of calamity. =Investment and retirement accounts disappeared. Insurance companies, their own files suspect, refused claims that couldn't be verified. And, of course, none could. With premiums going unpaid, insurance companies collapsed. They made noble announcements at the specially called press conference, but the public saw a helplessness in the excuses. Company executives joined the unemployed, as unskilled labor.

Payroll deductions for cars, houses, retirement, insurance, utilities and other commitments ended. Bank and credit unions couldn't even pay their staff, let alone foreclose on overdue accounts. Checks and credit cards were useless and cash was little better. People continued to use Credit Cards to the max when they could get someone to accept them. Michael had guessed right. The canned goods and items he had stockpiled were more precious than a Gold Card. You couldn't eat a gold card; you could trust a can of peaches.

Marketing firms were next as advertising failed to find its mark. People were hording money to be used only for necessities. Luxury items saw a downturn but the rich were still rich and could still write checks. Yachts, furs and elaborate jewelry still found buyers, but in greatly reduced numbers. Selling prices dropped as manufacturers tried to clear inventory. Those who bought on time found that their outstanding balance was higher than the resale price. They couldn't find a buyer willing to pay the balance due and yachts mysteriously sank as insurance scams abounded.

The Insurance industry suffered default. Their automated system had made fortunes from direct payment of premiums on the mandatory coverage of government workers. Workers were furloughed or fired and the automatic payments stopped. The company's profits were severely curtailed. Payments had always far exceeded claims. With the electronic failure, even those policies that remained cease to produce the routine monthly payments. Holders of large blocks of stock in the companies tried to sell quickly to sit out the crisis on a pile of cash until the market corrected itself. Many sellers found no buyers; others settled for pennies on the dollar. In a short time those attempting to sell could not even get pennies.

Car dealers, major appliances and items with a long life saw a severe decline as people kept whatever serviceable items they had rather than pay for the new models. Barter clubs seemed to be able to do repairs indefinitely. Car companies in particular found that people did not need to purchase automobiles every few years. Indeed, there were many more cars on the road than the country needed. Repeat business could not sustain the industry in the short run.

People who had expected that their income would only increase ran into balloon payments on mortgages that left them homeless when pay rates stalled. There was growing suspicion that lenders had intentionally promoted lending schemes that they knew the borrower could not meet. In effect, letting them make the payments up to the time that they repossessed the property for resale at a higher price. Anybody could learn to do it in a seminar. Getting' rich with real estate. Actually just a lot of paper equity.

The expectation of built up worth in equity proved an illusion. As equity was included in family worth estimations by the Federal government, many families found that they had virtually no family saving sitting in their homes. Well armed residents, often, just refused to leave. They were only middle class by virtue of their home equity. Without it they found that they were not only poor, but in some cases destitute. Though former Ultra allies, they were suddenly viewed as the 'other' kind of people, undeserving of any relief.

In an attempt to stimulate American business, the Congress increased the cost of foreigners to do business. Higher tariffs were placed on imported items. Buy American, a periodic patriotic slogan was revived. Assembly plants of American companies in Canada and Mexico, suffered. The large corporations had moved their facilities across the border for cheap labor, or to break the labor unions. It also allowed them to dodge pollution standards, labor laws and United States taxes. The parts destined for the assembly plants and retail and wholesale outlets failed to arrive. Many of the source nations had developed homegrown industries that appropriated American parts and facilities on their soil. A less threatening United States ceased to intimidate client nations.

The American boycott of Chinese goods left many dependent on products that were no longer produced at all in the States. Foreigners had never bought American products in large numbers. China among other began to nationalize American assets in retaliation for unfair tariffs. India found they could do very well without American investors or consumers. The new requirements, aimed at Asia, came to haunt North America in a way the Ultras' had not expected. Chinese cheap labor had undercut many American industries. Sheltered workshops for the blind provided the clocks used in government offices as a way to give the disabled gainful employment. That was until the Chinese showed that they could produce them cheaper. It was a double hit when most of the now unemployed blind were forced to seek charity when replacement jobs were not available. American paychecks were cashed and spent in China.

The situation was further aggravated by a foreign backlash against American products. Even more devastating for the U.S. economy was the absence of foreign investment. Americans found that many received their paychecks from foreign companies operating in the United States or multi-nationals based elsewhere to avoid U.S. tax. The three top American auto makers were in decline and the three major foreign car makers were in assent. The foreigners withdrew their money and jobs, irritated by the bigotry that was sweeping America. They had discovered that they didn't need American consumers all that much. The Americans generally demanded products on credit, right down to the consumer level. Americans were shocked to find how well the world could get along without them.

Another unintended consequence resulted from foreign brand names that were produced or assembled in America. Hundreds, then thousands, of Americans lost their jobs at Toyota, Hitachi, Sanyo and other foreign brands that patriotic citizens shunned. Further, America discovered that many of the gadgets that they had come to rely on were not available from an American owned company. The stimulus could not create these industries overnight and many had to buy products at prices inflated by punishing tariffs which routed profits overseas. American businessmen overseas had no room for negotiation.

Golf, tennis, fitness, fashion and other magazines of limited appeal found themselves losing readership as people found more immediate needs. There was no such thing as disposable income. Even the local newspapers, formerly making ends meet with advertising dollars, reverted to local subscriptions for survival.

Local neighborhoods learned how to fend for themselves. Any useful materials were seized for the benefit of the residents. Construction had stopped when Federal funding of local projects were canceled. A number of construction sites in the Black Lake development had been mothballed. Materials and some of the equipment was left on site. The neighbors appropriated anything of use; commandeering lumber, tools, concrete, fixtures, even construction machinery. Items and materials not of immediate use were stockpiled in caches for the use of the locals. Who owns it? The Lakers responded with gusto, 'Possession is nine-tenths of the law'. Developers could take their claim to court, but to little effect

Major sports teams, or rather the owners of major sports teams, had been able to blackmail local communities into subsidizing stadiums and private holdings with the promise of economic expansion. With attendance drying up, the community leaders were no longer willing to spend public funds to appease the gamers. The tax revenues that they had promised did not materialize and the millionaire owners lost their leverage. Sports stars salaries dropped dramatically.

Strikes broke out in most of the professional sports teams as the players tried to unite for a voice against the owners. To their dismay, they found that most people had little sympathy for them or the owners. The local dirt lot teams were dearer to the hearts of locals than some imported superstar that was whining about his lost seven figure salary. The stars found that they were worth far less than the million dollars paychecks that they took for granted. The stars from another state, living in Florida in the off season, lost their following. Local areas still had some pride in the local stars, but the days of recruiting nationwide for the best were a thing of the past. Most athletes, out of necessity, were willing to compete for little more than room and board.

Sports figures failed to attract the hero worship that gave them marketing appeal. Sports strikes soured fans. Advertisers canceled contracts that were no longer profitable. Many of the jocks tried unsuccessfully to renegotiate for more reasonable amounts, but endorsement weren't worth a dime. Stadiums subsidized by taxpayers for the profit of owners failed to attract the crowds, no matter how appealing the promotions. The heroes of the recent past were reduced to playing sandlot ball just to pay the bills.

Initially the emergence of malnutrition in many population centers went unnoticed. The trend became more pronounced when people began to succumb to illness aggravated by the lack of nutrition. Fear, rather than compassion, was the response by most people not directly affected. Mass starvation was more apparent in the major cities as people who had depended on the infrastructure simple gave up and sat complacent until the end came. Many of the elderly just gave up; younger, more active people were willing to turn to crime to alleviate their want. The few on-duty policemen could not be spared for something as trivial as a property crime. Juries and TV courts would not convict a mother for stealing formula for her sick baby. Kids stealing gasoline and a Big Mack were not perceived as criminals, except by the big business interests that depended on an orderly population. Pilfering at companies became rampant. Locked fire doors at poultry producers were openly torn away in as employees stole for survival.

A more troubling trend for urban developers were those who refused to pay rent and refused to move out. Landlords were not physically able to eject their tenants with the courts and police swamped or on furlough. Ultras didn't much care while it was the small 'get rich with real estate' investors that were inconvenienced. Problems escalated, though, when larger corporate accounts began to suffer. The strong arm of government enforcement (civil, county, state and federal) was not available to enforce corporate boards' property rights.

Agri-business experienced steep losses. Vandalism and theft overwhelmed local law enforcement, who were often sympathetic to the perpetrators. Agri-business executives and enforcement agents were threatened. Squatters and midnight harvesters overran large industrial acreage. Other large tracts lay untended and unproductive. Local law enforcement seldom sided with the few millionaire executives that complained.

The organizational structure failed when most people simply failed to cooperate. Respect for the ownership of large tracts of fertile land evaporated. Families move in and refused to be ejected; even in the face of hired company thugs. Squatters banded for protection against any outside threat and shanty towns became a common site on huge industrial farms. The rural landscape began to resemble a patchwork of medieval looking co-ops. Corrugated steel barriers and abandon vehicles became small walled compounds protecting small clannish groups. Without paychecks, local economies reverted to barter. A couple of bushels of corn could buy a couple of hours of carpentry or necessary tools or harvest workers.

Post World War II newsreels and After the Holocaust movies gave people a view of what a ravaged society looked like. The new holocaust lacked the destruction and devastation that war created; but want, depravation and refugees were apparent. The scenarios of bombed out infrastructure did not happen, but modern society was just as devastated when the internal respect for law broke down. Most Americans were shocked to learn just how fragile social order could be. The kind of refugee movement as seen in foreign disasters was inconceivable. *Grapes of Wrath* in reality.

In the U.S. regional disasters were always in reach of assistance from the rest of the country. Hurricane Katrina in the first decade of the twenty-first century showed people that regions could not necessarily depend on the strength of the rest of the country to come to their aid. When the entire country found itself an economic disaster area, there was no one left to respond to the crisis.

Hijackings made shipments of virtually any consumer goods a dangerous proposition. Shipping lines hired armed guards to escort truck convoys. Often the guards themselves rifled the shipments that they were hired to protect. Routinely, uniformed police and National Guard units appropriated goods for local jurisdictions. The cost of losses, fuel and the expense of security, spelled the end for most independent shippers. Even the U.S. postal service found many rural and urban routes too dangerous, or distant, to maintain. Bulk rates soared, junk mail vanished, home delivery ended. At best a local drop off point remained for citizens to collect their mail. Mail order trinket dealers saw sales fall as shipping costs made them unaffordable. They folded with a resulting job loss. Local commerce collapsed from austerity measures the people themselves had voted for.

Collection agencies did booming business at first. The business had become significantly more dangerous. Bill collectors assumed more the role of bounty hunter. They were unable to make any headway with phones and computers and found the only efficient way to collect was in person; assuming the debtor had the ability to pay. And that usually required that the collector be armed and prepared to use force. The bounty hunters and mercenaries found the hunt increasingly dangerous. A well armed and hostile population often shared the concerns of the families the collectors targeted and rose to a neighbors' defense. Evictions became nearly impossible with entire neighborhoods in desperate circumstances and up in arms.

Bounty teams, city and county officials, anyone attempting eviction, where met by peaceful mobs that impeded movement and blocked arrests by force of numbers; Martins' 'Peace in Common Concern' lesson. There were always a few Panthers around to protect the community from outside violence. Moses' lieutenants had learned well. Prison and the work farm were their boot camp. They could take care of themselves and their community. Lilly, the mother of the street, kept a civil social order as both inspiration and director of relief efforts.

In the southwest, outside the cities, the predominately Latin population drew together to defend their territory. Southern whites had their enclaves, as did southern blacks. The Midwest developed into two camps; the industrial/urban faction and the agricultural plains. The western mountains were sparsely populated and relatively inaccessible. California was a melting pot and factions coexisted in a patchwork of regional, racial interests. Texas with little to offer its' citizens, nevertheless, retained a regional pride and identity. The distressed areas of Appalachia to the east became a dangerous collection of clans. The east coast was a shadow of its former glory. Without shipping and industry, international trade and government business, it was hardly self-sufficient. The northwest, where the Homestead was safely tucked away, seemed to simply close its doors to the worst of the crisis. With thriving agricultural areas and abundant water, the region suffered but didn't wither.

FREEDOM

The sun rose with an eerie silence over the work farm. No breakfast siren, no sound of guards checking their equipment or trustees rousing sleepy inmates. As the suns' rays crept across the small work farm barracks and caught the corner of Michaels' eye, he woke. It took a few seconds to realize that something was not quite right.

He got up puzzled. Moses was gone. The door was wide open. Travis still slept. Michael stumbled outside, rubbing his eyes as they adjusted to the sun. Inmates were wandering across the yard or talking in small groups. No single file lines. Still confused Michael looked around the yard, the fence, the towers... not a uniform in sight. No guards. The gate was open and untended. He spied Moses crouching low on a mess table with several young black men sitting around him.

"They may be back," he was saying as Michael approached, "I don't think so."

"Maybe them Ultras waitin' outside," a young man said in a concerned voice, "Jus' waitin' to cut us down."

"Not likely," Moses replied, "they coulda done that anytime they want. Looks like they just went home. An' they invitin' us to do the same."

"Or, just don't care." Another man added. "Guard tell me last week, they ain't been paid in a month. Somethin' bout Uncle Sugar gone broke."

"May be," Moses said with authority. "We got to stick together and see this through."

It was a strange feeling. Michael had wanted to get off that farm for six months. Everyday seemed endless. Now the gate was open and there was no one to stop him, but he was in no hurry to leave. He wanted to understand. He could see across the fields where dozens of men were heading off across the hills.

"What you think, Mikey?" Moses asked.

"Don't know," Michael stuttered, "What happened?"

"Everybody just up and left," Moses said. "Hear they ain't been paid. They took they guns. Looks like da kitchen's been gone through. Most everythin' been carried off. Guards took all they could."

"What's this white boy, know?" a man, obviously scared and angry, blurted out. "How he …"

"He knows the white mans' world," Moses' stern look silenced him. "Tell me Mikey, if those white guards ain't been paid, you suppose our families got mealtickets?"

Michael turned instinctively and looked at the crates lining the storage area. It had not occurred to him before, but they had not seen a convoy accepting produce for delivery in a few weeks. He knew, and so did Moses, that the system must have broken down. "No," Michael thought of his family. How long had they been without? His mealticket from the farm would have been their sole support. Most of his assets had been confiscated with his conviction. But his wife, family and friends were smart and resourceful. They would have found ways to carry on. But for how long? He turned as if to bolt for home.

"Hold on Mikey," Moses said, "You go now, you just one more hungry mouth. We gotta organize." He stood up on the table and raised his arms. "Listen," he cried across the compound, "Brothers."

"You ain't talkin' to me," Travis was up and milling about with a few of the skinhead faction.

"Brothers," Moses ignored him, "We don't know what's happenin' on the outside. We need to take care of ourselves, then we can see about getting' home. Those guys ain't thinkin'," he gestured toward the tiny figures trudging up the hills in the distance. "Maybe you can find a car, maybe you can find food and water," he paused for effect. "I wouldn't count on it. It gonna take days on foot to get to the city and when you get there you wanna be empty handed? If those guards ain't been paid, then you can bet our families ain't gettin' their mealticket." Several men looked at each other with concern. They hadn't thought that far ahead. "We gotta take stock of what we got."

"Whatta ya mean 'We'," Travis stood defiantly with arms crossed. "Who put the niggers in charge?" A short pushing bout ensured. Moses was use to Travis' insulting tantrums, but his compatriots were not. Moses, with a deep calming voice, defused the standoff. Slow and low, "Everybody can do as they please, but we gotta know what we got to work with."

"T-ball, take a couple of brothers and see what in the storeroom"

"Not without us," Travis growled.

"Then send along some of yo' rednecks," Moses said. The frustration in his voice conveyed how petty this partisanship was in these circumstances. Travis looked embarrasses and unsure. He had never given an order before and wasn't sure if anyone would listen. He motioned tentatively to one of his friends and was relieved when the man moved off toward the storeroom with Moses' followers. Silently the Hispanic faction leader waved one of his gang along as well.

"ShortShank, you and a couple of guys check for cars, guns, anything could help."

"Mikey, where you stand?" Moses asked.

"We're all equal here."

"Well, you mind divided stuff up. You know writin' and figurin'. Get you some paper and pencils an' see what we got."

Of the few hundred men still in and around the compound, about a third were white, a third black and a third Hispanic. A dominate figure emerged from each group; former or current gang chiefs who seemed to have control of their faction.

In short order the building were emptied into the central court. Fifty pound sacks of grain, cases of military MREs, Meals Ready to Eat, and a variety of small quantities of other foodstuffs were found.

And of course the hundreds of bushels of fruit and vegetables that they had planted and cultivated over the past several months

Surplus products were sold or distributed to care for the inmate family mealtickets. There was a noticeable reduction in the number of truck convoys. Then in the last few weeks, they just stopped. The quantity of foodstuffs seemed to indicate that the food had not been forwarded to the folks back home. There were still crops in the fields unharvested, but no one was anxious to go back into the fields.

There were no guns, but a number of knives and gardening tools served as weapons. Most of the men armed themselves in some fashion. Michael sporting a clipboard and pencil found there was plenty of food and little else. The inventory, basically, amounted to a way to keep the strong from taking advantage of the weak. The inmates seemed to associate the paperwork with authority. In a way Michael found it was comforting to have hold of the pencil, like a touch of normalcy. A small transistor radio was found in a guards' desk drawer and the committee gathered around to listen. Their first news of 'the World' in six months.

"… banking crisis continues. Congress will issue vouchers up to $250,000 for those with FDIC deposits. But there is little confidence that the vouchers will be honored. The Tax Revolt continues and is growing. The Government announced today that funds were insufficient for government operations. The Government announced the abolition of the FDA, USDA, Department of Education, the EPA and other non-essential Government agencies for a savings to the taxpayer of hundreds of millions of dollars. Police and corrections officers have been issued vouchers to stay on the job and keep order, but retailers are hesitant to accept the government FDIC bonds."

"The suspension of government operations has saved tens of millions of dollars in the few weeks…." The commentator droned on reporting the crisis as government savings in keeping with the new style of reporting that editorialized any event to the Ultra advantage rather than risk their well coordinated wrath.

"Save me millions," Moses said sarcastically. "You can't eat savings." Talking about savings was an old marketing strategy that was refined into a method of getting people to spend money. In reality there was no savings, or any money to spend.

Vouchers were issued as a stop gap measure to provide furloughed workers with subsistence. "Congress has waived its salaries to show unity with the Federal workers and Americans overseas are included in the moratorium on spending." Meaning that they would not be paid. "Thirty states have, so far, announced that they will issue mealtickets to unpaid workers." Most citizens, who had accepted such inadequate provisions before the collapse, knew what that meant. Their families were virtually on their own until State and Federal Government could resume operations; and that meant taxes.

The radio reporter continued, "Lilly Mathias, mother of the assassinated Martin Mathias, has announced that urban supermarkets have been occupied to provide care centers for citizens in need."

'Henry R. Parrot must be furious,' Michael thought.

"Family homes have been converted into nutrition centers for the duration of the crisis. To ease Federal costs, all non-violent Federal prisoners are being released to community service at a savings of two billion dollars." The inmates knew immediately that this was government whitewash. All inmates, non-violent and otherwise, were confined on the farm and no one was showing any responsibility for the violent convicts or anyone else.

"In Hawaii, ships of the U.S. Pacific fleet have been seized by state forces and naval personnel at the direction of the Governor. Governor Yama has released a statement saying Hawaii will defend itself against unauthorized immigration from other states." Fuel costs had grounded most air traffic. "Ships en route have been warned to turn back."

"Chief Executive Officers of several fortune 500 companies have announced a resumption of quarterly tax deposits for the good of the country, but reserve the right to challenge the amount."

"Those bastards," Michael said, "They are still playing this like it's some kind of marketing game. Trying to look like a savior to the folks they screwed."

"… Farm coops in the Midwest breadbasket, blaming the suspension of agri-price support payments, are refusing to allow any produce to cross state lines unless paid for at the set price in advance. The area governors, citing the Federal governments' failure to resolve the situation, have joined with the farmers and mobilized state police and state National Guard troops to enforce the restrictions. President White attempted to federalize the state National Guard; however, most of the troops have defied the order and decided to remain under the direction of their governors.

"It's all local," Moses mused. "Brother Martin knew… Momma knows," Moses stared quietly into space. "Control the source."

"Moses," Michael said, "You okay?"

"Yah. Yah, Mikey," his trance broken, "I think I got a plan. Control the source, We sittin' at the source. ...course that comes later. First, people gotta be fed. Gotta get to my people."

Out in the courtyard the Reverend Orion Rob was preparing his flock for a journey. His white Christian faction had turned anti-government when the Government labeled him a cult and suspended his favored status. His head had been the one on the block to whitewash the religion in politics scandal. Rob, a defrocked Baptist preacher, had been the poster boy for the southern whites who blamed all the worlds' problems on equal opportunity. They had nothing to gain from 'equal' opportunity. They had enjoyed the unequal opportunity that their race and religion had bought them. Though convicted of fleecing his flock, he still commanded a following. To them it was just another example of an out of control government coming down on religion and white guys. For some reason they believed that they deserved the preferential treatment. When treated like everybody else they felt slighted.

"We haven't had such a victory over the liberal Government since brother Timothy blew up Government workers and their spawn." Rob was preaching. His skinhead mentality in a five hundred dollar suit and a tasteful toupee had bought him fame and, even in plain prison clothes, he projected the attitude of arrogant superiority. Travis and his group were clustered around, each with a pillowcase bulging with foodstuffs.

"North," Rob was saying, "to the north we will find peace and security. No for'ners pouring across the border, no ignorant urban masses stealing what God gave us, no Government of Babylon. The mountains will protect us and provide us with subsistence. As we go we can collect the families, arms, transportation and brothers and sisters in the Lord. Let us go brothers, for Armageddon is upon us." He turned and walked stridently out the gate as though beginning a pilgrimage. He was quite an actor. Travis did not join the group. Though he approved of the white pride philosophy, he couldn't take the religious zeal. The Aryans marched out singing 'Onward Christian Soldier'. Several dozen men, all white, departed with all that they could carry.

Moses' followers were busy packing away a pile of supplies, as were the Hispanics in another corner of the compound. A number of men were clearing the last of the storehouse. A number of the Latin inmates exited the compound and drifted south. Many had families in the agricultural lands, or further south in the Latin countries.

Some older men, white professionals, that didn't buy Reverend Robs' leadership, a few Hispanics and blacks that were uncomfortable with the gang flavor of the other two factions composed a sort of non-aligned group and by default they turned to Michael. With his clipboard he seemed to project some semblance of authority.

He organized his following as best he could. The men who were placed at the camp as a result of the Save-Our-Streets Vagrancy law generally had nowhere to go and no family. They were the homeless; generally older and, though not aggressive, they were an embarrassment to society and an annoyance to business. A new law enabled society to criminalize their situation and find them a socially useful occupation. That meant the work farm until they could find a job. But they couldn't look for a job while held at the work farm, so their sentence was essentially open-ended.

Sergeant Tom was an elderly, likeable man. In his teens he had joined the American Expeditionary force, fought and was traumatized in several overseas wars. On returning home he found the country obsessed with trivial matters. Resumes, time clocks and cultural debates seemed so irrelevant compared to the cold reality of war. Physically and mentally worn out, he had been cut adrift by the army and ignored by the country at large. He degenerated into a subsistence lifestyle. It was enough that he was not up to his ass in a rice paddy or frying in a Middle Eastern desert. The veterans' hospital where he had found some relief was ordered to eject all, so called, physically fit patients as a cost saving device by Ultra budget cutters, who had never served in uniform. These men, called heroes a few years earlier, were forgotten in the frenzy of cost cuts to put more money 'In Your Pocket'. He was ignored, until he became an inconvenient reminder and fell victim to the vagrancy laws.

Curiously enough the fate of American MIAs continued to obsess mythmakers and lined the pockets of opportunists and moviemakers. Home-based MIAs, like Tom, were feared and neglected. Many in his situation ended up on work farms and in a strange way Tom found it soothing to work with the land. He had become quite an expert at coaxing the seedlings through the earth. 'Creating life,' he called it.

Michael asked him his plans.

"To take care of the farm," he answered simply. "Somebody's got to grow stuff."

A number of men were unsure what to do. They were told what to do, and when to do it, for so long that they were just confused by the turn of events. Many just sat and watched all the activity. Others waited for some kind of leadership. Tom seemed a natural. Michael suggested that he run the operation. At first he refused. He did not want to have to give anybody any orders. Michael put it in the form of teaching. Teach those who wished to learn how to make things grow. That appealed to him much more and he consented to try.

"Tom," Michael had moved to the side to speak privately. "I don't know how things are out there. I'm thinking this may be the safest place. Food, water, shelter. I need to see my family. If things are real bad, I'll try to make my way back here. I'd like to think we'd be welcome." He handed Tom the clipboard as though passing the torch; the symbol of authority.

"Time on the street is cruel," Tom said rather glassy-eyed. "Time on the land is good, natural. Nobody should be denied a place to rest his head. You and your people will be welcome. I never had a home. A place where I didn't have to pay somebody just to be there. This will be my home. Yours too, if you need. Who am I to say who owns a piece of ground?"

A majority of the men were inclined to leave. Families, home, dreams of normalcy beckoned. But normalcy did not exist anymore. Those with no families, no homes, those who accepted the routine of the farm as normal chose to stay.

As Michael packed, he considered what the outside world had become; a cold, impersonal world where people would inform on friends and family for the price of a meal, or from fear of being labeled a co-conspirator. A place where police used arrests to finance their departments and pay their salaries through confiscation or pitiless dragnets. Neighbors informed on neighbors to curry favor, only to be informed on themselves. On the farm there were no informants; everybody was guilty.

Michael was nearly packed. He had concentrated on food and water. He expected that the trip to Black Lake would take about seven days on foot. Clothing, dishes and things like that could be had anywhere. Food was scarce out in the world and if his family was without a mealticket, food would be vital. He had several pounds of coffee for trade, if need be. A few dozen MREs filled out every available space in his make-shift canvas haversack. He also carried a few pounds of potatoes that he hoped he could save for planting. With his six figure Ultra income he had never considered something so petty. He could never have imagined that potatoes would someday be a staple food. How things had changed.

For the journey he brought some cherries, pears and apples; food for the trip, seeds for later. In smaller quantities he was able to get about a pound of semi-sweet chocolate, salt and dehydrated milk. He managed to find a gallon milk jug that could hold water for a few days; which he hoped he could replenish as the opportunity presented itself. In the dispensary, overlooked by most of the inmates, he found some aspirin, vitamins and even some penicillin pills. Good for trade if he didn't need to use it himself. All of the painkillers were pillaged.

He balanced his bundles on the shaft of a workfarm pitchfork wondering if he had packed too much. He could not afford to be slowed in his quest. With the pitchfork cradled on his shoulder, feeling like a coolie, he made for the compound.

Moses and a number of his followers were departing.

"Careful, Moses," Michael called. "Mountain folk ain't use to dealing with people of your complexion." With a broad smile and a wave over his shoulder, his former roommate was off. Michael felt the loss immediately. He already missed the good natured radical of another culture that taught him so much. The small caravan snaked its' way up the road toward the mountains to the west; toward the cities.

Tom had found a small folding table. He set it up on the porch of the deserted administration building. Seated on a fruit crate, he began to organize those who had decided to remain. Others just lounged in the sun, grateful for the relief from work details.

"What can you do?" Tom asked the next in the line that formed at his table.

"Retail Manager," the man replied.

"You're a farmer now. Next."

"Cook," the man said.

"Good. We need a cook. Check out and organize the kitchen. Next."

"Laborer."

"Farmer." Tom had taken to his new duties with the commitment of a soldier.

"Burglar."

"Farmer."

A man walked up sporting a USMC tattoo and smiled warmly. He had planted and harvested and shared postwar trauma with Tom for years. "Used to be a damn good soldier, now a bum."

"War's over Lance," Tom said soothingly, "and you ain't no bum. You a farmer."

"I worked in a metal shop," the next man said.

"Can you weld?" Tom asked.

"Sure can," the man seemed relieved that he had not been instantly labeled a farmer. That was a job for unskilled workers, like lawyers and such.

"See what kind of equipment we have. Fuel, generators, batteries and such. See if you can set up some kind of shop."

"My buddy here knows some stuff too..." he gestured to an older man in line.

"Good enough," Tom approved. "I'll see if we can get you some more help when I sort things out. Next."

"Carpenter."

"You still a carpenter. See what you need to make this compound a home. Keep the buildings standing. Okay?"

"Right, chief." The man saluted, which made Tom a little self conscious and uncomfortable.

"Entrepreneur," the next man said proudly, "Kind of a manager."

"A damn landlord," the man behind him said menacingly.

The mans' pride dropped away, replaced by a meek fear as he realized that he had no useful skills to offer.

"Can you manage a hoe?" Tom said plainly. The man meekly nodded and moved off. "Next."

"Panhandler," the next burly man said. "I was a medic in Nam. Odd jobs since.

"What do you know," Tom said reassuringly, "We have a Doctor."

A small caravan formed near the front gate. Hamilton joined Michael; a trusted friend since they had both survived being thrown to the wolves. Hamiltons' cellmate, Peter, tagged along. He was a good natured hulk of a fisherman from one of the coastal villages. More travelers expanded the circle. Little John, a special forces veteran that had shared some chilling stories with Captain Corbett, and Joshua a retired NCO, who had been offered the work farm in lieu of his pension. Jefferson, a sandy haired defense attorney that had run afoul of the courts, joined the group. Joey and Monk were headed for the Indian nations, as they called the reservation south of Black Lake. Tom noticed Michael moving toward the gate.

"Michael, if you come back this way, bring children. Families. I want to hear children laugh."

"Keep creatin' life, Tom," Michael called, waving.

"I expect you be sowin' some seeds yourself when you get back to that lady of yours." The crowd burst into laughter; a light-hearted laughter that had not been heard in the compound for some time.

HOMECOMING

Michael had filled a gallon milk jug with water, just in case. He didn't think water would be a problem but he didn't know what kind of hospitality they would get along the way. It would take days on foot and, with most vehicles useless for lack of fuel, he didn't count on a ride or a commandeered car. With gas rare and expensive, any travel was local, necessary grocery runs. Cars were more than likely to get hijacked. A momentary flash of self reproach crossed his mind. Here he was thinking of Grand Theft Auto in a very matter-of-fact way. "Necessity," he reassured himself after a history of condemning people who took just such a course when times were good for him and he could afford to be judgmental. After all, at the time, law enforcement was protecting his property. He suspected the desperately poor thought in those same pragmatic terms. 'So, this was what poverty was like. Just getting by'.

They were thirteen walking slowly, burden as they were, and strung out along the road. A few in a bit more of a hurry had forged ahead. The group caught up to them in a few hours of steady walking, as the more ambitious stopped to rest. Tired and disoriented, the former inmates joined the small band as they made their way toward the city.

The early trekkers had found no hospitality from the few settlements that they passed. The farms they passed were empty of people and anything useful. The larger farms had become sort of communal strongholds to fend off marauders. Large, threatening 'No Trespassing' signs were posted and armed guards blocked access roads from the deserted interstate highway.

After three days of no traffic and dark nights, they crossed through the mountain passes. The travelers began the hike down the western slopes to the rolling foothills. In their path lay Blackhawk. It was a small mountain town named after the Indian chief that led his tribe against the encroaching white man. Unlike the few small towns they had bypassed, Blackhawk was not off along some access road, but straddled the main highway. The road was blocked by two rusting cars and two men armed with rifles paced back and forth behind the roadblock.

"Stop where you are," one of them yelled as the travelers came within earshot. Michael heard the telltale sound of a rifle bolt chambering a round. One of the men ducked into a nearby building and emerged with several more compatriots, all armed.

Michael stood in the middle of the road as the other travelers put down their bundles for a rest. All seemed content to let Michael speak for them. Two men crossed the barricade and approached.

"You're convicts!" One of them declared. He had a flannel shirt and baseball cap. Cradled in his arms was a shotgun and a pistol was strapped to his waist.

"Yah," Michael answered briefly, "headin' for the city."

"We don't hold that against you," the man answered sincerely yet cautiously, "most of us have done time for some reason or other. Problem is we can't tell them who was railroaded from them who was put away for good reason, so we just turn you all away."

"The town is off limits," the second man added. He was much older and wore some type of makeshift uniform; the olive-drab 'pickle-suit' of the pre-Reagan army. The collar boasted a tarnished Majors' emblem. "You can go around. Step out of line and you'll be shot." A small crowd had collected at the roadblock. Women and children too. The first women or children Michael had seen in six months.

"We mean no harm," Michael said, "We just want to pass, Major." He used to title hoping the show of respect would ease the tension.

The steely eyed old Major showed no reaction. "No harm," He said slowly, "that's what that arrogant nigger said. We shot two of 'em. But you talk all proper. You civil or criminal?" That was the distinction in the lawbreaker class. The criminal offenses like murder, assault, robbery were recognized as a true threat to community safety. A civil offense usually meant the Government, the Ultras in particular, wanted your money or property. This type of criminal was generally viewed by the common folks as abused by the system and not particularly dangerous.

"Mostly civil," Michael answered. "Some criminal," he felt it necessary to play it straight with these folks. He figured that 'that arrogant nigger' was probably Moses and a few of his followers. Many urban criminals had seen the average Joe as just a victim. But times had changed. The average Joe was ready to shot if he felt threatened. And with no law enforcement to speak of, they could act on their fears without restraint. Michael hoped Moses had not been one of those that was shot. Probably not, Moses was smart enough to be careful until he knew the score. "We just want to get home," Michael said sincerely. "We got coffee." Michael tossed the pound package of ground coffee to the man.

The major caught the parcel, gave it a long sniff and, looking unimpressed, stuffed it in his jacket. "There's an old logging road that leads around the town," the Major volunteered. "Just to the left of that little hill. Stay on the road until you're past the town and nobody gets hurt. The road rejoins the main road about two miles beyond. Don't be around after dark. Understand?"

"Yah," Michael said, "We could use some water." Most of his companions had neglected water. They didn't seem to understand that something so basic may be hard to get. The infrastructure of society had always provided water at any faucet. It seemed incomprehensible that water could be a jealously guarded commodity.

"Not from us," the major replied. "There's a stream by the logging road. No fishin'. No huntin'. Just move on." He began walking back toward the roadblock, now bristling with guns. "Don't piss in the stream," he called back over his shoulder. "And mind, be gone by dark."

Around the edge of the small hillock they did indeed find a logging road. It was little more than a trail; dusty and rutted. As it skirted the edge of the town, Michael could see that each street, alley and entry point into the community was blocked and patrolled by armed men. Beyond the barricades the town looked remarkably normal. Children ran playing. People were in their yards chatting and tending gardens.

They found the creek, as the Major said they would, and all sat on the bank for a much needed break. Michael opened an MRE and ate sparingly.

"Hey, there's fish in here," the man named Peter was leaning out over the creek.

"Trout," Jefferson confirmed.

Peter slowly, carefully cupped his hands and eased toward his unsuspecting lunch. With a large splash, he bolted upright with the fish triumphantly in his grasp. A loud crack rang out. With the forest echoes, they couldn't tell where it came from, but Peter collapsed on the bank of the stream. The fish plunged back into the water. Hamilton ran to help but there was nothing he could do. Peter was trying to gasp something but could not make a sound except for a low gurgle. A large caliber bullet had torn into his throat severing his jugular. In a few short seconds, he was dead.

The group quickly got their things together to get moving. Peters' pack was unceremoniously pillaged by the others. In other times, Michael would have thought justice, mourning, burial, 9-1-1, police… Now he thought only, 'Townies made the mess. Let them clean it up.' Peter was left were he fell.

By late afternoon, they were back on the highway and starting down the mountain. A townie with a rifle slung on his back, riding a mountain bike followed them at a comfortable distance. After a few miles he turned back. Michael then felt enough at ease to begin looking for a place to spend the night.

They saw no sign of people or animals in the several farms they passed, and with no electricity, it got very dark, very fast. They settled down in a deserted farm house and built a small fire. There was no running water in the house but an old well in back still held water. Michael heated some water for the military coffee ration from the MREs. He was exhausted, yet troubled and unable to sleep.

He wondered how his family was doing. They had shelter but what if the mealtickets had stopped? The warehouse held plenty of food. But what if it had drawn the attention of foragers? Friends and neighbors would help. Neighborhoods came together in the hard times caused by the states rights legislation. He thought of the confrontation with the residents of Blackhawk. It didn't surprise him. He would have done the same, and communities everywhere were doing just that.

The Ultras' policy of divide and conquer had left most people fearful of any stranger and, with law enforcement absent, they would take this paranoia to deadly lengths. People took care of their own. The towns and midsize cities along the route presented an eerie ghost town impression. People fled or went into hiding when they approached. The fear encouraged by the major parties in an attempt to get their vote had worked all too well. Now, with elections just a memory, people weren't reassured. They were told by both sides of the dire consequences of an opposition victory. Regardless of who won, half of the people were left in sort of an opposition camp. Even the victors could not celebrate with a so-called enemy contingent in their midst.

Rural communities isolated themselves and traded their crops for anything useful. Government mealtickets and cash were useless. The new currency was food, clothing, tobacco, alcohol and weapons. Entrepreneurs, labeled middlemen by others in the community that needed their goods, found their suppliers unable or unwilling to restock their shelves. They raised prices and hoard goods and were generally held in contempt. They stood reciting old business clichés that weren't true in the best of times, much less now. Gaunt, sunken eyes and handfuls of useless cash could not buy respect or food. Pilfering and shoplifting was rampant. Scavengers surged into the suburbs and local National Guard units, operating in local interests, retaliated with deadly force.

As the group made their way down the mountain road and across the coastal plain, they entered the more populated areas that surrounded the big city. Things began to look almost normal. People looked them over suspiciously but they weren't armed and they made no threats. It seemed eerily appropriate that these suburbanites would cling to the status quo, even when the status quo no longer existed. They tried to continue their lives from a safe bubble, but circumstances had changed. The terrified residents reported widespread rioting and looting in the urban areas; a region to avoid.

Michaels' small group began to drift off to their own destinations. Several of the men had nowhere to go, but could not stand the thought of staying at the work farm. A few that Michael had considered untrustworthy, even dangerous, were bluntly told that they were not welcome to stay with the group. They were unceremoniously driven off. He reached the city below the Black Lake with half a dozen men still in company. Just outside of town in the wooded slopes was the Homestead.

Those that remained included Joshua. He was a former soldier, retired after twenty years before the military raised the service commitment to thirty years. On hearing that he would be required to do ten years of community service to retain his pension, he went berserk and burned down the local Recruiting Office. His wife escaped the sigma of the criminal family system, and rescued the children, through divorce. Arson; criminal.

Jefferson, a tall, young attorney had led the defense against a particularly abusive landlord. He turned the tables on the slumlord, won a countersuit and lost his freedom to a trumped up assault charge. The well deserved assault on the landlord, that he insisted was self defense, won him the admiration of his community. Assault; criminal

Hamilton, a small nervous fellow, was an accountant dabbling in bonds and tax shelters. He collected a fortune and was offered up by the Ultras when his estate planning tax scheme was declared tax fraud. He still could not acknowledge that he had engaged in anything other than good business. Fraud; civil.

Little John was a war veteran. As a former Special Forces trooper, John and Michael found mutual decompression; talking through past exploits. John had commandeered a hospital emergency room to get help for an overdosed friend. He was arrested for conspiracy, since his friend had obviously consumed an illegal substance. His friend died and John was charged with voluntary homicide; criminal.

Joey, a wiry young man of mixed Indian-Caucasian blood, was always cheerful and smiling. He was caught dealing drugs; unstamped cigarettes and alcohol from the reservation. The Native Americans, Joey preferred Indians, lost their casinos but still had their land and their river. They could also deal in cheap tobacco and liqueur. Contraband; civil.

The man known as Monk was brooding loner. He looked young in spite of his bald head. His dark complexion revealed some Hispanic ancestry. Monk had also been imprisoned for drug activity, but his offense was on a more international level. His former employers had marked him for death, not for anything he had done, but for what he knew. He had no urge to return to his own neighborhood. Joey had offered him sanctuary on the reservation. He seemed harmless and in desperate need of a friend. Drug dealing; criminal.

And Michael, fraud and tax evasion; civil.

Late in the evening, twenty miles short of Black Lake, they reached the reservation of Joey's ancestors. They hosted a great feast in the traditional style, with the first real steak the men had seen for months. Joey and Monk saw them off the following morning for their final destination; the Homestead at Black Lake.

Michael had instructed Suzanne not to wait for the round of business and bank failures. The day of his arrest she had taken every cent from checking, savings and the household piggybank. She max'd out their credit cards and shuttled all that it would buy to the Homestead. The Feds confiscated the stock holdings and the State appropriated his retirement accounts.

The Homestead at Black Lake was fully stocked and virtually invisible. From bank accounts to professional contacts to magazine subscriptions, the address that appeared was the house in the city. The Homestead was out of the spotlight; a local address that did not appear anywhere in the public domain.

Suzanne did not understand but trusted Michaels' judgment. Like most Americans she had been raised in a fully stocked economy. She could not conceive of a situation where the stores would have nothing to sell; where money was not as readily accepted; where supply and demand were not satisfied by a medium of exchange that everyone would accept. Michael had learned overseas during his military service that sometimes logistical systems collapsed. A person may have to defend his stash with force. The neighbors, at first curiously amused, began to follow her example as the news broadcasts presented stories that indicated the downward spiraling was likely to continue.

Michael had told his mother to join Suzanne at Black Lake and Suzannes' parents also sought refuge away from the city. At first to console their daughter, but it quickly became apparent that it was the safest place.

The warehouse was stocked with a variety of canned goods by the case. Dehydrated milk, coffee, sugar, salt, nuts, fruit and juices as well. Grains in bulk and seeds for a number of staple foods. Non-food items, too; batteries, matches, soap, candles, aspirin, canning jars, water purification tablets, band-aids, ammunition and food for the dogs. Thanks to Mosies' advice, they even had a cow. That violated the zoning laws, but there was no one to enforce such petty restrictions anymore. Suzannes' Easter chicks had grown into quite proficient egg producers.

Michael had the full range of camping gear. All the county folks did; for that getaway from modern life. That included the camp stove, lantern, compass, flares, and first aid kit. And also a generator that he bought after the power outage of the great Christmas snowstorm. It was just a simple little motor that ran as well on strong alcohol as gas and in the current climate it was priceless.

Michael found his neighborhood nearly deserted. Several houses had eviction notices on the doors. A seniors home here, a veterans' home there. As he rounded to corner, his step quickened. Walden Court looked virtually untouched, except for the yellow fluorescent eviction notices on several doors. He thought he could smell Suzannes' perfume. At the foot of his driveway he could see that his house too had a bright yellow eviction notice. The front door was locked and front windows were boarded. A six foot wooden fence surrounded the back yard. As he reached the foot of the driveway, he heard the distinctive howl typical of Cleos' breed. He rushed past the 'Beware of Dog' sign on the heavy gate and around the house to the rear deck. Enthusiastically barking, Caesar bounded over, nearly knocking him off his feet. Michael charged through the garden, on to the deck and in the back door.

Suzanne was sitting on the couch with Michaels' mother. Her parents sat across the room. He ran to her, dropping to his knees with his head in her lap. Tears welled up in their eyes as she cupped is face in her delicate hands.

"We thought you were dead," She stammered through tears of joy.

"I'm home now, sweetheart," Michael said.

"They said the work farms were disbanded." Her father James said, placing his hand on his son-in-laws' shoulder. "In Texas they went cell to cell and shot everybody. Some have put a bounty on released prisoners. There's no law anymore."

"The RBN (Religious Broadcast Network) says this is Armageddon." Michaels' mother had always been religious. "Reverend Patson says we need to renew our faith and tithe for God."

"That bastard!" Michael said with a savagery that shocked his pious mother. "Society is falling apart and he's still trying to make a buck."

"Money's no good." James continued, "the mortgage speculators wants food, liqueur, or...," He looked at Suzanne but didn't finish his thought. "He won't take money."

"Homestead's paid off !" Michael said agitated.

"The County raised taxes and auctioned off collection rights to speculators," James explained. "They send around these bounty collectors. Folks around here banded together... Mosie... that rancher fella across the road and his sons... even Jeremy..." The plump Gardner pulled aside his jacket to reveal Michaels' .38 in a shoulder holster. "...drove them off. They said they'd be back."

"It's okay. Let them come. They got no law enforcement backup anymore." Michael was holding Suzanne close when his traveling companions cautiously picked their way to the back door, escorted by a vigilant Caesar and Cleo. They eagerly eyed the kitchen. "These are my friends... Hamilton, Jefferson... Say hello... and this is Little John and Josh. Fellas, this is Suzanne. My mom Dorothy and Suzannes' folks, James and Ruth."

"Their criminals," Ruth said nervously. Suzannes' folks had never had the occasion to see a Con close up; a blue-collar criminal anyway.

"So am I," Michael said rather angrily. He instantly regretted his impatience. She didn't know any better. The Ultras' had her scared to death of this other breed, these barely humans that they had presented as the boogieman to get votes.

"You're welcome," Suzanne said sincerely to the nervous men in the doorway. Do we have enough food?" she asked Michael, speaking low so as not to alarm their guests.

"We can't feed 'em all," Ruth had heard Suzannes' comment and wasn't shy about speaking it out loud. "We aren't responsible for every lazy, vagrant..." she didn't finish as Josh approached menacingly. Ever present law enforcement had always meant she could be as rude as she pleased. She recoiled slightly as James tried to step between. Josh rudely pushed him aside and grabbed Ruth by the wrists, turning her palms face up.

"Lazy?" Joshs' expression was calm but firm, "Soft hands. And what kind of work do you do?"

"I keep home for my husband and children," she exclaimed proudly.

"My wife kept home," Joey continued, "Taking care of kids was unacceptable behavior; lazy; a burden to society. She was put to work and my kids were put in Shared Care."

"She doesn't know..." Michael intervened.

"My husband is a good provider," Ruth lashed back. Her role as Mother had never been questioned before.

"And what do you do, James?" Josh asked.

"I managed the Capitol grounds," He replied.

"A manager," Jefferson said, "That's about as useless as a lawyer these days."

"Actually, a gardener," Michael interjected.

"Well that's useful. But housewife? How much food does that put on the table these days?" Josh shot back to Ruth. "It seems you're obsolete. Maybe you could earn your keep on a work farm."

Michael had always detested the disdain his mother-in-law had for the less fortunate. She had married an American and by European standards he was a good catch. At the time even a blue collar American was believed to be a ticket to a comfortable life. She had continued to enjoy the special attention that her English accent had bought her when she reached the United States. She had always held herself out as special; cultured. Ruth had the accent of the Birmingham lower class. Most Americans were infatuated with a British accent. Michael, with time spent in the diplomatic corps, knew the dialect and knew a proper English gentlemen would recognize the accent as the equivalent of white trash; but Michael let her live the illusion of British sophistication.

Though he couldn't show it, Michael thoroughly enjoyed this exchange. "Enough," Michael called out. "Let 'em be Josh. Ruth, would you take charge of the kitchen? We have electricity?"

"A couple of hours a day for news and cooking." Suzanne answered. "Some radio still broadcasts."

"Eat the perishables first." Michael motioned the men to the kitchen with the remaining foodstuffs. "James, you're a gardener." He reached in his pockets and pulled out a handful of seeds. "Take care of these," he handed them to the pot-bellied, balding retiree.

"It will be a few seasons before these will produce anything," James protested. He and Ruth still expected to wake up some morning in the near future with everything back to normal by decree of the Veto-proof congress. They expected the cavalry to show up. What Michael knew was that the cavalry was busy pillaging the settlers.

A few neighbors had noticed the strangers in the neighborhood and gathered around to investigate. Michaels' neighborhood was luckier than most. As a new development, it was on a dead end road that led off another road built to serve the development. The project had city promises to make it a through street but funding had failed and it was never completed, much to the satisfaction of the local residents. That meant that there was no through traffic. No one had a reason to take the road that didn't lead anywhere, so the neighborhood was relatively free of the flow of refugees. The big cities were far off and the county easily held the local population.

The neighborhood block watches had given people a sense of security. Most of the crime they feared happened in the city; the poor on poor crime. Misreading of statistics had lined the pockets of security companies, who promised police protection that they couldn't provide. One in every six houses was burglarized every year. Though if the location was included; every house in a poor block, some more than once were hit, while remote small town neighborhoods went virtually untouched. But they were the ones with money to spend to ease their fears, so they were the target of the companies that peddled paranoia for profit. Their claim to a protective police presents was just a phone bank with no muscle or guns.

John, noticing Michaels' security sticker on the window, was giving the others a short lecture on security, or rather the lack thereof. Ruth was listening horrified. "N.D.S.S. that's Neighborhood Defense Security Systems. That means a silent alarm that sounds at the NDSS listening station. That's to catch them nasty criminals. You don't want to scare 'em off; you want to catch 'em. Now NDSS says police are notified in minutes. Quite true. Only NDSS has no power to dispatch police, so for fifty bucks a month you feel safe. A NDSS sticker means no loud noise to wake up the neighbors and at least half-an-hour before any cops show up. Hey Mikey, you know your house is a duck?"

"Not with a pack of work farm veterans on watch," Michael said smiling.

"Dear," Suzanne said, "We'll have power in a few minutes. It's time for news."

The fuzzy TV broadcast cleared enough to make out the reporter reading from his notes. The reception was rather weak. The cable systems, that replaced the open air broadcast, had failed. People who are not paid do not report for work indefinitely and those maintaining the lines had simply stopped servicing their routes. A few local stations dusted off old equipment and were on the air. Households with old style rabbit-ears and tin foil bowties pulled the signal out of the air.

"Henry R. Parrot, speaking to a group of business leaders today said, 'The Government got the message with tax receipts and vouchers turned in rather than money. He now urges people to resume their tax obligation for seniors, veterans and the kids." The announcer sounded unconvincing.

"That means he's losing money on his government contracts," Hamilton said sarcastically.

"In spite of the attempts by the Government and major investors to reinstitute the stock market, there are no investors. Technology stocks could not establish an opening price. Limited availability of energy is cited as a major drawback." Further, the uncertainty of owning stock that proved worthless in the face of executive pillaging had driven most investors to more safe, tangible goods. Better to own a few cases of oil than a few shares of General Motors stock. Besides Stock was worthless until it is sold to provide the purchasing power to buy something useful.

The announcer continued, "Meanwhile, troops continue the standoff with the, so called, Urban Republic squatters. Moses, brother of slain urban leader Martin Mathias, has resurfaced." Michael bolted to attention. "Mathias, with the support of his community has seized every supermarket and business in an area of several square miles. Reports indicate that, under the protection of armed gang members, the local stores have been turned in to feeding stations for the community. Though power and water have been cut off, the besieged residents show no sign of surrender." The broadcast continued with a roadblock interview with Moses. He stood with his frail looking mother, Lilly. Brothers in charge of his security, dressed in Panther black, covered his back.

"What are your goals in this standoff?" the reporter asked.

"Feed the kids," Moses' voice sounded strong and confident, "No one has a right to make our kids go hungry. This planet is our home. No one can make us pay for the privilege of being here. Landlords make sharecroppers of us and even try to cut our share. Food, clothing and shelter are basic human needs; our right. We will survive."

"That was from an interview with Moses Mathias, the leader of the urban squatters that have taken over the downtown businesses. Local National Guard troops have refused to move into the area. Supplies for several military bases came up short as providers held back their products rather than risk accepting Government vouchers. Desertion had become widespread and gangs of unpaid soldiers have, reportedly, commandeered what they need in some areas. President White has offered active duty soldiers incorporation into the *National Guard Community Nutrition Service*; returning them to service in their home states."

The Service was set up when large numbers of military families were found to need food stamps and subsidies due to low wages when the breadwinners were activated. Many men with no better prospects had joined the military to give their families a mealticket. But the military pay scale was not intended to support families at the lowest ranks and the military mealticket proved insufficient for young families. The hardship was even more pronounced when large numbers of these young soldiers found themselves deployed in overseas hot spots leaving their families behind. Or, in the worst cases, when the young head of household was killed or terribly wounded ending the security of a military career.

People sought the security of friends and family with impromptu communes. Jonathan and Janice, the neighbors next to Michaels' homestead had moved near other relatives leaving their house empty. The residents of Walden Court had respected the vacant house but necessity lead Michael to consider another use. He boarded his buddies in the empty house to the disapproval of some neighbors who still expected the status quo to return any day.

Michael is able to cloth the entire group with his excessive wardrobe. Jeans, overalls, socks, kerchiefs, gloves more than most of the men had owned in their entire lives. From work clothes to formal wear, Michael had the wardrobe to cloth the entire group. They had a fine time rummaging through the stacks, each finding an outfit that suited his tastes. Suzanne tailored each selected outfit for each new owner.

Ruth felt rather useless with her status as housewife challenged by the new arrivals. Her favorite pastime was bird watching. This was also viewed as useless. She found her expertise in weight watching, though, was something of a skill. Her knowledge of calorie counting emerged as valuable asset when it came time to ration supplies for their growing community. She became a kind of quartermaster for the group.

Michaels' attempt at planting an orchard had struggled when his country gentlemen phase wore off. The several dozen small trees clung to life and only blossomed when James took a personal interest in tending the budding saplings. By the time Michael and his band arrived, the small trees were heavy with ripening fruit. James had no idea that his private project would become an important source of food in the sparse times to follow.

Community protection was a real concern. This was not the hollow marketing gimmick promoted by the security companies during the good times. Roving bands of looters and random criminal gangs were a real threat. Michael asked Josh to handle security for Walden. A weapons inventory tallied a shotgun, a rifle, a pistol, 2 swords, several daggers, a functioning 1943 Russian rifle, a flintlock pistol, a cutlass, a mussel-loader, bow and arrows, a couple of axes, machetes, garden tools, routine kitchen cutlery, even a crossbow. Several of the neighborhood households also contributed to the weapons stash. Josh organized the able bodied into a 24-hours armed neighborhood watch. The residents, originally leery of the intruders, were comforted by the presence of the rugged looking guardian angels.

People couldn't count on police. With no prisons the only punishments for serious offenses was banishment or death. It bred in some men a no fear of consequences attitude.

The small workshop became Michaels' personal project. Supplies commandeered from the several uncompleted construction sites in the Black Lake development provided enough material for repairs, maintenance and basic building. Several residents contributed both hand and power tools; the hand tools being much more practical.

In local rounds to see how things stood in the community, Michael found that his jet skis had been appropriated by the Lake Siders for some kind of lake side constabulary on water. Michael understood and did not object.

Most Lakers had no experience with the justified urban paranoia. Living in a secured community they could be confident that the other residents meant them no harm; as they meant the other residents no harm. Even those they didn't know a few blocks away were no threat. They knew each other through their kids, births, marriages and Obituaries. They become familiar with the families even if they didn't know the individuals. Michael had the same community feel, growing up in a small Midwest town.

John was raised in an urban environment where there was a real danger from strangers. Safety and security meant only a few well known family and friends or gangster affiliation could be trusted for protection; survival.

The downtown farmers market continued to function as people came together to trade goods. The market was about seven miles from the Homestead and, with gasoline a valuable commodity worth saving for emergency, the trip was a two hour walk. With an armed escort, a party set out from the Homestead for the market. They had pooled their money, jewelry and items they felt they could spare and might have trade value.

The homestead was home for nine people now and the community of fifty or so inhabited the immediate vicinity. Black Lake hosted about half a dozen concentrations of families and friends of similar size making a community cluster of several hundred.

There were the Lakers of the lake side homes, the Foresters settled along the edge of the national forest, the Hilltop, River Banks and the Bay Siders group a little farther toward the coast. The various communities came together at central farmers markets, as they had in the before times.

The value of different commodities varied considerable from one stall to the next. Some vendors continued to value what had been treasured in the good times. Suzannes' jewelry, highly prized and purchased at exorbitant cost just a few years earlier, was traded for a bicycle and fertilizer. Suzanne kept a sharp eye out for the items with trade value. Potatoes were worth their weight in gold. This was something that the Homestead produced in abundance and a note was made for the next market run that this was something that had currency. Likewise, Jewelry and the like had some value to those who expected a quick recovery. Another note was logged; to trade this stuff off for something useful while it still had some value.

Simple, cheap utilitarian items were becoming scarce. Worth their weight in gold became an obsolete concept in that gold was not all that prized anymore, but people still had the ingrained idea that gold was wealth and it was worth trading. Trinkets amounting to several ounces of gold were traded for a bag of seeds.

Suzannes' herbal garden was a private project and the lovingly nurtured variety of spices and herbs cost more to produce than they would have cost to buy. After the collapse, however, the project was expanded and became a valuable resource for the group.

Josh became something of a horticulturalist. He had found some seeds somewhere and had started a little garden of his own toward the back of the homestead. He claimed to grow the weed for its value as fibers for rope and weaving, but everybody knew there was a more recreational, or medicinal, use. Ruth was shocked as she had no experience with anything so illegal that did not involve a balance sheet. Mike assures her that it is no more dangerous that her parsnips; physically, morally or spiritually.

LEISURE ACRES

Moses Mathias drew together the factions in the city; an ethnic melting pot, but mostly black. Yet his society did not seem at all exclusive. They began to arm and protect themselves and their neighbors. Easy targets and unconcerned neighbors gave way to mutual assistance groups who were willing to defend the helpless. Many returning veterans, welcome nowhere else, joined his following. The property, pooled from business and private holdings were parceled out.

At least the Mathias clan was content in their own area. Renegades, called in to retake the urban core had failed. When collapse came, they found themselves in suburban staging areas where pickings were rich and easy. The gangsters and renegades found few soft targets in the city and began to drift to the nearly helpless suburbs. They made themselves overlords of local fiefdoms.

Militiamen from the mountain training camps, after being decisively defeated by the street kid soldiers of the inner city were drifting back toward the wilderness areas foraging as they went. Many blamed the suburban recruiters for putting them in that situation and freely pillaged whenever they could. Local National Guard Units protected the communities where they served; no national commitment, just local concern. The families of the troops took up the rallying cry, 'National Guard to protect this Nation'. Local Veterans groups banded together to form local paramilitary units to make sure the renegades went on their way. A number of firefights erupted almost daily. When the threat passed the veterans could return to their homes. The local groups functioned like the minutemen of old. The suburbs found themselves under the protection of local armed forces.

Security communities were more at risk. There were few military age residents or extended families for defense. The isolated security communities were the first to be commandeered by roving paramilitary gangs. A security community's perimeter was never intended to keep out a determined assault. With their fences and guardhouses, they made a secure defensive base for the renegades. It was there to keep law abiding citizens law-abiding and to protect against the stray burglar. The residents who at earlier times felt secure from the stray criminals with their security guards, found their fortress like compounds only attracted unwanted attention. Lacking a police presence and a government to keep order, some communities were easily overrun. Gates could keep out the occasional prowler but were no obstacle to unchecked, well armed gangs of soldiers with no community attachment.

Walden Courts' Neighborhood Watch kept them secure from the random vagabond. Then a grey-haired scarecrow stumbled into their perimeter. Her name was Kate and she had escaped from kitchen duty at Leisure Acres, the security community just a few miles from the Homestead. The story that she told was frightening. A group of renegades, heavily armed, had invaded their community and created a military-like compound forcing the residents into a kind of forced labor to serve them. By day they send out squads to pillage and terrorize local communities; by night they secured themselves in the walled and gated compound. The elderly residents were helpless as the renegades commandeered their carefully preserved supplies. The old and sick found no sympathy and were often denied food and medicine, or just turned out.

The Black Lake residents knew something was wrong in the vicinity. Neighboring communities had been visited by squads of the violent men. Now they knew where they holed up at night. It was only a matter of time before they found their way to Black Lake. The Homestead group knew that they could not depend on police or military support, though they expected that they could count on help from nearby communities.

Some areas had earned a reputation for self defense. Moses' urban stronghold had shown a willingness to fight and was generally left alone by roving bands. Michael was determined that his neighborhood would not become a victim. Contact was made with those who wanted to defend their neighborhoods; the Lake Siders, the Hilltoppers and Foresters joined the effort. Among the Foresters was a former deputy sheriff and two of his troopers, who had kept their guns when they were put on furlough. Joey and Monk, contacted on the reservation, brought the Indians on board. Joey took an immediate liking to one of the kids in the neighborhood named Jeremy. The teen became his lieutenant and fast friend.

Jeremy, in earlier times, was a rebellious juvenile headed toward delinquency. He had terrorized the neighborhood pets with his sling shot. Michael had opened his target range to the boy in hopes of redirecting his excess energy. He had shown a remarkable proficiency with Michaels' powerful Crossbow. The 80lb. pull could send a dart through a half inch of plywood or human bone. Jeremy had delighted in prowling the target range that Michael had set up in his back woods. His skills in stealth and marksmanship made him a natural in the art of military intelligence. Jeremy excelled in the role of liaison with the reservation.

Michael would prefer to call it preemptive action but revenge brought out the emotional response that was needed from previously targeted communities. The soldiers from the Acres had made themselves a nuisance for several communities and it appeared they intended to dominate the areas as the own little kingdom. The original residents of the Acres, those who had not left when the troubles began, were herded into the community center while the soldiers appropriated their cottages. The lakeside communities were determined to act. They would no longer ignore or tolerate paramilitary bands that plagued the region.

Joey and Monk coordinated the Indians with Jeremy's bike hockey team for a reconnaissance of the Acres. Joey was proud, with his Native American ancestry, that he was the best in the group at handling the bow and arrows. The group was not at all sensitive in making jokes about this 'wild Indian'. Jeremy organized bike hockey games near the walls of the Acres. He succeeded in building a detailed report, under Joey's direction. The number of soldiers, weaponry and movement patterns were recorded in detail.

Everyday squads of soldiers left at dawn. Each of four groups went in different directions, returning before sunset with whatever they could pillage. That left about half of the fifty or so intruders in the compound during the day. Guards manned the walls at wide intervals. Their strength and lack of organized resistance made them overconfident and lax. As they systematically looted the area, their movements became predictable to anyone with a map.

Jeremy organized a band of young people who called themselves trackers. They followed the bands of renegades on their daily forays and made contact with the pillaged populations once the soldiers had left. A network of county-wide communities was formed. In a matter of days a small army of volunteers had come together to end the abused of the renegades.

Within a week the community volunteers agreed on a coordinated plan. On a given day the trackers, anticipating the movement of the foragers would plant a number of armed bands in the expected path of the roving bands. At the same time several of the women would approach the compound asking for food and shelter, offering medicine and booze.

The small group gathered around a table set up with a miniature mock-up of the Leisure Acres compound. Michael pointed out the key structures, "In the northeast corner was the Commons Building; a three story building and highest structure in the community."

"Most residents are sleeping on cots in the first floor commons," Kate explained. "Along the south wall is the Administration building." The two story structure was represented by two stacked blocks. The other structures were indicated by a series of small blocks that represented the residents' bungalows. "The center of the community was a large, open, grassy, park-like area." Kate had been an aide worker in Baghdad and had a keen sense of urban tactics. Her familiarity with Leisure Acres, combined with Michael and Johns' Special Forces training and Joey's reconnaissance, would provide the key to liberating the Acres.

"There are two guards at each of the north and south gates," Joey pointed to the points as he spoke. "There is another guard on each of the east and west walls. All small arms."

"Those not on duty, get together in the second floor rec room in the Commons Building." Kate added.

Michael leaned over the table, explained the plan. "The road through the north gate and the road from the south gate join here," he pointed at the junction roughly in the center of the miniature village. "... the gardeners' cottage has a clear line of sight to both gates. Kate and her team will be taken into the compound. We expect they will be taken to the Commons building where they can prepare the residents for what's to come."

"Here is how we expect this to go down." Michael had an eerie feeling that he had been here before; in the mountains of Pakistan, outside a mud village. "At the appointed time the returning bands... members of our confederacy will approach the gates. The bike hockey team will set off a satchel charge to blow the front gate. That should draw the attention of everybody in the compound. Once the gates were open, sharpshooters will take out the guards on the wall. The Lakers will take 'em under fire... keep up the racket... advance if the opportunity presents itself. The sheriff and his team at the east wall and the deputy's boys at the west wall will take out the guards in their area."

"I'll take the team at the north gate and attempt to gain entry quiet-like. We'll make our way across the plaza. Joey will lead his team to the gardeners' cottage and cover the roads. My team will swing west to the commons building to protect the residents. The team at the east wall will search the bungalows; get residents to safety and root out any thugs. The team at the west wall will enter the Commons building from the back door as my team from the north gate swings west and enter." Michael got very serious. "These aren't soldiers that we are dealing with. We can't give these thugs a break. Kill them," he paused for effect, "...if they are unarmed or surrender; spare 'em. If they want to run away, let 'em. Otherwise..."

"Michael," Kate had another concern, "some of them have companions." She let the meaning of that sink in before continuing. "Some as vile as the thugs… others by necessity or circumstances have joined the group."

Michael thought briefly and said as compassionately as he could, "…if they are armed; they are combatants."

Suzanne volunteered and Michael could not very well object. Once inside they would prepare the innocent for the coming assault. The order of the day; kill the renegades. There was no time to measure degrees of guilt. No means of incarceration for those guilty of lesser crimes. Shop keepers, accountants, mechanics and teachers were fully prepared to become judge, jury and executioner to insure their survival.

The trackers were in the neighborhoods that were expected to be targeted on the day selected. Residents were prepared and reinforced by neighbors of areas that had been hit or feared that they would be next on the list. Each of the bands would outnumber the renegade squads twice over. The locals selected the best areas to achieve surprise and lay in wait. Battery operated walkie-talkies kept the parties in touch to coordinate.

The northern arm was first to make contact. An old man, playing the part of a destitute street peddler was all it took to get the renegades attention. Several bottles of Jack Daniels and a few other spirits and they clustered around, roughly pushing the old man aside. The old beggar quietly disappeared unnoticed.

Monks' band was ready. A variety of weapons of different caliber opened up in an irregular rattle; a few shotgun blasts from a second floor window and all of the renegades lay bleeding in the street. A few moaned, showing signs of life.

"The head," Monk said matter-of-factly. "Don't damage the uniforms any more than we have to." No hatred, no remorse. They couldn't spare medical supplies or confine prisoners. Several of the locals became physically sick at the sight. As mad animals, those that were still breathing, were put out of their misery. The bodies were left for the locals to dispose of. Monk and his team immediately departed for Leisure Acres. Indian ponies provided by

Joey's tribe would cover the distance before the appointed time for the assault.

Meanwhile, the second renegade squad to the east approached a distinguished looking house with a large clear yard surrounding it. From the upper window two young women, pleaded for food. The thugs entered the front door to find the stairway blocked. They stood milling about perplexed. Little Johns' band targeted the intruders through the windows. John stepped into the doorway. "Fire," he ordered as he cut down the nearest soldier. Most were dropped before they could raise their weapons. One man got off a shot that shattered Johns' knee. The renegade was quickly silenced by the locals at the window gun ports.

A few locals stopped the bleeding and made John comfortable. John gasped between clinched teeth as the shattered limb was tended, "I can't go on. Hamilton, you take charge. You know the plan."

The third faction ran into problems. As the renegades approached the town square where the locals waited in ambush, a small band of refugees appeared on the road. The soldiers were soon mixed in with them, looting their meager bundles. The Forester deputy sheriff quickly revised the plan. He sent his trooper with half his team to work around the open square, through the trees, to the road behind the renegades. He then signaled Jefferson and a couple of Foresters with handguns concealed to follow him. They approached the cluster of people cowering before the intruders.

The burly leader moved to block their path as his men continued searching the refugees. "Where you going?" he demanded pushing Jefferson back a step, with the M16 pointed at his chest.

"My sister," Jefferson said meekly, "She needs food." He pointed down the road.

Momentarily the man lowered his rifle and looked. That was all the time the deputy needed to pull his gun and fire into the mans' face. The soldiers began firing indiscriminately. A local was hit. Refugees and locals dived for the ground taking what cover the shallow roadside ditch could offer. Another soldier went down. Then a burst of automatic weapons fire cut through two refugees and one of the Foresters. Jefferson was slightly grazed. The deputy sheriff ended the renegades' rampage with a shot at the base of the neck.

Children were crying. Wounded civilians screamed in pain. Three of the soldiers were withdrawing down the road, firing as they retreated. They reached the trees and were lost from sight. From the tree line a hundred yards away several more bursts of automatic weapons fire echoed down the town square. A few rifle shots, a shotgun blast and all was quiet except for the whimpering of a few scared and wounded locals.

The fourth squad approached a bridge leading to a little town in the west. A wrecked and apparently deserted van sat at the far end. The invaders had never met resistance before and suspected nothing. As they reached the middle of the bridge, Joey and several men rushed out from below the bridge, some moving right, others moving left. Mussel flashes erupted from the van and several second story windows ahead. Joey and his men raked the bridge with fire until there was no movement.

Michael waited restlessly in a small cottage a short way from the back gate of Leisure Acres. The dogs seemed to sense some adventure and sat alert but silent by his side. An hour before sunset Kate and her group moved toward the compound. Several dozen locals were in hiding in the neighborhood just out of sight of the community wall. Two men who claimed some ability in marksmanship were allocated to each of the half dozen guards on the wall. The front gate was the key location and Jeremy's crew prepared to blow the gate to distract the renegades, once Kates' group was safely inside.

Suzanne and her band would see that the innocents inside were under cover just before sunset when friends in renegade uniform would return. Those with Suzanne were young healthy women who could take care of themselves. Kate, though quite a bit older than the rest, joined the group. Her steady manner marked her as a leader. Michael had refused to let her go arguing that those inside must be able to move quickly and fight for themselves and others when the time came. Kate, though, with knowledge of the neighborhood was insistent. She would fight. She had escaped the old Soviet Union in her youth and was tough and courageous. She would go, with or without Michaels' approval. They dressed in meek and tattered clothes, carrying their passport; the bundle of medical supplies and a few bottles of liqueur. Hopefully, the thugs would be pretty drunk by the time the locals struck.

A few of Jeremy's street kids, dressed to look young and harmless worked their way toward the compound in an innocent looking game of bike hockey. The bike patrol casually cruised outside the main gate of Leisure Acres. The guards had become accustom to their occasional visits; actually intelligence gathering missions. Then Jeremy glided closer, doing a wheelie, pretending to show off. The guards looked on amused but not alarmed.

The ambush elements had returned to the scene as quickly as possible and took up their positions. Michael with the dogs and another team quietly crouched outside the rear gate with their weapons leveled at the two guards atop the wall.

Then Jeremy made his move. He moved in to within a few feet of the gate and unslung his backpack. It had a slow fuse and several sticks of the dynamite that Mosie had tucked away to clear stumps during the good times. "I found a bunch of Playboys," he yelled to the guards as he threw it to the foot of the gate. The guards chuckled and warned him off, but took no further action.

The explosion shook the wall and blew one gate off its' hinges. The other gate hung lazily at an angle. A hail of gunfire caught the surprised guards unaware and they were soon lying in lumps at the foot of the wall.

The ambush patrols rushed the gate and took cover at the wall. Several men mounted on the reservation ponies and the bicycle teams circled near the front gate. A few bull horns and bugles drew the attention of the militia men inside the compound to the front gate. Orders were screamed to phantom teams to disorient the defenders.

At the rear gate, Michael took careful aim with his crossbow and knocked one guard off the wall. A few arrows and a few return shots and the second guard was knocked down as well.

In minutes a dozen men scaled the wall and threw open the gate. The rattle of continued fire echoed from the front gate as Joey's team veered off toward the gardeners' cottage. Several of the thugs had rushed to the front gate on hearing the explosion and they began taking fire from the rear. They quickly took cover in the Administration Building.

Michael and his team turned west and rushed toward the Commons Building with Caesar to his right and Cleo to his left. He reached the door in a matter of seconds and ran into a startled thug emerging from the door. One of the team fired a shot that passed slightly over Michaels' shoulder and hit the thug in the chest. 'A little too close,' Michael thought.

Inside huddled along the wall the residents had taken cover under Kates' direction. Michael scanned the scene as a few of the team covered the broad stairway to the second floor Rec Room.

"Where's Suzanne?" he yelled. Almost simultaneously the team from the east, having eliminated the guard and scaled the wall, ploughed through the back door. Nervous trigger-fingers paused just in time to avoid friendly fire. Just as suddenly, a few thugs from the second floor began a fierce firefight from the top of the stairs. The team kept them at bay with suppressing fire. The thugs pulled back, taking cover and inviting an attack up the stairs. The team covered the stairs but advanced no further. The thugs weren't going anywhere and an assault up the stairs would have been bloody.

"Where's Suzanne," Michael yelled again.

"One of the thugs took her," Kate called back. "Toward the cottages."

Michael was already headed out the door as he called to the dogs, "Caesar, Cleo, find Mama!"

A few stray shots kicked up dirt around Michael as he recrossed the plaza. Caesar and Cleo had already caught up and passed him headed toward the lines of bungalows.

The fire at the front gate had slackened but continued. Michael could see muzzle flashed of gunfire from the Gardeners cottage, but they weren't aimed in his direction.

He rushed past the cottage and into the maze of bungalows. Caesar and Cleo were weaving between the buildings, hot on the scent. Cleo came to alert at the door of a cottage and Michael barged through the door. Suzanne was slumped on the floor with a torn blouse and bloodied fingernails. A gruff looking thug, with deep scratches across his face, stood over her with a rifle leveled at the doorway. Before Michael could react a searing blast tore into his shoulder knocking him off his feet. As the grinning thug leveled his gun for the kill, the window to his right crashed. Caesar caught him by the throat in mid air, taking him to the floor. Cleo vaulted over Michael and joined in. Though Michael could have called them off, he did not.

Suzanne, sounding calm and in control, gently said, "Caesar, Cleo, release."

The two dogs immediately backed off but remained on alert over the cringing thug. Suzanne rushed to Michael examining his shoulder. There didn't seem to be any serious damage; no bones or major arteries were hit. Securing the thugs gun with his good left hand, Michael marched the brute out of the building flanked by Caesar and Cleo and supported by Suzanne.

The gun fire in the compound had tapered off. Michael and Suzanne could only hope it was the townies that prevailed. When they emerged into the plaza, they could see a number of townies standing guard on some disarmed, downcast looking thugs. A few bodies littered the front gate area and many of the windows of the administration building and the common building was shattered.

"There may be a few skulking around yet," Jeremy said to Michael as he approached, "but they ain't dumb enough to try anything."

"How are the residents?" Suzanne asked.

"Kate's taking care of them in the Commons," Jeremy answered. "There's a problem in the Administration Building," he added.

Several of the thugs had holed up on the second floor with a few of the residents as hostages. In bold, blustering terms, they were demanding a range of unreasonable demands. Surrender of all weapons, promises of continued food, evacuation of the compound, hostages to insure compliance… They seemed to think they had some bargaining power, as when life was political theater in the good old days.

Michaels' impatience with the playacting was wearing thin. "Listen," he strolled boldly to the foot of the wide sweeping stairway.

The thug who seemed to be in charge, strutted into view at the top of the stairs with an assault rifle cradled on his hip. "Talk to me townie."

Michael continued, "Who do you think you're dealing with? We ain't no police negotiators. We're not politicians or public officials who have to worry about elections or keeping our jobs. Give up this standoff and you can keep your lives. Kill the hostages and you've lost your cover. Then we kill you. We can't stop you from killing them, but you can't stop us from killing you. So, we all live, or some of us… most assuredly you… will die. We don't deal with terrorists."

"You can have my gun when you pry it from my cold dead hands," the thug screamed the worn out cliché. There was something familiar in that voice. Michael couldn't quite place it, but he had heard it before. Something about the inflection; the self-righteous contempt. Michael studied the camouflage clad figure at the top of the stairs. Through the green grease paint the fat, bigoted face of Russ Limpaw emerged.

"Then it's a deal." Michael turned to walk away, "some of us, and all of you die." As he walked away, he heard the mechanical clank of the bolt of an automatic weapon chambering a round. Limpaw slowly took aim. Shooting a man in the back was not something beneath him, figuratively or literally, in politics or war.

A single shot rang out. Michael flinched but did not feel the sting of a bullet. He took a mental inventory of his limbs and torso. No wounds, other than those he already knew about. He slowly turned to face Limpaw.

Limpaw slumped to his knees, the superior sneer washed from this face. He heavily rolled down the steps. Behind him another of the camouflaged renegades held a smoking gun. He looked emotionlessly at Michael and let his gun drop.

"Hi, Mikey." It was the innocent looking Chip Libby wrapped in soldiers' garb. "You always seemed to find your way into a Fortunate Fraction. You'll have no more trouble," he said. "Give it up boys," he called back to those under cover behind him," then slowly added, "It's un-American." The surviving militiamen were not as prepared as their bosses to go out in a blaze of, supposed, glory. When they saw that they could expect to live, they gave up any resistance.

Michael was amazed how easy it was. These violent buffoons were not willing to die for their cause or their community, as were the Townies. Their motive was self-preservation and that was understandable, but it made for a weak coordinated defense. These were not the type of men motivated to self sacrifice if necessary like police or firemen or Lakers. The moral of the story seemed to be that military forces could not defeat a community effort. As an insurance policy the weapons dropped by the renegades were collected and stockpiled; just in case they might be needed in the future.

The disarmed renegades still looked defiant. Michael calmly and honestly gave them the facts. "If you return, it will be to a civilized community that is not afraid to defend itself. Remember the way it was? Most people obey most of the laws most of the time. I'm guilty of speeding, smoked some... But we all get along, by remembering about casting that first stone. But like some rabid dog, you plague us again and we... will... kill... you. No hate, no hesitation, no remorse we... will... kill... you."

Not one of the companions chose to follow the renegades. A few of the renegades, that the residents had cleared of any overt acts of abuse or violence, were allowed to remain. Among the fallen women was an unkempt Sarah Colt; trying to cling to those in power to the last minute. Michael was disgusted and would have preferred to send her on her way, but he did not insist. Kate put her to work washing dishes. She would find a difficult life among those she lorded over as Limpaws' intimate deputy. There were no recriminations. Some of the companions were willing, some seduced, some forced. All were welcomed into the fold. Chip elected to stay, considering himself fortunate just to be accepted. He considered it a second chance to join a Fortunate Fraction. One based on mutual concern rather than power.

"It's not neighborly to inflict unrepentant renegades on another community without warning. We wouldn't want them doing that to us," Michael reasoned. The offenders seemed a lot less dangerous disarmed but, never the less, Joey's pony express spread the word that there were outsiders in the area. Any interference with the locals and the whole community would come down on them. Local people were coming together for the common good. Black Lake sent out representatives to establish contact and express good will. Radio links and regular broadcasts had to be established. A logistical network emerged from the ground up, not from central authority down. Community spirit was on the increase and banditry in decline. The renegades posed little threat to a united people.

PILGRIMAGE

"Moses…" the short wave radio crackled in the urban headquarters. The small radios, considered primitive by before-times standards became the primary means for different regions to communicate. Cell phone towers cease to function and satellites had fallen or failed. "Moses? You there, brother?"

Moses rushed into his communication center in time to hear a voice from the past emerge from the static. He grabbed the headset with a big smile, "Mikey? Hey, brother, how you doin'."

"Not bad," Michael was pleased to hear the familiar voice.

"Where you at?" Moses asked.

"About sixty miles south of you," Michael answered. "Listen, brother, we got a deal for you."

" This ain't one them Ultra get-rich-quick-schemes is it?" Moses joked.

"Ain't no such thing as an Ultra anymore," Michael shot back. "Here 'tis. We got something I think you can use. And I suspect you got something we can use."

The Lakers had discovered a flaw in Michaels' self-sufficiency plan. It was easy enough in the make-shift blacksmith shop to produce hoes, shovels and the like, but something as delicate as a sewing needle was an industrial marvel; beyond their capability. They could produce food in abundance, but items as simple as plates, cups, scissors, thread and all the bounty that the big box stores stocked in volume, were becoming scarce.

"You see," Michael continued, "we got this little lakeside community with lots of land and no industry… "

"Ain't nobody got no industry anymore," Moses responded.

"But you got warehouses full of that Urban-Shop-All inventory."

"We do got that." Moses confirmed.

"Well, we got plenty of chickens, fruit and seeds, but we're short of pots-n-pans." Michael proposed his trade, "just the kind of stuff from those USA stores in your territory."

"Ain't 'dat somethin'. You become a farmer, Mikey. Wouldn't Tom be proud?"

"Yah, well it's easy to beat swords into plowshares, but try to make a needle and thread. I never knew how complicated it was to make somethin' as simple as a pencil. These days that's high tech."

"We need simple stuff that you guys probably got. You got more than you need on the shelf, I expect. Plates, shoes... We got food and seeds to trade. What do ya think Moses?"

"Sounds like a deal," Moses agreed. "Tell ya what, Mikey, you have your people talk to my people. Get a list of stuff... I'll scrounge around here and see what you might need. You folks have transport."

"Just our backs... a few animals... some carts and bikes," Michael said.

"Okay, let's do this," Moses concluded. "One thing, brother, be careful in the suburbs. Seems nobody ever taught those people how to take care of themselves. They're running out of everything and getting desperate. Lots of those Parrot-type militias still layin' low out in the suburbs. Our people just stay clear."

The next step was to send a delegation to the cities to the north and south, and the open farmlands east of the mountains. The Lakers were fearful of what they might find, of what may find them. Those were a different people and they didn't just mean color. Fear and bigotry, promoted by the Ultras in the before times, lingered on. The others were viewed as gangsters, criminal; not civil offenders. This was why they had invested heavily in police and tough on crime politicians. Michael knew better. He had done time on the farm and knew most were just people in desperate straits; situations that most of the suburbanites had never had to face.

Suzanne and Ruth worried when he volunteered to lead the effort. He was a former Ultra; white, unlike those people. Michael assured them he would be careful. He would be armed. That would sound reassuring, through Michael understood that the arms were protection from any renegades and jittery suburbanites along the journey; not protection from Moses and his people. They wanted peace and security; same as the Lakers.

A peace offering was arranged. The northern route was expected to take about three days and the route to the southern city led by John would be about the same. The crown jewel of the offering was fresh fruit; something the cities probably had not seen for weeks.

Another delegation led by Jocy and his sidekick Jeremy were dispatched with a radio to make contact with Tom at the old work farm site over the mountains to the east. With spring, the snow in the passes had melted. Michael expected that they would welcome some settlers in that sparsely populated area and the land could easily support their work.

Friendly communities were known to populate the environs up to about thirty miles north and south. There, folks were knows through cooperation at Leisure Acres and meetings at the farmers market. Hopefully, those folks would be able to provide information to facilitate the next step of their journey.

The caravan formed on the unused interstate highway. It would provide a straight clear route to the city. One of Mosies' horses pulled a wagon loaded with fresh fruit, seed corn and a variety of produce. A few of Joey's tribe rode ponies dressed in the style of their ancestors. Several backpackers carried loads of seed that had been carefully husbanded by James and his gardeners. Some bicycles were rigged in the style Michael had seen in Asia as a push cart, with a crossbar over the handlebars to carry more goods. Caesar did his part; pulling the Homesteads' little green lawn wagon filled with trade goods. The expedition of about a dozen, also, carried a few firearms they hoped they wouldn't have to use.

John put together another similarly equipped expedition to the city to the south. Joey and a few trackers prepared to cover the more difficult route to the farms across the mountains with a spare short wave radio for Tom.

After two days travel, Michaels' group could see the skyline of the darkened city. An eerie quiet greeted their approach. The suburban bands around the city were peopled by dazed looking scarecrows that blandly watched them pass. They could see a number of campfire-like arrangements where cooking was carried on in primitive fashion. It looked like a hard life. He knew he could help, but passed on his way. Michael felt a weird déjà vu of the time when he was part of the fortunate fraction. He wondered if his settlement at Black Lake was a sample of the new fortunate fraction. He felt guilty passing them by, but the trade arrangement with Moses had to be completed if everyone were to benefit in the long run. Was he rationalizing. He experienced something of the same attitude that he had as part of the fortunate?

Each community along the route was able to provide accommodations and knowledge of the next step. Portion of a variety of seed was shared at each stop. The dividing line was reached at the outskirts of the city. The color line had yet to be breached to any extent. Former suburbanites feared Moses and his people and the urban dwellers didn't trust the people they viewed as their former oppressors. The dividing line resembled ramparts. Both groups with limited space for agriculture and large numbers of people were close to desperation. Each blamed the others for the collapse and neither seemed to know what to do about it.

The suburbanites accepted Michael with due caution and were amazed that he intended to plunge into the urban other-land. The strip malls and mom & pop stores on the city fringe were thoroughly pillaged.

Here a small orchard, there a family garden, but no provision for the number of people that found themselves in need. The weak, the medically fragile and the hopeless had succumbed to the new austerity. A deadly selfishness was apparent. Michael, again, thought of his membership in earlier times in the fortunate fraction. He understood the fear. At the time he saw fear used as a tactic. Now he suspected it was not just a tactic. Those people were honestly afraid; and with good reason. He now knew that the fortunate fraction was an illusion. Mutual caring was a more sustainable tactic. But he suspected that he would never be free of the guilt of his callous former life.

If the opposing camps began to compete for self preservation, the mutual distrust would be fatal. The cork had to come out of the bottle. The Urban masses would have to reach the open spaces. They had the manpower, the former rural population had the space; vast rural areas that had formerly been run as industrial agri business tracts. Without the huge machinery and logistical network of agri-industry, they had devolved into local family plots. Much went uncultivated and unused.

There was plenty of space for the Urbanites. But neither urbanites nor rural folks trusted each other. The suburbanites, trapped in between, would only see the human wave of migration; like locust in their eyes competing for already scarce commodities. The wise move would be to let them pass, not try to stop them. Moses could see that the solution would be in the former industrial agri lands, not in suburban pillage. Not just for his people but for the depleted suburbs as well.

The trouble was convincing the fringers that they just wanted to pass and not grab more territory around the urban strongholds. But then, many urbanites did want to grab suburban territory. Territory that, unbeknownst to the urbanites, had already been picked clean. The pass-through strategy would take trust, and trust was hard to come by.

It would take a united effort; an infrastructure that would take care of all. The Ultra era of me-first-and-foremost had bred a suspicion of any group not of your own. The United States had become disunited over the course of a number of political seasons of selfishness exploitation. Nobody trusted anybody.

There was no barrier or checkpoint, but a band of desolate ground a few hundred yards wide skirted the urban core. Deserted buildings with broken windows faced the no mans' land. There had been widespread attrition in the cities. Population density was reduced to a subsistence level with urban gardens, the brainchild of Martins' movement. The travelers penetrated the outer circle. They were surprised to find large scale agriculture in all non-paved openings.

The stores in Moses' reach were commandeered and rationed and reasonable intact. But with no resupply, the goods were beginning to run short. Few had planned for the time when before-time goods would be exhausted.

Groups of black clad, black men walked peacefully and watchfully through the parks and neighborhoods. Then travelers began to see groups of shadowy silhouettes monitoring their caravan. They neither helped nor hindered the groups' progress. These were the Panthers who functioned as the urban security force. They had, evidently, been informed that Michaels' group would be making their way into the city.

The city looked almost deserted. There was no automobile traffic and only the occasional bicycle or pedestrian going about their business. The buildings looked dirty and neglected. Growth seemed to ooze from the rooftops. The eaves looked ragged and overgrown. Michael thought of the before-times at Black Lake when he had to mount the roof of the Homestead twice a year to scrap off the moss and clear branches and leafs.

It slowly dawned on him that he was not witnessing overgrowth and neglect, but rooftop gardens. The urbanites had laboriously moved tons of earth to the flat rooftops and planted gardens. The growth had yielded lush vegetable harvests and the occasional color and fragrance of flowers. There were window boxes in abundance.

There was something else, also. The sloped roofs were lined with solar panels and at places large tanks were secured on the upper floors. Obviously intended to collect rain water, pipes ran into the buildings below; running water powered by something as simple as gravity.

The visitors felt more and more conspicuous. For once, they were the minority. Most of the travelers had always been in the majority in their community.

As they moved into the urban jungle a figure appeared from the shadows. The middle aged black man in the uniform black dress of the Panthers approached Michael.

"You Michael?" he asked.

"Yah." Michael answered briefly.

"This way," he turned and casually walked away.

Michael could see, here and there, in windows and doorways, the spectral figures watching them. The landscape was an odd mixture of gutted building and small green gardens. Occasionally, they could glimpse a cow grazing on an unattended patch of stray grass amid the pavement. Evidently, the result of Martins' 'holy cow' campaign.

They were led to an unassuming row house; indistinguishable from the dozens of houses lining the street. Their silent guide pushed open the door and stood aside. Michael entered and let his eyes adjust to the darkness.

Slowly objects took shape, but the first thing he could make out was a familiar, toothy smile.

"Hey, Mikey," Moses sounded sincerely happy to see his former cellmate, "World's turned upside down, huh?"

"That's a fact, Moses," Michael offered his hand in greeting, but Moses grabbed him in a big bear hug.

"Fact is, life ain't much different for us poor folk." Moses said jovially. "We never did have much, but we get by."

Several Panthers lounged around the room, looking suspiciously at the new arrival. "You hungry?" Moses asked. "We got plenty of canned food," he held up an open tuna fish can that showed evidence of snacking.

"Not me, but this little guy could use a meal," Michael pulled a special present from his coat that he had brought just for Moses. The little husky puppy was the pick of Caesar and Cleos' first litter. "His daddy's damn near a hundred pounds and he's got his mommas' blue eyes."

Moses looked at the large paws that looked out of proportion to the little furry bundle. "He's gonna be a monster," he said while he shared a bit of tuna. "I think I'll call him Mikey."

"I'm honored," Michael said half joking, but flattered none the less.

"Now let's do some business." Moses sat down with the puppy on his lap and produced two Cuban cigars; handing one to Michael. "My people got most everything on your shopping list. Some stuff... bicycles... shoes... no can do. But most everything."

Michael remembered a list that Suzanne had handed him as he was leaving. A wish list of nonessentials that he had promised to ask about. He had not even read the list in his haste and just now opened the page. "We have a few more things I wanted to ask about."

"Ask away, Mikey."

Michael began to read, "Lipstick..." Moses broke into a smile. "make-up... Nail polish..." The stony faced Panthers in the room began to lose their composure. "... Tampons..." The Panthers burst into laughter. He ceased reading and folded up the list "Hey, can't you just give this to your ladies?"

Controlling his laughter, Moses called, "Suede, take a look, baby. See what we got."

The exchange went off without a hitch. The urbanites got fresh fruit and vegetables and seed for future gardens. Orchards could be planted in any available patch of unpaved ground throughout the city. The Lakers got needles and pins, pots and pans, pencils, thread and a wide variety of items that Michael had considered to common to stock at Black Lake. The urban ladies even presented him with a selection of different shades of lipstick.

RE-RURALIZATION

Radio traffic became routine between the Lakers and the urbanites. Simple hand cranks generated enough electricity to provide power. Tom, at the work farm, had received his radio and began making occasional contact, but he seemed self-sufficient and content; and always had very little to say. He still preferred getting his hands dirty to fooling with tech equipment.

The route between Black Lake and the city saw occasional traffic and exchanges of visitors became routine. The route to the farms was a different story. The farms were a good bit further to travel, and involved a trip over mountains. However, the concrete jungle was becoming depleted. It could not support large numbers of people indefinitely.

"The trade thing is workin' out alright," Moses had an idea to share with Michael. "That ain't enough. I don't want my kids to grow up on pavement. Climb trees, swim and fish. We need to get the people to the land. There, they can take care of themselves. You suppose 'ol Tom at the work farm would welcome us?"

"No doubt about it," Michael said.

"We got a few dozen families that would go today if it wasn't for the crazies. They afraid of bein' robbed along the way. We ain't got enough Panthers to go along for security. And they would look too militant. You know, threatening. Could be dozens of travelers... young... helpless... with just household stuff. You gotta talk to those paranoid suburbanites. Tell 'em it's not an invasion; we just want to pass through. They'll listen to you."

"Why? 'Cause I'm white?" Michael joked.

"Exactly. Tom don't care. There's lots of blacks and Latinos in those parts. They use to mixin'. But the suburbs... white folks get scared, they get dangerous. And some a them mountain folk really crazy."

"I'll see what I can do about safe pass-through," Michael promised. "I know the communities between you and me. Over the mountains is a different story. Remember Blackhawk?"

The conversation with Tom lasted just a few minutes. Michael was prepared to wheel-n-deal, the way they had with the urbanites. 'We can give you this for that.' Tom wasn't interested. He didn't reject the idea of refugees sharing the land; he just didn't want anything. Michael wanted to give him something; just out of gratitude, if not for payment. Tom insisted there was nothing he needed.

The initial exodus moved from the city to Black Lake. Black Lake was about half way between the major cities, just off the connecting interstate. Not far from the junction was the road that led over the mountain passes to the agricultural lands to the east. The Urban caravan carried little of value but their hopes for a better future.

The camouflaged figures, laying in wait, were not interested in pillage. Motivated by fear; they were more bandit than patriot. Parrots' former USA security guards and the Ultra commandos were also interested in revenge for the humiliating defeat of the urban assault effort and the subsequent collapse of the world they knew. Word of the action at leisure Acres had spread with the return of the Lakers, Foresters, and Hilltop groups to their neighborhoods. Inspired by the success over brute force, communities organized. The hills were refuge to the thugs. They were unlike the community based troops of the before time. In the before time, National Guard were community members; husbands and fathers. These thugs were intruders; not of the community. They were interested in status, power, adventure and revenge. Locals understood that their safety and security lay, not with the militias, but with standing up for themselves and the innocent travelers. Communities were determined to respect the ancient tradition of hospitality. The uninvited intruders would not be allowed to interfere with the peaceful refugees. The militias posed more of a threat then the urban travelers.

The thugs planned an ambush. They were about to be ambushed themselves. The entire region turned out in force to expose their plans and warn the travelers.

The commandos may have had super firepower, but a vast majority of suburbanites refused to cooperate. They had enough of the commandos' arrogance and abuse. Any lethal actions by the militia would incur the wrath of the masses of people they claimed to be protecting, making any move socially unacceptable. Most of the common folks no longer brought their fear tactics.

When it was sons, daughters, husbands and fathers wearing the uniform, the communities could be proud; no matter what the mission. Raised on stories of 'our brave boys in uniform', the self-styled soldiers believed just putting on a uniform would make them one of the brave boys. However, when the militant thugs put on the uniform, average folks found themselves at risk. The intruders did not have the community support they seemed to expect. The mission of these bands was entirely self-serving and the residents viewed them as bandits with no ties to the community.

The local Rotary clubs, Lions clubs and veterans organizations took leave from their community works projects, armed and organized. They would return to the good works of orphans, the disabled and disease, but for the time being the greatest good they could do was to defend their community with force, and insure safe passage of the urban refugees that were approaching. There was a sense of normality; the right thing to do.

The would-be ambushers were surprised by the fireworks that exposed their plan. Left over fireworks from an uncelebrated Fourth of July alerted the caravan to something ahead. The Panthers fanned out as lookouts on the flanks. They were met by the suburban teams that no longer feared the thugs in the bush. Should the renegades harass any locals, there would be consequences.

Revealed and outnumbered, the militia groups meekly melted into the foothills and forests. A few shots were exchanged, but the attack was averted. They might remain dangerous to the stray traveler or farmhouse, but the community and travelers were free from their intimidation. The strength of numbers and mutual assistance and concern bore fruit.

Talk, trade and treaties followed the joining of the urban settlers and the suburban residents. Some of the suburbanites, encouraged by the stories of open farmland to the east, joined the travelers. What had begun as resettlement of a few dozen families, turned into an expedition of several hundred; a reverse migration from west to east.

Michael stood amazed as the caravan pulled into Black lake. A few black clad Panthers led the way with Josh and Jeremy. The ethnic mix of the urban settlers followed. The group had attracted quite a tail of suburban recruits. When the goal of the expedition was explained to each community in route, they not only allowed unmolested passage, but had safeguarded and then joined the travelers. A number of families had fallen in behind the lead group. A few horses pulled community wagons.

Several dozen urban families with their carts and bicycles were joined by dozens of suburbanites, with their possessions carried on their backs. A number of young people joined to scout out the prospects for family members too young or too old to commit to the unknown. Adventurous youth and family groups walked side by side. Even juniors little red wagon was piled high with precious personal property to take to the new promised land. The caravan snaked into Black Lake and circled picturesquely into the park to prepare for the mountain crossing.

Campfires were lit and a few guitars were soon plucking folksy tunes. Water barrels were filled and treats were handed out to the kids. Caesar and Cleo relished in giving the youngsters rides in their little wagon. Several of their pups found families.

Singing erupted spontaneously. Joyous songs from the past. Children, that never learned anything more than TV theme songs, learned long forgotten ballads. Religious services were held at the people level. There was no Reverend Rob or Reverend Patson to threaten damnation and ask for donations. Services were sincere thanks for the new opportunity that awaited them.

The trip through the mountains to the farms beyond was more precarious. The winter snows in the pass had melted and the way was clear. The trek would still be a weeks' journey for the group traveling at walking speed. Michael went along, feeling like a sort of diplomat and old west wagon master. Joey and Jeremy became regular trailblazers. They preceded the group with gifts of greeting to the people of the mountain towns; including Blackhawk. They expressed the peaceful intentions of those who followed. Assurances that the pilgrims wanted only to continue to the farms in the east reassured the suspicious peoples they met along the way. A few stray families with their worldly possessions joined the caravan as they snaked their way through the mountains. Some families from the caravan were invited to settle in the communities they passed.

Even the people of Blackhawk took down their barricades and let the train pass through town. The atmosphere was that of a parade. They had not been able to socialize on this scale since the collapse and they greeted the opportunity. Trade flourished and smiles were traded.

The terrain became eerily familiar as Michael descended the mountain road toward the site of the work farm. The mountain peaks rose in the west and the broad plain stretching to the east had not changed. The farm was still nestled in the valley, looking like an oasis of civilization in the middle of a pristine prairie.

There was something different, however, about the work farm. The rows of uniform, military-like barracks still lay in rows as Michael remembered. Some had a new coat of paint and homey touches were added here and there.

The most striking change was the absence of the perimeter wire. Not as much an absence, as a reconfiguration. It no longer surrounded the compound. Small wire pens were scattered about with chickens, cattle, sheep and a few horses. Each seemed attached, or dedicated, to a small cluster of buildings.

As Michael slowly took in the changed settlement, he noticed similar structures dotting the prairie at intervals toward the horizon. It reminded him of farm country in his youth, with family farms spread out across the landscape. A community, but with elbow room.

The party advanced along the dirt track that led through the front gate. There was no gate, or fence, or towers. A number of small farm style windmills occupied the space where the towers had stood. Each drew water that gurgled into large tanks. Troughs channeled the water in long fingers through irrigation channels into the surrounding fields.

People went about their business, eyeing the visitors curiously. There were several women with children in their charge, but most were the same generic inmate faces and garb that Michael found almost indistinguishable during his stay on the farm. The plain white cotton prison suits were still in general use, but many were modified to suit each individual.

Tom sat behind his folding table on the porch of the Administration Building. It looked to Michael as though he had not moved in these many months.

"Michael, it's good to see you," Tom said, but he wasn't looking at Michael. He was smiling at the sight of the urban settlers and their children. "Make yourself at home." He turned to Michael, "There ain't as many rules as you might remember," he joked.

"Hay, Tom," Michael answered, "Hope we won't be much of a burden."

"Hell no," Tom said sincerely, "We got more land than we got people to work it."

"Oh, we'll earn our keep," Michael reassured him. "I think we have some stuff you can use."

"No doubt. Mostly what we need is people to fill up this empty space." Tom swept his arms indicating the vast prairie all around them, "We got plenty of farm sites still open. We'll work on getting shelter for everybody. Have a good old fashion barn raisin," he smiled. "And you guys gonna have to get yourselves a team together. We got a game tonight."

"A team?" Michael asked.

"Yah," Tom said enthusiastically, "We got an honest to God baseball league. You don't have to be big like football, or tall like basketball. Big people, little people, a stick and a ball. Everybody plays. We got four generations playing on one team."

The farm had become a real community. A family need only find a suitable piece of land and plant seeds. Building went on with a picnic atmosphere. Generally, shelter for the refugees was prepared in a matter of days.

Tom and the remaining inmates had brought in the so-called 'work farm widows and orphans'. Those who had been left behind in the bad 'ol lock-em-up days. All could enjoy the laughter of children and the comfort of family. The entire extended communities took responsibility for care and education of the young. Old and infirmed were given the dignity of respect and basic necessities. Laws amounted to community councils and true juries of your peers. Representatives were elected in town hall fashion. Family elders met in clannish groups, clan leaders met in tribal councils and discussed regional affairs. People had found peace.

The fertile prairies were thriving. Not all regions of the country were as fortunate. Areas of the country devoid of an essential element simply withered away. Sparse terrain supported only sparse populations. Arizona, New Mexico, Nevada and large parts of California became virtual deserts. Depleted farmland in the deep South could support only small family groups. Others had migrated or succumbed to the ravages of war and want. Isolated vacation getaways, without mass transportation, reverted to their scenic isolation.

The crush of the cities eased as those that could migrate to the more spacious regions, did. Los Angeles, Chicago, New York and Dallas were a pale memory of their former glory. Las Vegas, Phoenix, Salt Lake City and Houston virtually disappeared; consumed by desert and climate. New Orleans and Washington D.C. were reclaimed by the swamps. Many midsize cities reverted to a dog-eat-dog Wild West climate. Much of the territory in between was lawless and nearly empty. Most of the world went happily along. The developed countries viewed the United States as the United States once viewed places like Somalia or postwar Iraq. Parts of America were suddenly third world.

Processed food was quickly consumed and many, with no clue about how to produce their own sustenance, withered away.

Entire regions of the Country could not support a large population; Arizona without air conditioning, Nevada without water, Los Angeles without food imports, Texas without oil money. Alcohol was scarce and enjoyed but not abused. Drugs, legal and otherwise, were generally unavailable and were not very much missed.

American seemed surprised that nobody seemed particularly interested in invading them. They had heard from politicians for a generation that foreigners wanted what we had. The Ultra Commandos and assorted militias, eager to test their military skill, waited in vain. There were no Moslem fanatics, swarms of Asians or African hordes waiting to invade. It turned out that foreigners just wanted to be left alone.

Not only were there no invaders, those foreigners that did come were prepared to offer some degree of assistance. People in want accepted the sincere relief from foreign charities. American capitalists that had been very strict about this-for-that were a little suspicious of an unqualified helping hand; pure charity. Not a public relations ploy or a marketing gimmick, but honest compassion. Suspicion and pride aside, it was gladly accepted. Some essential motor traffic between regions resumed.

The population of the country was cut to about a third of the before time levels. Disease, starvation and violence had taken a huge toll. Many people found that their skills were useless and simply could not cope with the changes. Lawyers developed blisters working the land for their survival. High tech geniuses played with their electronic toys in the off hours between planting and harvesting.

Long caravans, resembling wagon trains of the old west, became routine. Some wagons, backpackers, even dog-carts traveled together in a continuous exchange. Violence was nearly nonexistent, as the pilgrims generally watched out for each other. A person with a stash of something the urbanites might want would make the trek to the city. There was safety in numbers. Urbanites with some treasure, or scarce manufactured goods, struck south to trade for food or seed. Everyone could count on the courtesy of hospitality and food on the well traveled trails. There was suddenly plenty of houses and no landlords. Food and a place to rest was a right; not a commodity.

Curiously enough money, regular U.S .Currency, rose in value. Once it was no longer rolling off the press, it was scarce, easily recognizable and served as a universal medium of exchange. Coins rather than paper was preferred. It felt more like real money; treasure.

Rudimentary local radio stations kept people informed of important news and small newsletters began to circulate with local interest stories and notices of a variety of goods. Community bulletin boards with notes such as, 'Have Shovels for Sugar' and 'Will do plumbing for fabric' and 'recipes to share' appeared.

Churches and community centers, being the biggest buildings in most areas became public meeting places. Gone were the mammoth industries that provided even the common items of civilization. Michael was reminded of the Fall of the Roman Empire; a collapse so dramatic that within a few generations, the Romans were incapable of maintaining, let alone constructing, such marvels as aqueducts or heated baths. He knew the principles of aerodynamics, but he could hardly build an airplane.

It took a large well coordinated array of skills with the coordination of materials to produce an automobile or electricity. Just the scientific knowledge alone was not enough. The assembler could not assemble without the parts fabricator. The fabricator could not make parts without the refined metal. The metalworker could not mold parts without mined ore. And the miner could not extract the raw material without massive machines that were produced using this same sequence of activities. When the system collapsed, it resulted in a catch-22 situation. The system could not be rebuilt without the machines, and expertise; the machines and expertise could not be restored without the system in place. The processes had been built up over a few generations to the point of efficiency and mass production. Any element missing and the whole system ground to a halt. Though the knowledge may be there, the sequence of steps had huge gaps that could not be readily repaired. The system would have to be rebuilt from the bottom up.

Furthermore, the specialized workers needed to repair the damage, could not devote the time and energy to such activity when they had to worry about feeding their families. Steelworkers and electricians spent their time nurturing vegetable gardens. Food, clothing and shelter took priority when there was no industry or paycheck that allowed them to secure those products from other sources. A common medium of exchange, cash, allowed them to use their specialized skills. In the absence of a sophisticated society, a micro biologist wasn't worth a sack of apples.

A complex society that allowed people to make a living off their pet cause, cease to exist. The obesity epidemic in America was over as was the weight loss industry. No one got a salary for working the anti-smoking cause. Electronic marketing cease to exist. Abortion was nobody's business, except those involved. Political organizations focused on local and grass roots issues. Common law and common sense, and a memory of better times, inspired the ideas of law and justice.

Daycare and schooling for the young was a mission that was taken for granted by those involved in the childrens' lives. Local people took responsibility for basic education. The absence of 24-hour news meant settlements were much more tranquil. An act of violence half way across the continent was not news to disrupt and cause concern locally.

Air travel was almost non-existent, except for a few mail runs with small crafts. The days when a letter could travel point-to-point over thousands of miles in a few days for under a buck was just a memory. It was amazing, though, how easily people could get along without cars, gas and electronics. It was as though the urban giants just exhaled and the land took in the people.

Life on the Homestead on Black Lake was a happy one for Suzanne and Michael. They were content; part of nature and the environment. For those that remained in the outlying areas, life was simple and Spartan, but good. The pressure was off. People knew and trusted their neighbors. The world did not belong to them; they belonged to the world.

Printed in the United States
By Bookmasters